D0336041

General Editor: Richard Dutton, Professor of English
Lancaster University

This series offers stimulating accounts of the literary careers of
the most admired and influential English-language authors.
Volumes follow the outline of writers' working lives, not in
the spirit of traditional biography, but aiming to trace
the professional, publishing and social contexts which
shaped their writing.

A list of the published titles in this series follows overleaf.

Published titles

George Orwell

A Literary Life

Peter Davison

First published 1996 by
MACMILLAN PRESS LTD
Houndmills, Basingstoke, Hampshire RG21 6XS
and London
Companies and representatives
throughout the world

ISBN 0–333–54157–X hardcover
ISBN 0–333–54158–8 paperback

A catalogue record for this book is available from the British Library.

10   9   8   7   6   5   4   3   2   1
05   04   03   02   01   00   99   98   97   96

Printed and bound in Great Britain by
Antony Rowe Ltd
Chippenham, Wiltshire

 Published in the United States of America 1996 by
ST. MARTIN'S PRESS, INC.,
Scholarly and Reference Division
175 Fifth Avenue, New York, N.Y. 10010

ISBN 0–312–12820–7

Dedicated to my wife, Sheila,
with love and gratitude,
to mark the fiftieth anniversary of our first meeting,
30 May 1945

Contents

Introduction

Jacintha Buddicom first saw Eric Blair when he was 11: he was standing on his head, the better to be noticed, he said.[1] If studies and biographical accounts are anything to go by, for a man who wished no biography to be written about him, he has been well and variously remembered. In addition to two excellent biographies, Bernard Crick's *George Orwell: A Life* (1980, 1982, and 1992) and Michael Shelden's *Orwell: The Authorised Biography* (1991), and earlier, Peter Stansky and William Abrahams, *The Unknown Orwell* and *Orwell: The Transformation* (1972 and 1979), on my shelves alone are studies by Keith Aldritt, John Atkins, Laurence Brander, Jacintha Buddicom, Tosco Fyvel, Bernard Gensane, J. R. Hammond, Rayner Heppenstall, Christopher Hollis, Tom Hopkinson, Lynette Hunter, Robert A. Lee, Peter Lewis, Jeffrey Meyers, Daphne Patai, Alok Rai, Sir Richard Rees, Patrick Reilly, John Rodden, David Smith and Michael Mosher, Alan Sandison, Ian Slater, William Steinhoff, Edward M. Thomas, John Thompson, W. J. West, Raymond Williams, Ian Willison (his UCL Librarianship Diploma Thesis (1953) is invaluable), George Woodcock, David Wykes, and Alex Zwerdling, plus essay-collections and memoirs edited by Audrey Coppard and Bernard Crick, Miriam Gross, Irving Howe, Christopher Norris, Peter Stansky, Stephen Wadhams, Courtney T. Wemyss and Alexej Ugrinsky. There are books I do not have and there are countless essays (notably those by Maung Htin Aung, Elisaveta Fen, Robert Pearce, and Nicolas Walter). One might conclude that standing on one's head *does* get one noticed. More to the point, it is obvious that Orwell has been and continues to be an abiding source of interest, to friends, enemies and objective scholars. At the same time doubt must arise as to whether there is very much more to be said.

This study is chiefly concerned with what influenced Orwell – people, reading, circumstance – and his relationship with publishers and editors. It is drawn from experience of editing *The Complete Works of George Orwell*. The first nine volumes of this edition give corrected texts of nine of Orwell's books. In their hardback editions, published by Secker & Warburg, 1986–87, textual notes and collations record what happened in print to what Orwell wrote; how, for example, *A Clergyman's Daughter* was savagely cut and *Keep the*

Aspidistra Flying modified because (with some justification) the
publisher, Victor Gollancz, feared legal action of a kind that would,
today, be impossible. Orwell later rejected these two novels as pot-
boilers. But also, in part I believe, because of the way in which, to
use his word, they had been 'garbled' by his publisher. The first
volume of this edition, *Down and Out in Paris and London*, has a long
introduction explaining the genesis of the editions, touching on 'what
Orwell really wrote'. Volume Five, *The Road to Wigan Pier*, reproduces the 32 pages of plates which appeared in the first editions in
England and the USA but never thereafter until 1986, and Victor
Gollancz's anxious Foreword addressed to members of the Left Book
Club in 1937. The eighth volume, *Animal Farm*, has Orwell's proposed Preface to his Fairy Story, his Preface to the Ukrainian edition, and Orwell's own adaptation of *Animal Farm* for radio. The
Penguin editions of these texts, 1989–90, have shorter notes on the
textual problems (and some have introductions by distinguished
writers); the Penguin *Road to Wigan Pier* reproduces the plates for
the first time in a paperback edition, and its *Animal Farm* includes
Orwell's two Prefaces. (Penguin's one-volume *Complete Novels of
George Orwell*, published in 1993, evidently due to an unfortunate
oversight, reprinted the garbled instead of the corrected texts; the
editor, on Orwell's behalf, had better try standing on his head.) In
addition, in 1984, a Facsimile edition of all that remains of Orwell's
draft for *Nineteen Eighty-Four* was published.

Editing of everything else of Orwell's that has been traced –
essays, letters, broadcasts, diaries, reviews of books, plays and films
– was completed in February 1993 for publication in eleven 600-
page volumes. In January 1994, when a little over 40 per cent of the
text had been set and proofread, the publishers, Harcourt, Brace,
New York, 'withdrew from the contract' (without telling the editor).
In September 1994, Secker & Warburg agreed to take over publication and it is hoped that the eleven volumes will appear in September 1996. These volumes are very fully annotated. The close
examination of every word Orwell wrote, every event and person
he referred to, has thrown up new insights into George Orwell,
especially through his relationships with his publishers and those
with whom he worked. For example, from the minutiae recorded in
these volumes it is possible to work out what Orwell earned in the
crucial years between his leaving the Indian Police and the publication of *Animal Farm*; to doubt the myth that he was paid an advance
of £500 for writing *Down and Out in Paris and London* at a time when

a miner was lucky to earn between £2 and £3 a week;[2] from the seemingly unprofitable BBC years, how he set up what we would now call an 'Open University' for students in India, and encouraged creative writing and practical drama in the sub-continent; the true significance of censorship of his work as a writer and as a broadcaster; the importance of the pamphlets he collected in shaping his political ideas; and, from what could be a much longer list, how his and Arthur Koestler's efforts to reveal the slaughter of Polish prisoners by the Soviets failed to find a publisher. Perhaps no item in the *Complete Works* is more significant than the analysis of the deposition laid before the Tribunal at Valencia in 1937 charging Orwell and his wife with Espionage and High Treason, a document which, though he never knew it existed, explains vividly how he came to write *Animal Farm* and *Nineteen Eighty-Four*.

This study is not intended to review all that has been written about Orwell and it certainly cannot replace the many books written about him, least of all Crick's and Shelden's biographies; nevertheless, it may complement them, filling in gaps, making some corrections, and providing, from its particular standpoint, a literary biography of this great writer and man. Although by and large a chronological order is followed, this has not been adhered to strictly. If it might prove more helpful, there is reference forward and back, as, for example, the account of Orwell's wish to amend *Burmese Days* and the long-term implications of Dorothy's loss of faith. Because my chief concerns are directed to what influenced Orwell's writing and the publishing history of his work in his lifetime, I have deliberately concentrated on the period up to the publication of *Animal Farm*.

Rather than rehearse in detail the events of Orwell's life, which are well recorded by his biographers, a fairly detailed chronology has been provided. Unless a particular point is being made about the use of the names Eric Blair and George Orwell, the author is always referred to by his pen-name. His first wife, Eileen, is referred to as Eileen Blair.

References to Orwell's books are to the editions in the *Complete Works*, edited P. Davison, published by Secker & Warburg, 1986–87. The pagination is almost always identical with that in the Penguin Twentieth-Century Classics edition, 1989–90. The volumes are numbered in chronological order and references are by volume number (in roman), page, and, if necessary (after a diagonal) line, so: II.37/5 means line five of page 37 of *Burmese Days*. Secker editions have Textual Notes and apparatus; Penguin editions have A Note on the Text; these are not identical with the Secker Textual Notes and Penguin editions do not list variants. There is a 32-page introduction to the Secker *Down and Out in Paris and London*. References to *The Collected Essays, Journalism and Letters of George Orwell*, ed. Sonia Orwell and Ian Angus, 4 volumes (Secker & Warburg 1968; Penguin Books, 1970), are by volume and page number of the more conveniently available Penguin edition. Many items referred to are not in these four volumes but will be found in the fully-annotated *Complete Works* edition, vols 10–20, due for publication by Secker & Warburg, 1996. These items are individually numbered; they (and their notes) are referred to by italicised numerals, e.g. *2736* and *2736 n. 3*. Owing to the delay in the publication of these volumes occasioned by the withdrawal of the original publisher part-way through the enterprise after some 42 per cent of the text was set and proofread, this book will appear before all the volumes of the *Complete Works* have been set. It may occasionally happen, therefore, that these numerical references may prove to be slightly at variance with the edition when it does appear. It is hoped that, though this is a nuisance, it will not prove seriously so.

Secondary works frequently referred to are indicated as follows after their first reference. Full publication details are given in the Bibliography.

Brander: Laurence Brander, *George Orwell*, 1954.

Crick: Bernard Crick, *George Orwell: A Life*, 3rd edn, 1992.

Eric and Us: Jacintha Buddicom, *Eric and Us: A Remembrance of George Orwell*, 1974.

Hodges: Sheila Hodges, *Gollancz: The Story of a Publishing House, 1928–1978*, 1978.

Norris: Christopher Norris, ed., *Inside the Myth; Orwell: Views from the Left*, 1984.

Orwell Remembered: *Orwell Remembered*, ed. Audrey Coppard and Bernard Crick, 1984.

Rees: Sir Richard Rees, *George Orwell: Fugitive from the Camp of Victory*, 1961.

Rodden: John Rodden, *The Politics of Literary Reputation*, 1989.

Shelden: Michael Shelden, *Orwell: The Authorised Biography*, 1991.

Wadhams: Stephen Wadhams, *Remembering Orwell*, 1984.

Willison: Ian Willison, *George Orwell: Some Materials for a Bibliography*, 1953.

I owe much the the Orwell Archive, University College London, especially to Gill Furlong; to Mark Hamilton of the Orwell Estate for generously permitting me to quote from Orwell's work; and to Ian Angus, who, with Sonia Orwell, edited the four-volume selection of Orwell's essays, reviews, and diaries, although not involved in the writing of this book, has been of the greatest help in my editing of the 11-volume edition, and I have been conscious of, and grateful for, his influence and advice over the past decade. I am also grateful to Professor Richard Dutton, the General Editor of this series, for his enormous patience in waiting for my manuscript and, in contrast, his responding so quickly and helpfully, and also to John M. Smith at Macmillan for spotting errors I had not noticed. Finally, my thanks are due to the students of De Montfort University, Leicester, to whom for two years I had the pleasure of teaching Orwell's work. In introducing Orwell to them I reintroduced him to myself.

PETER DAVISON
De Montfort University, Leicester

Chronology

Note: This is not a comprehensive chronology; for example, most reviews are not included.

7 Jan 1857   Orwell's father, Richard Walmesley Blair born, Milborne St Andrew, Dorset. Joined the Opium Department of the Indian Civil Service, 4 August 1875 and rose to the rank of sub-deputy agent. On sick leave for 15 months for reasons unknown from 20 August 1885.

19 May 1875   Orwell's mother, Ida Mabel Limouzin, born, Penge, Surrey. Married Richard Blair, 1896.

21 April 1898   The Blairs' first child, Marjorie Francis, born at Gaya, Bengal.

25 June 1903   Eric Arthur Blair born in Motihari, Bengal.

1904   Ida Blair returns with Marjorie and Eric to England and settles at Henley-on-Thames, Oxfordshire.

Summer 1907   Richard Blair on three months' leave in England.

6 April 1908   Eric's younger sister, Avril Nora, born.

1908–1911   Attends a day-school at Henley run by Anglican nuns (as did his sisters).

Sept 1911–Dec 1916   Boards at St Cyprian's, a private preparatory school at Eastbourne, Sussex.

1912   Richard Blair retires from the Opium Dept, and returns to England. The family moves to Shiplake, Oxfordshire (probably early in December).

Summer 1914   Makes friends with the Buddicom family, especially Jacintha.

2 Oct 1914   First appearance in print: Poem, 'Awake! Young Men of England', *Henley and South Oxfordshire Standard*.

1915   The Blairs move back to Henley-on-Thames (to autumn 1917).

21 July 1916   Poem, 'Kitchener', which Orwell himself submitted, published by *Henley and South Oxfordshire Standard*.

Lent Term 1917   At Wellington College as a scholar.

May 1917–Dec 1921   At Eton as a King's Scholar. Contributes to *The Election Times* and *College Days*.

13 Sept 1917   Orwell's father commissioned as 2nd Lieut; posted to 51st (Ranchi) Indian Pioneer Company, Marseilles. His

mother soon after let the Henley house and moved to Earls Court, London, to work in the Ministry of Pensions.

9 Dec 1919 Orwell's father relinquishes his commission on completion of war service. He was by then almost 63. He joined his wife, then living at 23 Mall Chambers, Notting Hill Gate.

Dec 1921 The Blairs move to Southwold on the Suffolk coast.

Oct 1922–Dec 1927 Orwell serves in Indian Imperial Police in Burma; resigns while on leave in England, Autumn 1927.

Autumn 1927 First expeditions to East End of London to examine the conditions of the poor and exploited.

Autumn/Winter 1927 Lives in Portobello Road, Notting Hill, London.

Spring 1928 About this time lives for a while as a tramp.

Spring 1928–late 1929 Lives in working-class district of Paris; writes a 'ballade' (after Villon?), several articles and short stories, and either one or two novels. Five articles are published in French translations in Paris and one in English in London. His other writing from this period has not survived. In autumn 1929 works as a dishwasher and kitchen porter in a luxury hotel, probably the Crillon but there is circumstantial evidence suggesting the Lotti.

6 Oct 1928 'La Censure en Angleterre' appears in Henri Barbusse's paper, *Monde* – his first professional publication.

29 Dec 1928 'A Farthing Newspaper', *G.K.'s Weekly* – first professional publication to appear in England.

29 Dec 1928 'La grand misère de l'ouvrier britannique', *Le Progrès Civique*, 3 Parts (also 5.1.29 and 12.1.29).

7 Mar 1929 Admitted to Hôpital Cochin, Paris, with 'une grippe'. Discharged 22 March.

23 Mar 1929 'John Galsworthy'. *Monde* – first literary article.

4 May 1929 'Comment on exploite un peuple: L'Empire britannique en Birmanie', *Le Progrès Civique*.

1930–31 Uses his parents' home in Southwold as his base, writing there but going off to tramp and live with down-and-outs in London.

1930 Begins writing for *The Adelphi*; by October has completed 'Days in London and Paris', a 35 000-word version of *Down and Out in Paris and London* in diary form. Submitted to Jonathan Cape who reject it as 'too short and fragmentary'.

Apr 1931 'The Spike', *The Adelphi*.

Aug 1931 'A Hanging', *The Adelphi*.

Sept 1931 Revised version of *Down and Out in Paris and London* rejected by Jonathan Cape.

Autumn 1931 Picks hops in Kent. Writes four short stories which have not survived. Starts to write *Burmese Days*.

17 Oct 1931 'Hop-Picking', *New Statesman & Nation*.

14 Dec 1931 Submits revised version of *Down and Out*, now called 'A Scullion's Diary' to Faber & Faber. Rejected by T. S. Eliot, 15 February 1932. (Crick, p. 621 n. 44).

26 Apr 1932 Writes to Leonard Moore (of Christy & Moore) following the submission to him by Mrs Sinclair Fierz of the ms of *Down and Out*. Moore becomes his literary agent.

Apr 1932–July 1933 Teaches at The Hawthornes, a private school for boys aged 10–16, Hayes, Middlesex. Writes and directs a school play, *Charles II*, Christmas 1932.

3 Sept 1932 'Common Lodging Houses', *New Statesman & Nation*.

19 Nov 1932 Puts forward several names, including 'George Orwell', as his pen-name but continues to write (and especially review) as Eric Blair until December 1936. Would prefer title to be 'The Confessions of a Dishwasher' because he would rather answer to 'dishwasher' than 'down and out', but accepts Gollancz's decision of a title that will help the book sell.

9 Jan 1933 *Down and Out in Paris and London*, by George Orwell (the first use of that name), published by Victor Gollancz. Published on 30 June 1933 in New York; as *La vache enragée*, Paris, May 1935; and as *Trosecníken v Parízi a Londýne*, Prague, 1935.

Mar 1933 Poem: 'Sometimes in the middle autumn days', *The Adelphi*.

May 1933 Poem: 'Summer-like for an instant the autumn sun bursts out', *The Adelphi*.

Autumn 1933 Teaches at Frays College, Uxbridge, Middlesex. Finishes *Burmese Days*. In December, ill with pneumonia in hospital; gives up teaching.

October 1933 Poem: 'A dressed man and a naked man', *The Adelphi*.

January–October 1934 Lives with his parents in Southwold. Writes *A Clergyman's Daughter*.

Apr 1934 Poem: 'On a Ruined Farm near His Master's Voice Gramophone Factory', *The Adelphi*.

25 Oct 1934 *Burmese Days* published by Harper & Brothers, New York. (Published 24 June 1935 by Gollancz, London, with

alterations required by the publisher; as *Tragédie Birmane*, Paris, August 1946; *Giorni in Birmania*, Milan, November 1948; *Tragédia Burmában*, Budapest, 1948.

Oct 1934–Mar 1935   Takes a room at 3 Warwick Mansions, Pond Street, Hampstead, London.

Oct 1934–Jan 1936   Part-time assistant (with Jon Kimche), at Booklovers' Corner, 1 South End Road, Hampstead.

11 March 1935   *A Clergyman's Daughter* published by Gollancz. Published by Harper & Brothers, New York, 17 August 1936.

Aug 1935   Begins writing for *The New English Weekly*. Moves to Kentish Town, London.

16 Oct 1935   Lecture: 'Confessions of a Down and Out', South Woodford Literary Society.

In 1935   Submits ms, 'Pacifism', to ILP Publications Committee; rejected because too absolutist and too long (Bob Edwards).

23 Jan 1936   'Rudyard Kipling', *New English Weekly*.

End Jan 1936   Completes *Keep the Aspidistra Flying*.

31 Jan–30 Mar 1936   In North of England to collect material for a book commissioned by Gollancz on the depressed areas.

2 April 1936   Moves to The Stores, Wallington, Hertfordshire.

20 April 1936   *Keep the Aspidistra Flying* published by Gollancz. Published by Harcourt, Brace, New York, December 1955.

May 1936   Starts *The Road to Wigan Pier* and begins reviewing for *Time and Tide*.

9 June 1936   Marries Eileen O'Shaughnessy.

4 Aug 1936   'An Outsider Sees the Depressed Areas', talk at *The Adelphi* Summer School, Langham, Essex.

Autumn 1936   'Shooting an Elephant', *New Writing*.

November 1936   'Bookshop Memories', *Fortnightly*.

12 & 19 Nov 1936   'In Defence of the Novel', 2 Parts, *New English Weekly*.

December 1936   Poem: 'A happy vicar I might have been', *The Adelphi*.

15 Dec 1936   Delivers ms of *The Road to Wigan Pier*.

Christmas 1936   Leaves to fight for the Republicans in Spanish Civil War.

January–June 1937   Serves in Independent Labour Party contingent with the POUM militia on the Aragón front.

8 March 1937   *The Road to Wigan Pier* published by Gollancz in trade and Left Book Club editions. Published by Harcourt, Brace, New York, 1958.

c. 28 Apr–10 May 1937   On leave in Barcelona during Communist attempt to suppress revolutionary parties (including the POUM).

20 May 1937   Wounded in the throat by a Fascist sniper at Huesca.

23 June 1937   Escapes with Eileen from Spain into France (at Banyuls).

1–7 Jul 1937   Arrives back at Wallington; starts to write *Homage to Catalonia* shortly thereafter.

Jul 1937   *New Statesman & Nation* refuses to publish Orwell's article on the POUM or his review of Borkenau's *The Spanish Cockpit*.

13 Jul 1937   Deposition presented to Tribunal for Espionage & High Treason, Valencia, charging the Orwells as 'rabid Trotskyists' and agents of the POUM.

29 Jul 1937, 2 Sept 1937   'Spilling the Spanish Beans', 2 Parts, *New English Weekly*.

Aug 1937   'Eye-Witness in Barcelona', *Controversy*.

5 Aug 1937   Addresses ILP Conference at Letchworth, Herts, on his experiences in Spain.

12 Nov 1937   Invited to join *The Pioneer*, Lucknow.

Mid-Jan 1938   Completes *Homage to Catalonia*.

8 Mar 1938   Falls ill with tubercular lesion in one lung; gives up idea of working as leader-writer for *The Pioneer*.

15 Mar–1 Sep 1938   Patient at Preston Hall, a sanatorium at Aylesford, Kent.

25 April 1938   *Homage to Catalonia*, having been refused by Gollancz, is published by Secker & Warburg. Published by Harcourt, Brace, New York, 1952; as *Omaggio alla Catalonia*, Milan, December 1948.

June 1938   Joins the Independent Labour Party. Writes pamphlet, 'Socialism and War'; submitted to Hogarth Press; in November abandons attempts to have it printed. The pamphlet has not survived.

24 June 1938   'Why I Join the I.L.P.', *New Leader*.

2 Sept 1938–26 Mar 1939   In French Morocco (mainly at Marrakech); writes *Coming Up for Air*.

December 1938   'Political Reflections on the Crisis', *The Adelphi*.

11 April 1939   Returns to Wallington.

Late May–mid-Dec 1939   Writes *Inside the Whale*.

12 June 1939   *Coming Up for Air* published by Gollancz. Published by Harcourt, Brace, New York, January 1950.

28 June 1939   Orwell's father, Richard Blair, dies of cancer, aged
          82; Orwell at his bedside.

24–31 Aug 1939   Stays with L. H. Myers in Hampshire.

Sept 1939   'Democracy in the British Army', *Left Forum*.

3 Sept 1939   War breaks out. Shortly after, Orwell leaves Inde-
          pendent Labour Party because of its opposition to the war.

Christmas 1939   'Marrakech', *New Writing*.

Feb 1940   First contribution to *Horizon* ['Lessons of War', a review].

2 Feb 1940   Talk (subject not known) to 'Women of Today'.

Mar 1940   'Boys' Weeklies', *Horizon*.

11 Mar 1940   *Inside the Whale and Other Essays*, Gollancz; includes
          'Charles Dickens' (written 1939) and 'Boys' Weeklies' as well
          as title essay. Published in Italian by Mondadori, Milan, 1949.

29 Mar 1940   First contribution to *Tribune*.

Apr 1940   Projects long novel in three parts; probably not started.

May 1940   Moves to Regent's Park, London. Joins the Local De-
          fence Volunteers (Home Guard).

18 May 1940   First of 25 theatre reviews for *Time & Tide* (until
          9 August 1941).

25 May 1940   Lecture on Dickens to Dickens Fellowship.

June 1940   Laurence O'Shaughnessy, a Major in the RAMC and
          Eileen's dearly-loved brother, killed at Dunkirk while tend-
          ing the wounded. According to Elisaveta Fen, Eileen's 'grasp
          on life loosened considerably' thereafter.

Aug–Oct 1940   Writes *The Lion and the Unicorn*.

17 Aug 1940   'Books in General' [on Charles Reade], *New States-
          man & Nation*.

Autumn 1940   'My Country Right or Left', *Folios of New Writing*.

5 Oct 1940   First of 27 film reviews for *Time & Tide* (until 23
          August 1941).

Dec 1940   'The Ruling Class', *Horizon*.

6 Dec 1940   Broadcast (with Desmond Hawkins): 'The Proletarian
          Writer', BBC Home Service.

20 Dec 1940   'The Home Guard and You', *Tribune*.

Jan 1941   'Our Opportunity', *Left News* (see 3 Mar 1941).

3 Jan 1941   First of 15 London Letters for *Partisan Review* (pub-
          lished Mar/Apr 1941).

19 Feb 1941   *The Lion and the Unicorn* published by Secker &
          Warburg (the first of the 'Searchlight Books' edited by Orwell
          and T. R. Fyvel).

3 Mar 1941   'Fascism and Democracy' and 'Patriots and Revolu-
          tionaries' [= 'Our Opportunity']. chs 8 and 10 of *Betrayal of
          the Left*, Gollancz.

Early Apr 1941   Moves to St John's Wood, London.

23 May 1941   Talk: 'Literature and Totalitarianism', Oxford University Democratic Socialist Club.

May–June 1941   Series of four broadcast talks, BBC Overseas Service, published in *The Listener*, as 'The Frontiers of Art and Propaganda' 29.5.41; 'Tolstoy and Shakespeare' 5.6.41; 'The Meaning of a Poem' 12.6.41; and 'Literature and Totalitarianism' 19.6.41.

Aug 1941   'Wells, Hitler, and the World State', *Horizon*.

18 Aug 1941–24 Nov 1943   Talks Assistant, later Talks Producer, in the Indian section of the BBC's Eastern Service.

Sept 1941   'The Art of Donald McGill', *Horizon*.

21 Nov 1941   First of over 200 newsletters written by Orwell for India, Malaya, and Indonesia, some in English (many broadcast by him), many translated into Gujarati, Marathi, Bengali and Tamil.

22 Nov 1941   Talk: 'Culture and Democracy', Fabian Society.

8 Jan 1942   Radio talk: 'Paper is Precious'. (All BBC programmes are for the Eastern Service of the BBC unless stated otherwise.)

15 Jan 1942   Radio talk: 'The Meaning of Scorched Earth' (script lost).

20 Jan 1942   Radio talk: 'Money and Guns'.

22 Jan 1942   Radio talk: 'Britain's Rations and the Submarine War'.

29 Jan 1942   Radio talk: 'The Meaning of Sabotage'.

Feb 1942   'Rudyard Kipling', *Horizon*.

8 Mar 1942   First contribution to *The Observer*.

10 Mar 1942   Radio talk: 'The Re-discovery of Europe' (*The Listener* 19.3.42)

15 May 1942   'Culture and Democracy' in *Victory or Vested Interest?*, published by George Routledge & Sons.

Summer 1942   Moves to Maida Vale, London.

11 Aug 1942   'Voice 1', first of six broadcast literary magazines for India edited by Orwell.

9 Sept 1942   Lecture at Morley College, Lambeth.

9 Oct 1942   Orwell gives first instalment of a story by five authors broadcast to India.

2 Nov 1942   Imaginary radio interview with Jonathan Swift. (*The Listener* 26.11.42).

29 Nov 1942   'In the Darlan Country', *The Observer*.

9 Jan 1943   'Pamphlet Literature', *New Statesman & Nation*.

22 Jan 1943   Radio talk: 'George Bernard Shaw'.

23 Feb 1943   First (anonymous) contribution to 'Forum' (on India) for *The Observer*.

Mar 1943 'Looking Back on the Spanish Civil War', written Autumn 1942, published in *New Road* (Abridged).

5 Mar 1943 Radio talk: 'Jack London'.

19 Mar 1943 Orwell's mother, Ida Blair, dies.

2 Apr 1943 'Not Enough Money: A Sketch of George Gissing', *Tribune*.

9 May 1943 'Three Years of Home Guard', *The Observer*.

4 June 1943 'Literature and the Left', *Tribune*.

13 June 1943 Radio talk: 'English Poetry since 1900'.

18 June 1943 Verse: 'As One Non-Combatant to Another: A Letter to "Obadiah Hornbrooke" [Alex Comfort]', *Tribune*.

11 Aug 1943 Radio: featurised story: *Crainquebille* by Anatole France.

24 Aug 1943 'I am definitely leaving it [the BBC] probably in about three months' (letter to Rayner Heppenstall).

Sept 1943 Review: 'Gandhi in Mayfair', *Horizon*.

9 Sept 1943 Radio play adapted from *The Fox* by Ignazio Silone.

6 Oct 1943 Radio: featurised story: 'A Slip Under the Microscope' by H. G. Wells.

17 Oct 1943 Radio talk: *Macbeth*.

18 Nov 1943 Radio talk: *The Emperor's New Clothes* by Hans Andersen.

18 Nov 1943 *Talking to India* published by Allen & Unwin, edited and with an Introduction by Orwell (and including 'The Rediscovery of Europe').

21 Nov 1943 Radio talk: *Lady Windermere's Fan*.

23 Nov 1943 Leaves BBC and joins *Tribune* as Literary Editor (until 16 Feb 1945). Leaves Home Guard on medical grounds.

Nov 1943–Feb 1944 Writes *Animal Farm*.

26 Nov 1943 'Mark Twain – The Licensed Jester', *Tribune*.

3 Dec 1943 First of 80 personal columns titled 'As I Please', *Tribune*, 59 published to 16.2.45; remainder, 8.11.46 to 4.4.47.

9 Dec 1943 Begins reviewing for *The Manchester Evening News*.

24 Dec 1943 'Can Socialists be Happy?' by John Freeman (= Orwell?), *Tribune*.

21 Jan 1944 Poem: 'Memories of the Blitz', *Tribune*.

13 Feb 1944 'A Hundred Up' (centenary of *Martin Chuzzlewit*], *The Observer*.

May 1944 Finishes *The English People*.

14 May 1944 The Orwells' son, adopted June 1944, born; christened Richard Horatio Blair.

Summer 1944   'Propaganda and Demotic Speech', *Persuasion*.

28 June 1944   The Orwells' flat bombed; they move to Inez Holden's flat, George Street, off Baker Street, London.

16 Jul 1944   'The Eight Years of War: Spanish Memories', *The Observer*.

7 Sept 1944   'How Long is a Short Story?', *The Manchester Evening News*.

22 Sept 1944   'Tobias Smollett: Scotland's Best Novelist', *Tribune*.

Oct 1944   'Raffles and Miss Blandish', *Horizon*.

Early Oct 1944   Moves to Canonbury Square, Islington, London.

19 Oct 1944   'Home Guard Lessons for the Future', *Horizon*.

Oct [Nov?] 1944   'Benefit of Clergy: Some Notes on Salvador Dali', *Saturday Book*, 4 [Orwell's article physically excised].

22 Dec 1944   'Oysters and Brown Stout' [on Thackeray], *Tribune*.

15 Feb–end Mar 1945   War correspondent for *The Observer* and *The Manchester Evening News* in France and Germany.

28 Feb 1945   'Inside the Papers in Paris', the first of Orwell's articles from Paris for *The Manchester Evening News* as war correspondent.

Mar 1945   'Poetry and the Microphone', *New Saxon Pamphlets* (written autumn 1943).

4 Mar 1945   'Occupation's Effect on French Outlook', the first of Orwell's articles for *The Observer* as war correspondent.

29 Mar 1945   Eileen Blair dies.

31 Mar 1945   Signs first of his 'Notes for my Literary Executor' (and see Post-June 1949).

8 Apr–24 May 1945   Returns to France, Germany and Austria as war correspondent.

Apr 1945   'Antisemitism in Britain', *Contemporary Jewish Chronicle* (written early February 1945).

8 June 1945   Broadcast for Schools: *Erewhon*, BBC Home Service.

15 June 1945   Broadcast for Schools: *The Way of All Flesh*, BBC Home Service.

25 June 1945   Warburg reports that Orwell had written 'the first twelve pages of his new novel' [*Nineteen Eighty-Four*]. 'But, of course, disclaims knowledge of when it will he finished.' Orwell told by Warburg that Cass Canfield, Head of Harper Brothers and of the OWI's Paris Office, was 'greatly impressed' by Orwell's *Observer* articles.

Jul 1945   'In Defence of P. G. Wodehouse', *Windmill* (written February 1945).

3 Jul 1945   Agrees to write four long articles for *Polemic*.

5 Jul 1945   'Authors Deserve a New Deal', *The Manchester Evening News*.

21 Jul 1945   'On Scientifiction', *Leader Magazine*.

28 Jul 1945   'Funny but not Vulgar', *Leader Magazine*.

Summer 1945–Dec 1948   Writes *Nineteen Eighty-Four*.

Aug 1945   Elected Vice-Chairman of the Freedom Defence Committee.

17 Aug 1945   After many rejections, 4500 copies of *Animal Farm* published by Secker & Warburg with a further 21 000 in his lifetime. (Published by Harcourt, Brace, New York, 1946 (50 000 copies), and made American Book of the Month Club choice, 540 000 copies.) By the time Orwell died, *Animal Farm* had been published in Portuguese, Swedish, Norwegian, German, Polish, Persian, Dutch, French, Italian, Gujarati, Ukrainian (with Orwell's Introduction, November 1947), Danish, Estonian, Spanish, Korean, Japanese, Telugu, Indonesian, Icelandic, and Russian editions.

10–22 Sept 45   First visit to Jura, Scotland; stays in fisherman's cottage.

Oct 1945   'Notes on Nationalism', *Polemic*.

8 Oct 1945   Forces Educational Broadcast: 'Jack London', BBC Light Programme.

14 Oct 1945   'Profile: Aneurin Bevan', [anon.; chiefly by Orwell], *The Observer*.

19 Oct 1945   'You and the Atom Bomb', *Tribune*.

26 Oct 1945   'What is Science?', *Tribune*.

Nov 1945   'The British General Election', *Commentary*.

2 Nov 1945   'Good Bad Books', *Tribune*.

9 Nov 1945   'Revenge is Sour', *Tribune*.

23 Nov 1945   'Through a Glass Darkly', *Tribune*.

14 Dec 1945   'The Sporting Spirit', *Tribune*.

15 Dec 1945   'In Defence of English Cooking', *Evening Standard*.

21 Dec 1945   'Nonsense Poetry', *Tribune*.

Jan 1946   'The Prevention of Literature', *Polemic*.

4 Jan 1946   'Freedom v. Happiness' [review of Zamyatin's *We*], *Tribune*.

12 Jan 1946   'A Nice Cup of Tea', *Tribune*.

18 Jan 1946   'The Politics of Starvation', *Tribune*.

24, 31 Jan, 7 Feb 1946   Sequence of three articles: '1. The Intellectual Revolt', '2. What is Socialism?', '3. The Christian Reformers', *The Manchester Evening News*.

31 Jan 1946   Letter: 'Indian Passengers' [a protest at racial discrimination], *The Manchester Guardian*.

1 Feb 1946   'The Cost of Radio Programmes', *Tribune*.

8 Feb 1946   'Books v. Cigarettes', *Tribune*.

9 Feb 1946   'The Moon under Water' [characteristics of a favourite pub], *Evening Standard*.

14 Feb 1946   *Critical Essays* published by Secker & Warburg. (Published in New York as *Dickens, Dali & Others*, by Reynal & Hitchcock, 29 April 1946; as *Ensayos Críticos*, Buenos Aires, July 1948.)

15 Feb 1946   'Decline of the English Murder', *Tribune*.

8 Mar 1946   'Do Our Colonies Pay?', *Tribune*.

29 Mar 1946   Radio Play: 'The Voyage of the *Beagle*', BBC Home Service.

Apr 1946   'Politics and the English Language', *Horizon*.

12 Apr 1946   'Some Thoughts on the Common Toad', *Tribune*.

26 Apr 1946   'A Good Word for the Vicar of Bray', *Tribune*.

Mid-Apr 1946   Gives up journalism for six months to concentrate on writing *Nineteen Eighty-Four*.

May 1946   'Second Thoughts on James Burnham', *Politics*; as pamphlet, *James Burnham and the Managerial Revolution*, Socialist Book Centre, London, July 1946.

3 May 1946   Death of Marjorie Dakin, Orwell's older sister.

3 May 1946   'Confessions of a Book Reviewer', *Tribune*.

23 May–13 Oct 1946   Rents Barnhill on the Isle of Jura, Scotland.

Summer 1946   'Why I Write', *Gangrel*.

8 Jul 1946   Contemplates starting on *Nineteen Eighty-Four*.

9 Jul 1946   Radio play: 'Little Red Riding Hood', BBC Children's Hour.

20 Sept 1946   Has 'done about fifty pages' [of *Nineteen Eighty-Four*].

Sept–Oct 1946   'Politics vs. Literature', *Polemic*.

14 Oct 1946–10 Apr 1947   At Canonbury Square, Islington.

29 Oct 1946   BBC Pamphlet No 2: *Books and Authors* (containing Orwell's talk, 'Bernard Shaw's *Arms and the Man*), and BBC Pamphlet No 3: *Landmarks in American Literature* (containing Orwell's talk, 'Jack London'), published by Oxford University Press, Bombay.

Nov 1946   Jack London's *Love of Life and Other Stories*, with Introduction by Orwell (written November 1945), published by Paul Elek.

Nov 1946   'How the Poor Die', *Now* [revised from version originally written for *Horizon*, late 1940?].

22 Nov 1946 'Riding Down from Bangor' [review of *Helen's Babies*], *Tribune*.

Jan 1947 'Arthur Koestler', *Focus* [written Sept 1944].

14 Jan 1947 Radio play: *Animal Farm* [Orwell's adaptation], BBC Third Programme.

Mar 1947 'Lear, Tolstoy and the Fool', *Polemic*.

4 Apr 1947 Seventy-eighth and last 'As I Please' [though Orwell only intended to suspend writing his column].

11 Apr–20 Dec 1947 At Barnhill, Jura, writing *Nineteen Eighty-Four* and often ill.

31 May 1947 Sends Frederick Warburg version of 'Such, Such Were the Joys'; final version probably completed about May 1948.

Jul/Aug 1947 'Toward European Unity', *Partisan Review*.

August 1947 *The English People* published by Collins in the series, *Britain in Pictures*; as *Det engelske Folk*, Copenhagen, February, 1948; *Die Engländer*, Braunschweig, December 1948.

Sept 1947 Gives up lease of The Stores, Wallington.

31 Oct 1947 So ill has to work in bed.

7 Nov 1947 First draft of *Nineteen Eighty-Four* completed.

30 Nov 1947 'Profile: Krishna Menon' by David Astor, with Orwell, *The Observer*.

20 Dec 1947–28 Jul 1948 Patient in Hairmyres Hospital, East Kilbride (near Glasgow), with tuberculosis of the left lung.

Mar 1948 Writes 'Writers and Leviathan' for *Politics and Letters*; when that fails, published in *New Leader*, New York, 19 June 1948.

May 1948 Starts second draft of *Nineteen Eighty-Four*. Writes 'Britain's Left-Wing Press' for *The Progressive*, and 'George Gissing' for *Politics and Letters* [published in the *London Magazine*, June 1960]. Probably makes last handwritten amendments to final typescript of 'Such, Such Were the Joys'.

13 May 1948 *Coming Up for Air* published as first volume in Secker's Uniform Edition.

28 Jul 1948–*c* Jan 1949 At Barnhill, Jura.

22 Aug 1948 'The Writer's Dilemma' [review of *The Writer and Politics* by George Woodcock], *The Observer*.

Autumn 1948 Writes 'Reflections on Gandhi' for *Partisan Review* (published June 1949).

Oct 1948 'Britain's Struggle for Survival: The Labour Government after Three Years', *Commentary*.

Early Nov 1948 Finishes writing *Nineteen Eighty-Four*.

15 Nov 1948   *British Pamphleteers*, Vol. 1, published by Allan Wingate, with Introduction by Orwell (written spring 1947).

4 Dec 1948   Completes typing fair copy of *Nineteen Eighty-Four* and posts copies to Moore and Warburg. Has serious relapse.

Dec 1948   Gives up lease of flat in Canonbury Square, Islington.

24 Dec 1948   Makes final entry in his last Domestic Diary.

c 2 Jan 1949   Leaves Jura.

6 Jan–3 Sep 1949   Patient in Cotswold Sanatorium, Cranham, Gloucestershire, seriously ill with tuberculosis.

Jan 1949   *Burmese Days* published as second volume in Uniform Edition.

Mid-Feb 1949   Starts but never completes article on Evelyn Waugh for *Partisan Review*.

Mar 1949   Corrects proofs of *Nineteen Eighty-Four*.

9 Apr 1949   Sends off his last completed review: of Winston Churchill's *Their Finest Hour*, for *The New Leader*, New York.

Apr 1949 onwards   Plans a novel set in 1945 (not written). Writes synopsis and four pages of long short-story, 'A Smoking-Room Story'. Makes notes for an essay on Joseph Conrad.

May 1949   'The Question of the [Ezra] Pound Award', *Partisan Review*.

8 June 1949   *Nineteen Eighty-Four* published by Secker & Warburg (26 575 copies published in his lifetime). (Published by Harcourt, Brace, New York, 13 June 1949; two editions, each of 20 000 copies in his lifetime); American Book of the Month Club selection, July 1949, about 190 000 copies.) By the end of 1950 it had been published in Danish, Japanese, Swedish, German, Dutch, French, Norwegian, Finnish, Italian and Hebrew.

Post-June 1949   Signs second 'Notes for my Literary Executor' (see 31 March 1945).

August 1949   Plans a book of reprinted essays.

3 Sept 1949   Transferred to University College Hospital, London.

13 Oct 1949   Marries Sonia Brownell.

18 Jan 1950   Signs his will on eve of proposed journey to Switzerland, recommended for his health's sake.

21 Jan 1950   Dies of pulmonary tuberculosis, aged 46.

26 Jan 1950   Buried, as Eric Arthur Blair, All Saints, Sutton Courtenay, Berkshire.

1

Getting Started

THE FAMILY

The first influences to affect Orwell's development as a writer can be traced to his parents and to his childhood friends, especially the Buddicom family. In a crude way, these influences may be described as negative and positive respectively. Orwell's relationship with his parents was at best uncertain but it is important to stress that this did not stem only from the personalities of his parents. Orwell's father, a dutiful, modest, Victorian, minor Indian civil servant, must have found it galling that his son seemed to waste the efforts his parents and Orwell's preparatory school, St Cyprian's (and Orwell himself) had made to get him to Eton as a King's Scholar. He must have found incomprehensible his son's rejection of service to the Empire in preference for a poverty-stricken life as a would-be author. With the benefit of hindsight we can tell how serious Orwell was in his determination to make himself a writer, and his long, hard apprenticeship can be seen to have a pattern and purpose. At the time, to his father, his son must have seemed (to describe him anachronistically in contemporary terms) little better than a layabout, little different from the way many now contemptuously view New Age Travellers, or squatters. If this seems excessive, over thirty years ago and only a decade after Orwell's death, his close friend and literary executor, Sir Richard Rees, wrote that 'A retired Indian civil servant cannot be expected to enjoy seeing his son become a voluntary down-and-out.' Mabel Fierz told Ian Angus in 1967 that to his father, Orwell was a dilettante – for a man trained in the traditions of service such as Richard Blair, a severe condemnation.[1] Orwell had been trained (especially at St Cyprian's) in that same tradition of imperial service; it would only become clear in the last year or two of Richard Blair's life how his son had transmuted that tradition of service, applying it to a wide field. Orwell's early experience of his parents, especially his father, was not unusual at that time for people in their walk of life, especially when distance and

1

time split families, but the effect on Orwell of the circumstances of his upbringing was profound.

Orwell was born in India (coincidentally only some 250 miles from where his second wife, Sonia Brownell, was born) but he came with his mother and older sister, Marjorie, to settle in England in 1904 when he was about one year old. Between then and June 1912, when his father retired at the age of 55 and came to live with his family, Orwell saw his father for only three months, when he returned home on leave in the summer of 1907. The advent of a father, a stranger, into Orwell's life at the age of 8 must have seemed, at the least, awkward. Jacintha Buddicom described Mr Blair as 'not *unkind*' (her italics); he never beat his son, she said, 'but he did not understand, nor, I think, much care for children – after all, he hardly saw his own till he was fifty. He always seemed to expect us all to keep rather out of his way, which we were reciprocatively glad to do.'[2]

Towards the end of Orwell's life there is a curious interjection in his essay about his preparatory school, 'Such, Such Were the Joys' (*3409*). How factual and how imaginative this essay is will be referred to later, but this passage departs at a tangent from the main subject and is of a different order of 'truth' from the rest of the essay: it is surely heartfelt. Orwell has just remarked that the appropriate emotion required of him towards the headmaster and his wife was gratitude: 'it was my duty to be grateful . . . but I was not grateful'. He continues:

> It was equally clear that one ought to love one's father, but I knew very well that I merely disliked my own father, whom I had barely seen before I was eight and who appeared to me simply as a gruff-voiced elderly man forever saying 'Don't'. It was not that one did not want to possess the right qualities or feel the correct emotions, but that one could not. The good and the possible never seemed to coincide.[3]

Although there are one or two passing references to his parents, it is the only direct reference to his father in the whole of this long essay. This passage is the more significant because it is, like a question Orwell asked Sir Richard Rees, so far as Rees could recall, 'apropos of nothing'. Orwell asked Rees out of the blue, 'I hope you love your family?' Rees's understanding of Orwell was based on intimate knowledge and warm friendship. He comments:

I may be wrong in thinking there had been nothing to lead up to this remark, but in any case I knew him well enough to be able to interpret it. He was thinking of the Oedipus complex, the fear of castration by the father or absorption by the possessive mother and all the other psychological bogeys that have inspired so much of modern art and literature, and he was repudiating them. Rashly perhaps, because he was not always completely successful in loving his own family. He was estranged from his father for a number of years, and I can understand that the elder Mr Blair may have felt that he had reasonable grounds for complaint.[4]

In 1917 Richard Blair joined the army. He was commissioned on 13 September and joined the 51st (Ranchi) Indian Labour Company in Marseilles; he was by then 60 and, reputedly, the oldest second-lieutenant in the British army. His son was 14. As his father was in charge of the army's mules, Orwell may, as Bernard Crick suggests, have found this posting ludicrous and even embarrassing; no one at Eton recalled him mentioning what his father was doing in the army.[5] He did not complete service in the army until the very end of 1919 and then he joined his wife at her flat in London.

As Orwell spent much of his time at boarding school, his acquaintanceship with his father can only have been slight. From the time Orwell came to England in 1904 until he returned from Burma in August 1927 – that is, between his ages of one and 24 – Orwell saw his father for three months in 1907 (when he was four); a total of less than two years of school holidays spread out between 1912 and 1917; and nine months in 1922, from the time he left Eton until he sailed for Burma; a total of less than three years. Father and son only rubbed against one another thereafter when Orwell came to stay at Southwold, the longest period being from January 1934, after Orwell had been discharged from Uxbridge Cottage Hospital, until October 1934, when he took a part-time job at Booklovers' Corner. It was then that he wrote *A Clergyman's Daughter*.

It is not difficult to imagine that his father and mother – especially his father – would find *Down and Out in Paris and London* difficult to comprehend and that his father would find *Burmese Days* a prime example of *trahison des clercs*. Even his mother, whose family had close commercial links with Burma, might have been less than pleased by the novel's anti-imperialist tone. They must have been puzzled that he seemed to be struggling so hard to eke out a living which produced books that were far from bestsellers. The

Wigan experience, too, must have seemed to them distinctly odd. Mabel Fierz, who was to be instrumental in getting *Down and Out in Paris and London* published, recalled that Orwell was devoted to his family, but that that they were disappointed in him because he had thrown up his job with the Burma Police. This disappointment 'was a great sorrow to him, that he never came up to his father's expectations. It always hurt him.'[6] But, as Sir Richard Rees records, Orwell was able to tell Rees 'with deep satisfaction' that he and his father 'were reconciled before his father's death', Orwell closing his father's eyes in the traditional way by placing pennies on his eyelids (and then, embarrassed, not knowing what to do with the pennies after the funeral, throwing them into the sea: 'Do you think some people would have put them back in their pocket?', he asked Rees).[7] In a letter of 4 July 1939 (555), Orwell told his agent that latterly his father 'had not been so disappointed in me as before', and he described how the last words his father had heard before he lapsed into final unconsciousness were those his sister read to him from a favourable review of *Coming Up for Air*.

There was nothing particularly unusual for a boy of Orwell's class, with a father working in the service of the Empire, to be brought up in the way he was, but it meant, in terms of parental affection, that a great burden fell upon his mother. How well was she able to satisfy that need?

Orwell's mother was a lively and independent woman. Her diary for 1905, when Orwell was two, shows she led a very active social life. Crick and Shelden record visits to London, to see her sister, Nellie Limouzin, to the theatre (to see Sarah Bernhardt), Wimbledon, Kew Gardens, the Mansion House, and so forth. She played tennis, golf and croquet outdoors, and bridge indoors. Certainly on one occasion she had to come dashing back to Henley because her son was, once again, ill. But, in August 1905, she did go with her children to Frinton-on-Sea for a long holiday.[8] It would be quite wrong to imply that Orwell suffered neglect. It is dangerous to take what is written in a novel as autobiographical, even with an author as closely dependent upon his own life for inspiration as was Orwell, but there is no reason to doubt that the memory of Upper Binfield recalled by George Bowling is also Orwell's of Shiplake and Henley: 'If I shut my eyes and think of Lower Binfield any time before I was, say, eight, it's always in summer weather that I remember it.'[9] (It was when he was 8, of course, that Orwell's father returned home to retire.) Jacintha Buddicom says of the family relationships:

The Blairs, though certainly not demonstrative, were nevertheless a united family, and their home seemed to us to be a happy
one. I do not think Eric was *fond* of his father, although he respected and obeyed him, but without any doubt he was genuinely fond of his mother and sisters, especially Avril. . . . He was
always very kind to Avril when they played with us, and equally
kind to Guiny.

Guiny (Guinever) was Jacintha's younger sister, a year younger
than Avril.[10] But Orwell's relationship with his mother was not so
transparently simple.

At the very end of his life, in his last Literary Notebook (3724, pp.
10 and 11), there is a passage in a curiously detached tone that
starts, 'The conversations he overheard as a small boy, between his
mother, his aunt, his elder sister (?) & their feminist friends. . . . he
derived a firm impression that women *did not like* men. . . . Somehow,
by the mere tone of these conversations, the hatefulness – above all
the physical unattractiveness – of men in women's eyes seemed to
be established.' The third-person mode distances the dying author
from these remembrances of forty years earlier, but it is not difficult
to picture Orwell as a little boy, sitting quietly listening, hearing but
not fully comprehending, increasingly aware of his own male hatefulness to his mother. He goes on:

It was not till he was abt 30 that it struck him that he had in fact
been his mother's favourite child. It had seemed natural to him
that, as he was a boy, the two girls should be preferred to him.

The third-person mode may be dictated by Orwell's noting this as
possible material for a future novel (he had two in mind in the last
year of his life), but he is, nevertheless, still mulling over his childhood in his mind. The entry in the Notebook stands out the more
because of the style in which it is written and because it is immediately followed by a cool analysis of the use of the cliché, 'I hold
no brief for –.' Why 'till he was abt 30'? That was when *Down and
Out in Paris and London* was published: did his mother then think
her son had finally achieved something?

Even more telling are two short passages towards the end of
'Such, Such Were the Joys', written (or finalised) not more than a
year before that entry in the last Literary Notebook.

A child which appears reasonably happy may actually be suffering horrors which it cannot or will not reveal. It lives in a sort of alien under-water world which we can only penetrate by memory or divination.

And shortly afterwards, a sentence that might serve as a commentary on Jacintha Buddicom's description of Orwell's fondness for his mother (she does not use the word 'love'):

Looking back on my own childhood, after the infant years were over, I do not believe that I ever felt love for any mature person, except my mother, and even her I did not trust, in the sense that shyness made me conceal most of my real feelings from her.

Like the reference to his father, this is the only direct reference to his mother in 'Such, Such Were the Joys'.

It is impossible to pinpoint what may have caused Orwell's unease. Many middle children seem to be affected by their position in the family (though for that parents can hardly be blamed).[11] What little that can be pointed to suggests that Mrs Blair was adept at finding that her children were an encumbrance. Her diary for 1905 demonstrates that she enjoyed life away from her home and children; Avril recalled that very often their mother 'used to park us out'.[12] Orwell spent the Easter and summer holidays in Shropshire with Jacintha Buddicom's brother, Prosper, at the Buddicom's Aunt Lilian's (57.3; and see below, p. 8). On 14 November 1917 Mrs Blair asked Mrs Buddicom if she would take Orwell and Avril as paying guests for Christmas because she was 'very awkwardly placed'; on 5 November 1918 she wrote to say that 'Eric and Avril . . . have implored me to ask you [if they could spend the Christmas holidays with you] & I promised I would.' She was invited to spend Boxing Day with the Buddicoms but did not reply; after a reminder she added a PS to a letter of 13 December to say she couldn't accept and, when then asked if she would care to come for Christmas Day, replied that that too was impossible.[13] Staying with the Buddicoms *was* fun, but despite their being said to implore their mother (a not unknown technique in such circumstances), it was tantamount to a rejection, as many who have experienced being off-loaded in this way could bear witness. At Christmas 1920 he went to stay with his father's cousins near Ipswich from 30 December (57).

What sprang from this upbringing, so far as Orwell's relationship with his parents was concerned, was coolness between him and his father until just before the latter died; unawareness until he was 30 that he was a favourite of his mother; and the birth of a deep-seated and long-abiding sense of failure. Coupled with this was (as is characteristic of so many children in like emotional circumstances, if often suppressed) a desire to please those nearest in blood to them who seem to have disregarded them or even to have rejected them. The first motive Orwell gives for his determination to become a writer in 'Why I Write' (CEJL, i.23–30) is 'Sheer egoism. Desire to seem clever, to be talked about, to be remembered after death, *to get your own back on grown-ups who snubbed you in childhood*, etc. etc. It is humbug to pretend this is not a motive, and a strong one.' (The italics are mine).

Orwell harps on failure in 'Why I Write'. In the second paragraph he says, 'I knew that I had a facility with words and a power of facing unpleasant facts, and I felt that this created a sort of private world in which I could get my own back for my failure in everyday life'; note again, 'get my own back'. Later in the essay, speaking of the time after he had returned from Burma, he says, 'I underwent poverty and the sense of failure.' He carefully does not say he was poor but that he *underwent* poverty, as if it were a deliberate suffering, a passion. Then, towards the end of the essay, he speaks of the relative success (as he saw it – it was, of course, an immense artistic and financial success) of *Animal Farm* and his hope that, after a gap of seven years, he would write another novel fairly soon. This would be *Nineteen Eighty-Four*. And he comments: 'It is bound to be a failure, every book is a failure.' Failure is mentioned several times in section V of 'Such, Such Were the Joys', culminating in that last sentence, referring to the time when he had left St Cyprian's and was bound for what he thought would be the relative freedom of Wellington (where he stayed a term before going to Eton). There was, he said, 'a bit of happiness before the future closed in upon me. But I knew the future was dark. Failure, failure, failure – failure behind me, failure ahead of me – that was by far the deepest conviction that I carried away' [from St Cyprian's]. Whatever may be exaggerated or distorted about St Cyprian's in this essay, these emotions ring true. In opposition to failing, winning is also described in 'Such, Such Were the Joys', but Orwell relates winning (in school terms) to those who were 'bigger, stronger, handsomer, richer, more popular, more elegant, more unscrupulous than other people': virtue, so qualified, consisted in winning.

Until he left St Cyprian's, Orwell's conditioning, with one

exception, was such as to make him feel, fairly or not, that he was, if not unloved, passed over; easily 'parked out'; inferior; and, inevitably, a failure, even that 'winning' was itself reprehensible. However, his conscious determination to be a writer and his subconscious determination to prove himself to himself and to please his parents and seek their approbation, gave him immense driving force that sustained him through years of privation and disappointment. Whether that would have been possible without the 'one exception', the positive influence of the Buddicoms, and especially Jacintha, may be doubted.

THE BUDDICOMS

Even before meeting the Buddicoms, Orwell had determined he would be a writer. In 'Why I Write', he recalled, 'From a very early age, perhaps the age of five or six, I knew that when I grew up I should be a writer.' Orwell met his neighbours, the Buddicoms, in the summer of 1914, just before the outbreak of the First World War. He was 11; Jacintha, with whom he was especially friendly, was two years older and survived him by fifty-three years, dying in 1993. Her brother Prosper, with whom he often played, was born in 1904 (and died in 1968) and her sister, Guinever (Guiny), was born in 1907. Orwell and Avril played constantly with the Buddicoms. Of the many varieties of recollections of the past, two kinds stand out. One views the past with love and enjoyment; the other in bitterness; both only tell a part of the story. Jacintha Buddicom's *Eric and Us* and Orwell's 'Such, Such were the Joys' represent these extremes. There are reasons why Orwell may have adopted the tone he did (see pp. 103–4) and Jacintha may, because of her personality, present an over-comfortable picture of the past, but her delightfully evocative account through its warmth and shared pleasure in simple things, reveals what was missing in Orwell's own home and suggests much that was to prove positive in Orwell's development as a writer.

Orwell needed no encouragement to read as a child, but he and Jacintha also shared reading and that was to have a long-term influence on Orwell. It was in the Buddicoms' home that Orwell came across H. G. Wells's *A Modern Utopia* (1905). So attached was he to it that Jacintha's father, Robert, gave Orwell his copy. She remembers Orwell, aged between 11 and 13, telling her that one day he might write a book like *A Modern Utopia*, an intention that might, with only a little romantic exaggeration, be seen as the moment when *Nineteen Eighty-Four* was conceived. Another book which they loved to read together was Beatrix Potter's *Pigling Bland* (1913). It was really Guiny's book but, as she recalls, though Orwell and she were too old for it, 'we adored it all the same. I remember his reading it to me twice over from beginning to end, to cheer me up one time when I had a cold. And we used to call each other Pigling Bland and Pigwig in moments of frivolity.'[14] As she points out, *Pigling Bland*, with its pigs walking on their hind legs like humans, lies behind *Animal Farm*. *A Modern Utopia* and *Pigling Bland* both turn up much earlier in Orwell's career as a writer. When he was at Eton, Orwell was involved in the publication of the school journals, *The Election Times*, *College Days* and *Bubble and Squeak*. The contributions to these journals are unsigned but one story which can confidently be assigned to Orwell is 'A Peep into the Future', *The Election Times*, No. 4, 3 June 1918 (32).

'A Peep into the Future' looks forward to a time when Science will rule all. The 'Grace' before a meal was 'Science bless us', and after, 'Blessings of Science'; the response was 'Bless her'. The dietary principle in operation was that one got enough to eat but 'not too much or too rich'. This was enshrined in a text signed by the Headmaster: ' "Full stomach, full coffin", Sir Pigling Hill, 1919.' Pigling looks back to Beatrix Potter and Hill to the science student of that name in H. G. Wells's 'A Slip Under the Microscope'; the hungriness to St Cyprian's: in 'Such, Such Were the Joys' Orwell writes of food at the school being 'not only bad, it was insufficient', and the maxim repeated at St Cyprian's was 'it is healthy to get up from a meal feeling as hungry as when you sat down'; the futuristic elements look forward to *Nineteen Eighty-Four*. There is, too, a remarkable ending to the story – remarkable in that it, too, looks forward to Orwell's last novel. Professor Pigling Hill describes women as 'greatly inferior to males both in strength and physical courage', except when fighting for their children. As he does so, a deep voice is heard: 'Ho! har they, indeed?'. A 'mighty woman' was to be seen standing in the arch above the space where the chapel organ had once stood, 'massive hands on her hips, a heavy chin stuck out aggressively', spelt with one 'g'. *The Election Times* was handwritten and Orwell, even in the manuscript of *Nineteen Eighty-Four*, still spelt 'aggressive' with one 'g' (and 'address' with one 'd'). The mighty woman strode up to Pigling Hill, seized him

by the collar and slapped him so hard that he lay motionless on the
ground. The boys gag and bind the Professor and 'The reign of
Science was at an end.' 'The End' is written at the conclusion of
the story (as it is at the end of another attributed to Orwell, 'The
Adventure of the Lost Meat-card'); this was characteristic of Orwell
who so finished off nearly all his books and even some essay col-
lections. This mighty woman who appears out of the blue antici-
pates the singing woman of *Nineteen Eighty-Four*. She is described
as 'a monstrous woman, solid as a Norman pillar, with brawny red
forearms' (IX. 144), and later, Winston Smith hears her singing just
before he and Julia are arrested:

> her thick arms reached up for the line, her powerful mare-like
> buttocks protruded, . . . she was beautiful . . . a woman of fifty,
> blown up to monstrous dimensions by childbearing. . . . The solid,
> contourless body, like a block of granite. . . . (IX, 228)

Orwell was one of those writers whose reading and experience
provided a permanent reservoir upon which he could draw over
remarkably long periods of time. Thus, deep down in the recesses
of his mind when he was preparing notes for his Literary Executor
during the last six months of his life (3727), he recalled that he had
not made an alteration to the text of *Burmese Days* when revising
that book for publication by Penguin Books in 1944. Yet the change
he wanted, 'knelt' for 'sat', *had* been made, but much earlier, when
he had been forced to revise the book after its first publication in
New York so that it would meet British legal objections. The Gollancz
edition of 1935 was, in Orwell's eyes, 'garbled' (and he had no
stronger condemnation for the deliberate marring of what an author wished to say), so he instructed his Literary Executor to ignore
the readings of that edition. His forgetting he had already once
made this change is explicable because he so fiercely rejected the
Gollancz edition that it was to him as if it had not been published.
Despite the novel's convoluted textual history, there remained in
the recesses of his memory, until the very end of his life, the thought
that a single word had to be changed. The word is hardly vital
except in its importance to Orwell, the writer. In the text as revised
in accordance with Orwell's wishes, the passage reads:

> Flory sat in the same pew as these two. . . . 'Shut your eyes and
> count twenty-five,' whispered Ellis as they knelt down, drawing
> a snigger from the policeman. (II.282)

Orwell's capacious memory shows also in his ability to quote from memory, as for his essay on Dickens. As is common to those who do not need to resort to the originals, there are often tell-tale memorial substitutions; the variants are listed in the notes to the Dickens essay (596).

Jacintha Buddicom mentions a number of authors, very different in kind, in whom Orwell was interested and to whom he was introduced at her home. The authors who surface later in his writing, some frequently, include Shakespeare, Dickens, Wells (Orwell would dramatise 'A Slip Under the Microscope' for a broadcast to India, 6 October 1943, 2297), Poe, Charles Reade (Jacintha's name derives from his play, *The Double Marriage*, 1867, based on his novel *White Lies*, 1857; the origin of Guinever's name is also literary but more obviously so), Kipling, E. A. Hornung, R. Austin Freeman, E. F. Benson, M. R. James, Barry Pain, and Harry Graham. From this time also stems Orwell's interest in Richard Garnett's *The Twilight of the Gods* and G. K. Chesterton's *Manalive* (copies of both of which he lent or gave Jacintha) and *The Fairchild Family*.[15]

The text and illustrations to *Eric and Us* (the latter showing the various houses where the Blairs and Buddicoms lived) reveal the delightful side of Orwell's life at that time: bicycle races, French cricket, fishing, shooting, reading, pencil-and-paper and card games, roulette, going to the cinema, making bombs; they all go to show how enjoyable for Orwell was the company of Prosper and Jacintha.

A more significant activity was Jacintha's and Orwell's exchange of poems. A fair amount of Orwell's early juvenilia, as well as that written at St Cyprian's and Eton, has survived, for example, a mystery, 'The Vernon Murders' (27) and a playlet, 'The Man and a Maid' (28), both probably written between 1916 and 1918, the latter possibly intended as a Christmas entertainment. No claims for budding talent can be made for this work but Orwell's two surviving poems for Jacintha, 'The Pagan' (autumn 1918; 33) and a sonnet, 'Our minds are married, but we are too young' (Christmas 1918; 34) are, at the least, touching. Both, with a short poem they jointly composed, 'Friendship and love' (summer 1921; 62), are printed in *Eric and Us*, which also illustrates the draft manuscript of 'The Pagan' (plate 24) and the setting where Orwell wrote his sonnet (plate 28). Orwell's Christmas sonnet for Jacintha starts:

> Our minds are married, but we are too young
> For wedlock by the customs of this age

When parents' homes pen each in separate cage
And only supper-earning songs are sung.

Mabel Fierz thought that Orwell would have liked to have been a poet 'but he felt he wasn't equipped for it'.[16] Nevertheless, he wrote and published poetry until 1943 and a draft of a poem was among his papers at his death.

Whatever may have been lacking in Orwell's home was well supplied by the Buddicoms. He wrote three letters to Jacintha from Burma but she only answered the first, regretting later in life that she had not replied to the others. When he returned from Burma he stayed for a fortnight in Shropshire with Jacintha's Aunt Lilian, Prosper and Guiny, but Jacintha, 'the one he always talked to, was not there'. Jacintha's aunt gave her a very unfavourable report on the new Eric. Aunt Lilian said words to the effect that 'you haven't really missed anything, because he's not at all what he used to be, and I don't think you'd like him very much now'.[17] They never met again but did exchange letters when Orwell was ill at Cranham Sanatorium in 1949; Jacintha did not marry. Although the companionship of the years to 1922 did not continue thereafter, one of Orwell's letters to her in the last year of his life (15 February 1949; *3551*), repeats the private language of their salutation and farewell of thirty years earlier.

ST CYPRIAN'S AND ETON

Orwell left St Cyprian's with bitter memories, but he worked, or was worked, hard enough, and showed sufficient native ability to win a King's Scholarship. At Eton he did little solid work and there was no question of his going to Oxford or Cambridge even had his parents been able to afford that. What he did do at both schools was write. There is a certain irony, in view of his dislike of St Cyprian's and his enjoyment of his time at Eton, that his two poems written at his preparatory school were disciplined and were published in a commercial newspaper, whereas his stories and doggerel written at Eton were jejeune, often parodies, and published in private journals. At St Cyprian's, Orwell and Cyril Connolly both wrote poetry and criticised each other's work. The poems, as Connolly says, were often derivative (which is hardly surprising) of Stevenson, Longfellow, or Connolly's favourite, Robert Service.[18]

At the end of the twentieth century, it is easy to smile at the naive patriotism of his two St Cyprian poems but his contemporaries thought well enough of them. *The Henley and South Oxfordshire Standard* was no *Art and Letters* or *Egoist*, and the selection of Orwell's first poem, 'Awake! Young Men of England' (23) was prompted by Mrs Vaughan Wilkes, the headmistress of St Cyprian's, but she had a good eye for those with talent as her school's record in winning scholarships to public schools showed. Though not then the critic he was to become, Cyril Connolly showed enthusiasm rather than envy for 'Kitchener' (24):

Who follows in his steps no danger shuns,
Nor stoops to conquer by a shameful deed,
An honest and unselfish race he runs,
    From fear and malice freed.

Connolly wrote home that Blair 'did a very good poem, which he sent to his local paper where they took it' (*24.1*). Orwell was then just 13 and it is significant that whereas his first poem had been submitted by Mrs Wilkes, he was confident enough to submit the second one himself. It might also just be significant that it was published a column or two away from a report on the problems posed by tramps.

Orwell maintained he did not exert himself in the classroom at Eton, but as his friend from BBC days, Laurence Brander, pointed out, 'It should be noted that his slacking was comparative. He held his place half-way up a form of scholarship boys.'[19] He was active in what did engage his attention – the Wall Game and football 'in the field', and in the production of school periodicals, especially *The Election Times, Bubble and Squeak* and *College Days* (of which he was a successful Business Manager). It is not possible to be certain precisely what he wrote but his role as Business Manager indicates that he was, with the editor for Nos 3, 4, and 5, Dennis King-Farlow, one of the two leading lights who got the various issues off the ground. Three things can be said. Many of the items reasonably attributable to Orwell are parodies: 'The White Man's Burden' (42; after Kipling); parodies of 'La Belle Dame Sans Merci' (44) and 'The Ancient Mariner' (55); 'The Photographer' (50; after 'The Burial of Sir John Moore at Corunna'); 'The Wounded Cricketer' (51; subtitled 'Not Walt Whitman'); 'Wall Game' (40; after Kipling's 'If'); and 'A Summer Idyll' (46; probably after Zane Gray).

Secondly, on the debit side, the frequent resort to parody suggests Orwell needed something to prompt his pen. That characteristic was to be apparent throughout his career as a writer. As a schoolboy it was the literature he read that served as a source of inspiration; in later life he would draw heavily on autobiographical experience to an extent that sometimes makes it difficult to tell what is fact and what is fiction. Indeed, it might be claimed that he brought writing on the fictional-factual edge to a high art. However, one of the best contributions which can be attributed to Orwell, 'Eton Master's Strike' (41), is not a parody. It springs from one of those hoped-for incidents beloved of boarding-school boys: a rebellion by the masters.

Thirdly, but on the credit side, it is possible to see in these contributions the beginnings of Orwell's mordant wit, that sardonic humour that was so often mistaken by those at whom it was directed. Years later, his colleague at the BBC, John Morris, found that humour difficult to accept so that each always seemed to irritate the other.[20] In these parodies can be seen the beginnings of that Orwellian wit which would flower in the ironical Fairy Story *Animal Farm* and the bitter satire of his last novel. Although Orwell's humour could be sharp, David Astor, the distinguished editor of *The Observer* (and for whom Orwell wrote), told me that, when he was depressed, he would seek out Orwell because Orwell's humour so cheered him up[21] – a reaction to Orwellian humour that may surprise some people brought up only on *Nineteen Eighty-Four*.

If, relatively speaking, a great deal of attention has been paid here to Orwell's early years, the justification is to be found in what Orwell himself wrote in 'Why I Write' when explaining why he had given 'all this background information': 'I do not think one can assess a writer's motives without knowing something of his early development. His subject-matter will be determined by the age he lives in . . . but before he ever begins to write he will have acquired an emotional attitude from which he will never completely escape' (CEJL, i.25).

2

Foreign Fields

BURMA DAYS

Orwell left Eton in December 1921. On 7 April 1922 he applied to join the Indian Imperial Police and to compete in the 1922 examination. In January 1922 he enrolled at a crammer's in Southwold to prepare for the examination. Orwell came seventh out of 29 successful candidates, his best marks in the seven papers being (out of 2000): Latin 1782; Greek 1703; English 1372; and French 1256. He only just passed the horseriding test with 104 marks out of 200 (100 being the pass mark).

The value of Latin, Greek and French might seem remote from the needs of a policeman in Burma, Orwell's choice of where he would serve. However, it showed he had one ability that he was able to turn to good use in Burma, France and Spain: a capacity to learn languages. He learned Burmese and Hindustani and even mastered a particularly difficult language, Shaw-Karen. One incentive to do this was the 1000-rupee bonus given for each examination passed. He had eight different postings in Burma, the last being at Katha, from 23 December 1926 until he left Burma on 12 July 1927, when he took home-leave of five months and 20 days.[1]

One of the most interesting writers on Orwell in Burma is Professor Maung Htin Aung, onetime Professor of English at Rangoon University, the University's Honorary Vice-Chancellor, and his country's Ambassador to Ceylon in 1958. In 'Orwell and the Burma Police' he shows that, in his first year at the Training School, Mandalay, Orwell was paid £23 a month plus £5 Burma allowance and £9 overseas pay: £37 a month or £444 a year. This, as Maung Htin Aung points out, compared very favourably with the pay of locally-recruited men: 'Constable £1, Cadet £5, Inspector £10, all without allowances'. The rationale for this difference in treatment of local and 'heaven-borns' (as the British were described) would quickly have struck Orwell. By 1925 his pay would have risen to £58 a month – £696 a year. Only in 1943, when he joined the BBC and was paid £640 a year, would he approach anything like his

15

Police salary. In his five years' service he would have earned about £3000 plus language bonuses. Maung Htin Aung describes Orwell as 'an efficient police officer'; it is certain, he says, that the tiger-hunt described in *Burmese Days* and the shooting of an elephant are based on experience; and that Orwell did witness a hanging, probably at Moulmein jail (where he served from 19 April 1926 until he was transferred to Katha).

Maung Htin Aung's 'George Orwell and Burma' includes a particularly important description of an incident in November 1924, when Orwell was serving at Twante, about 40 miles south-east of Rangoon. Orwell was coming down the steps of Pagoda Road Railway Station. A group of schoolboys was fooling and one bumped into Orwell and sent him flying down the stairs. Orwell struck the boy on the back with his heavy cane. The schoolboys protested and some undergraduates of University College, Rangoon, joined Orwell in his first-class carriage – 'in Burma, unlike India, first-class carriages were never taboo to natives'. They argued until the train reached Mission Road Station, where the undergraduates got out. One of those undergraduates was Maung Htin Aung himself, then in his first year at the College. Two things arise from this incident. First, and most obvious, is that it serves as the basis for Orwell's fiction: in *Burmese Days*, Ellis strikes a boy across the eyes with a cane and that leads to a full-scale riot (II.251–66). More important than Orwell's response as a writer was his reaction in the railway carriage: argument. Maung Htin Aung also shows that the introduction of senior Burmese to European clubs – a major cause of controversy in *Burmese Days* – was a live issue at that time. His father, U Pein, a district magistrate, was, in 1923, the first Burmese to become a member of such a club. He went only once a month 'and always considered it an unpleasant social duty'.[2]

When Orwell arrived in Burma he was imbued with the Spirit of Empire, of imperialism. Although Connolly says in *Enemies of Promise* that Orwell was 'an intellectual and not a parrot for he thought for himself', and that he 'rejected not only St Wulfric's' – Connolly's pseudonym for St Cyprian's – 'but the war, the Empire, Kipling, Sussex, and Character',[3] he exaggerates, although Orwell may have spoken in that manner. In any case, Orwell's indoctrination in imperialism at St Cyprian's was of such a strength that it was not shaken off until Orwell experienced, and practised, imperialism in action in Burma. As Connolly put it, St Cyprian's demanded stoic fortitude, its message was 'Character, character,

character', 'the path of duty was the way to glory' (from Tennyson's 'Ode on the Death of the Duke of Wellington'), the poetry of Kipling and Newbolt ('Admirals All', 'Drake's Drum', 'The Fighting Téméraire', 'Vitaï Lampada'), and preparation for a 'vocation in India, Burma, Nigeria, and the Sudan, administering with Roman justice those natives for whom the final profligate overflow of Wulfrician character was all the time predestined'.[4]

I should here, I hope without self-indulgence, like to offer a personal diversion. My own education at the ages of 8 and 9 was similar in this respect to Orwell's at St Cyprian's, twenty or so years earlier. I can attest to the initial impact of a fiercely imperialist education and, however consciously rejected, its permanent, subliminal effects. Tags like 'There's always to be seen/ A little strip of green/ On the left of the thin red line' (a reference to the Rifle Brigade) refuse to leave my memory. And the incredibly blinkered, unquestioning, technique of learning lasts for ever, it seems. Thus, not only did we learn dates of the English monarchs by rote, but the method of testing was recitation at speed: the fastest accurate repetition gained top marks. No better example of the immediate and long-lasting limitations of this technique was to be found in our introduction to Russian history and geography. Although the events of 1917 had taken place only eighteen years earlier, they were not even mentioned. They came to me, fresh and coincidentally, only when I read *Crime and Punishment* when I was 14 or 15. (As for Orwell and his fellows, the limitations of the teaching method and syllabus were compensated for to a large extent by an encouragement and opportunity to read widely and imaginatively.) What Russia (*pace* the USSR) meant to me in 1935 was a (vain) attempt to recall the stations on the Trans-Siberian Railway, from Leningrad to Vladivostock. Again, what mattered was how fast one could recite these tongue-twisting names. The only stretch I can now recall is the rather musical 'Omsk, branches to Tomsk and Semipalatinsk'. The true limitation of this technique was that the rhyming-off was all-sufficient. I never looked up this railway until I came to think of Orwell and imperialism. When I did, I only then discovered that the Trans-Siberian Railway began at Moscow, not Leningrad, and that, so far as I can tell from my atlas, the branch to Tomsk does not even go from Omsk. Thus, not only was the recitation of names itself pointless, but it inhibited genuine inquiry and even inculcated false information. I cannot believe, however much Orwell rejected imperialism (as he certainly did), that elements of St Cyprian's did not similarly linger on in his subconscious throughout his life. Reference to a single poem, a favourite in preparatory schools of the period, will illustrate the pervasive influence of such an education.

In the autumn 1940 issue of *Folios of New Writing*, Orwell concluded his essay, 'My Country Right or Left' (CEJL, i.587–92) by comparing John Cornford's poem, 'Before the Storming of Huesca', written just before he was killed in Spain, with Sir Henry Newbolt's 'There's a breathless hush in the Close tonight' ('Vitaï Lampada'), one of *the* most memorised of poems in the 1920s and 1930s. The emotional content of the two poems is almost exactly the same, Orwell says. 'The young Communist who died heroically in the International Brigade was public school to the core. He had changed his allegiance but not his emotions.' This, he concludes, shows how one kind of loyalty can be transmuted into another, and 'the spiritual need for patriotism and the military virtues' for which 'the boiled rabbits of the Left' can find no substitute. Then, in a review of Edmund Blunden's *Cricket Country* (20 April 1944, 2455), he refers again to Newbolt and, as the context is cricket, he must have had in mind 'Vitaï Lampada' with its concluding line, 'Play up! play up! and play the game!' Not everyone who learned 'Vitaï Lampada' did 'play the game' in its broadest sense, but it can not only be demonstrated that Orwell sympathetically retained some elements of his St Cyprian's education, reject though he did the principle of imperialism, it can surely be claimed that, with his passion for 'decency' in social behaviour, he put into the best practice that last line of Newbolt's old warhorse.[5]

Whatever of imperialism Orwell brought to Burma, as he says in *The Road to Wigan Pier*, by the end of his five years in the Indian Police, 'I hated the imperialism I was serving with a bitterness which I probably cannot make clear' (V.134). Later he says: 'I watched a man hanged once; it seemed to me worse than a thousand murders. I never went into a jail without feeling (most visitors to jails feel the same) that my place was on the other side of the bars' (V.136–7). Note the touch of generosity in the aside, 'most visitors to jails feel the same'; Orwell makes no claim that such a response is peculiar to him. He was later to confess that he had bullied subordinates. All this haunted him intolerably: 'I was conscious of an immense weight of guilt that I had to expiate.' Once again he reverts to his sense of failure: 'At that time failure seemed to me to be the only virtue'; success, because it reinforced imperialism, seemed 'spiritually ugly, a species of bullying' (V.138). The short-term result was the writing of *Burmese Days* and the essays, 'A Hanging' and 'Shooting an Elephant'. Here attention might usefully be paid to what were to prove Orwell's first attempts to make himself a professional writer. These are six poems, a scenario and dialogues from an untitled play, and 19 pages of sketches that seem to be preliminaries for *Burmese Days*. (Some scholars believe these sketches are an early draft of *Burmese Days*. Though Flory features in them, if they are from a draft it must be a very early, tentative state of the novel.)

It is not possible to date this material precisely. He probably wrote most or all of it in Burma or on the ship on the way home, but it is possible he wrote some items immediately on his return. Some of the paper used was Burma Government paper stock. This is so unpleasant that it is unlikely that anyone as well-paid as Orwell would bother to carry with him a stock upon which to write aboard ship (where decent paper is usually freely available to passengers) or in England. The poems were probably written in Burma. One might have been inspired by Jacintha Buddicom (64). The first and last of the five stanzas read:

My love and I walked in the dark
Of many a scented night in June;
My love and I did oft remark
How yellow was the waning moon,
How yellow was the moon.

The suns and moons are much the same,
But all their golden charms are fled,
And she and I look back with shame
To think of all the things we said,
The foolish things we said.

One poem is comic ('Brush your teeth up and down, brother,' 68), another is a 'Romance' (65):

When I was young and had no sense,
In far off Mandalay
I lost my heart to a Burmese girl
As lovely as the day.

She turns out to be a prostitute. (Orwell served in Mandalay from 27 November 1922 until he was posted to Maymyo a year later and again from 17 December 1923 for five weeks.) The most interesting poem is 'The Lesser Evil' (69). In this Orwell adopts the persona of a parson who visits 'the house of sin'. The first and last of the eight stanzas are:

> Empty as death and slow as pain
> The days went by on leaden feet;
> And parson's week had come again
> As I walked down the little street.

> The woman waited for me there
> As down the little street I trod;
> And musing upon her oily hair,
> I turned into the house of God.

A 'parson's week' is from a Monday to a Saturday in the following week (thirteen days inclusive), when a parson takes the intervening Sunday as a holiday. The penultimate line requires 'on', not 'upon', but though Orwell revised the poem he did not change this word. He did rewrite stanzas four and five and the original and revised versions show Orwell's development. As first written, these stanzas read:

> The woman oiled her hair of coal,
> She had no other occupation.
> She swore she loved me as her soul,
> She had no other conversation.

> The only thing that woman knew
> Was getting money out of men.
> Each time she swore she loved me true
> She struck me for another ten.

These became:

> The house of sin was dark and mean,
> With dying flowers round the door;
> They spat their betel juice between
> The rotten bamboos of the floor.

> Why did I come, the woman cried,
> So seldom to her beds of ease?

When I was not, her spirit died,
And would I give her ten rupees.

Orwell's idea of his being a parson would be taken up again in 1935 in the well-known poem that he published later as the conclusion to 'Why I Write': 'A happy vicar I might have been'. The 'parson' element in Orwell particularly struck Laurence Brander. In his study of Orwell, written shortly after Orwell's death, he several times describes Orwell as 'a preacher', or preaching, most strikingly in the paragraph that concludes his discussion of *The Road to Wigan Pier*.[6] The poems written in Burma, and Orwell's continuing occasionally to publish poetry until 'Memories of the Blitz', early in 1944 (2409), show how keen he was, like Gordon Comstock of *Keep the Aspidistra Flying*, to be a poet.[7]

There are five prose passages which can all be related to *Burmese Days* (71–5). They are written on a variety of papers. Some are on Government of Burma paper; one on paper that has no markings and cannot be identified; another is watermarked 'Aviemore', a paper produced from 1922; and a typed copy of one item (in manuscript on Burma paper) is watermarked 'British Emblem', a paper first available in 1928 (or possibly a few months earlier). Although the typing must have been done after Orwell returned to England, what was typed may well have been written in Burma. The items cannot be shaped into a recognisable sequence. Although Flory and the Lackersteens appear, and Kyauktada where they lived, there is no storyline relationship to *Burmese Days*. John Flory's epitaph (71), in which he ponders where he will be buried, has been suggested as being intended as the work of a man in prison, possibly awaiting execution.[8] It is more likely that Flory is dying in the jungle, among those who could not form the letters for his epitaph. The use of the place-name Nyaunglebin (not Nyauglbiu as it is sometimes reproduced), in another extract, 'An Incident in Rangoon' (74), in which Flory's office-assistant and his friend spend a weekend gambling, suggests not prison but the jungle; it means 'Four Banyan Trees' and is a common name for a Burmese village. Flory's end is thus akin to what might have been Mr Lackersteen's fate had not his wife limited his intake of alcohol and warded off women. To that extent these may be seen as trial runs for *Burmese Days*, but a more interesting possibility is that they formed the basis for one of the two novels Orwell wrote in Paris but destroyed.

Two of the items, 72 and 73, are extracts from John Flory's autobiography and are in the first person. The first begins, 'I said at the end of the last chapter that I was trying to make love to Mrs Lackersteen, although Lackersteen was my best friend, and although I liked him much better than I liked his wife.' The opening indicates that the extract was once part of a longer text but its subject matter, despite the names, is quite different from that of *Burmese Days*. The nearest Flory comes to thinking of love in connection with the Mrs Lackersteen of the novel is when he ponders on the possibility of finding someone who will share his life in Burma – 'but really share it, share his inner, secret life, carry away from Burma the same memories as he carried. . . . A friend. Or a wife? The quite impossible she. Someone like Mrs Lackersteen, for instance?' (II.72–3). It will be *Miss* Lackersteen, Mrs Lackersteen's niece, Elizabeth, whom Flory will ineffectually and fatally woo.

The second of these extracts starts, 'I was born in Buckinghamshire in 1890', the county, incidentally, in which the paper used for the typed version was manufactured by Thomas and Green Ltd. The writer goes on to say that his father was an Indian civil servant who had married his mother in 1882. He was sent to Burma in 1883 and the wife and children went back to England in 1888. There is a succession of births and a death culminating in the writer's birth following his father's return to England on home leave in 1889. Although put back a few years, there are slight similarities to the Blair family's experience but the father of the story retires in 1903 and dies suddenly in 1908: Orwell was born in 1903 and Avril in 1908, but Orwell's father retired in 1912 and died in 1939. There is, possibly, a loose family significance in the sentence: 'I saw my father twice in the next ten years, for about six months at a time.' Orwell saw his father twice from 1903 until 1912, for the first year of his life and then for three months in 1907.

'An Incident in Rangoon' (74), could be a free-standing short story. Its opening is of interest: 'Here for awhile I abandon autobiography and commence fiction writer.' This is a stylistic device that Orwell would adopt later in his writing career, without his being so specific as to his intention.

Only two pages of the last item of this sequence, an extract from 'A Rebuke to the Author, John Flory' (75), survive. The rebuke is a warning to Flory not to get entangled with a Eurasian girl, however respectable. The passage concludes with Flory's superior saying to him:

'Always remember, my boy, that we must think of others before ourselves. Esprit de corps! Never forget it. Esprit de Corps! All white men hang together. That's all. Run along, now. Be a good boy, eh?'

It might have been the headmaster of St Cyprian's or Mrs Wilkes speaking.

Finally, when in Burma, Orwell made another attempt to write a play (76). The text is handwritten on Government of Burma paper, is incomplete, and lacks a title. It has an indirect connection with *Burmese Days*. Orwell gives a patent medicine the name 'Pereira'; when, for Gollancz, he had to substitute a name for 'Walters' in the novel, he chose 'Pereira' (II.23/1). What survives is a scenario for scenes one and two (four pages) and seven pages of dialogue from these scenes. Francis and Lucy Stone are in despair. (Orwell would use the surname, 'Stone', for the church schoolteacher in *A Clergyman's Daughter*.) Their four-year-old child needs an operation; that will cost a hundred guineas (roughly £4–5000 today) and they have no money, only debts. Then Stone is offered a well-paid job writing advertisements, the kind of work Gordon Comstock will so abhor in *Keep the Aspidistra Flying*. In the scenario the advertisements are said to be for Pereira's Salvation Balm, but in the dialogue this is changed to Pereira's Surefire Lung Balm, possibly prompted by Orwell's persistent bronchial weakness. This he refuses to do because he knows the medicine to be a swindle. When his wife protests he says she might as properly work as a prostitute to raise money. The second scene, which the scenario says is to be mainly in blank verse (but which is mainly in prose in the dialogue surviving), is set in a prison. The cast is made up of Stone, The Christian, The Poet, The Poet's Wife, and The Jailor, a particularly violent character. The sounds of revolution can be heard off-stage; prisoners are being executed in the next cell. The plotting and characterisation are stilted and possibly influenced by Expressionist drama. It is not difficult to see why Orwell abandoned writing this play but he retained his interest in writing drama. He wrote *King Charles II* (154), to be performed by his pupils at The Hawthorns at Christmas 1932 (and this appears as the play, *Charles I*, that Dorothy produces in *A Clergyman's Daughter*). Later Orwell was to show much interest in 'featurised dialogues', as he called them, when at the BBC in the early forties, and, when he left the BBC, he not only adapted *Animal Farm* for radio in 1947, but wrote a version of *Little Red Riding Hood* for Children's Hour, and *The Voyage of the Beagle* for the Home Service, both in 1946.

Orwell left Burma on leave on 12 July 1927, leaving the ship at Marseilles and making the rest of the journey overland through France. He returned to England fiercely anti-imperialist and anti-racist; as he put it in *The Road to Wigan Pier*, 'I hated the imperialism I was serving with a bitterness which I probably cannot make clear' (V.134). He had matured, if not in the way he might have chosen, and he had made a number of attempts to turn himself into a writer. So keen was he to pursue a future as a writer that he resigned his commission earlier than he need, sacrificing almost £140 – perhaps the equivalent of about £5500 in early 1990s values.[9] Although he had several hard years ahead of him, he was now able to begin the course of action, in living and writing, that would lead to his becoming a writer of worldwide renown. Consciousness of Burma never left him. He was always ready to take up the cudgels on behalf of its (and India's) independence, and at his death he was writing a novella, 'A Smoking-Room Story' (3721), which took Burma for its setting.

DAYS IN LONDON AND PARIS

When he returned from Burma, Orwell stayed for a while with Jacintha Buddicom's Aunt Lilian in Shropshire and spent September with his family in Cornwall. He there decided not to return to Burma and left the Indian Imperial Police on 1 January 1928. In the autumn of 1927 he started his series of expeditions into the East End of London and then, at an unknown date in the spring of 1928, he went to Paris to concentrate on writing.

Obviously to almost any writer, and especially to Orwell, all experience is grist to the mill. For Orwell, once he had left Burma and determined to make himself a writer, the most significant experiences in his life were his plunge into 'the lower depths' in England and Paris, the journeys to the north of England in 1936 and to Spain in 1937, and perhaps the BBC years, 1941–43, the significance of which has been underrated. The biographies of Stansky and Abrahams (to 1937), Crick and Shelden, and the many studies and memoirs, more than adequately give an account of Orwell's life and so having, it is hoped, established 'what made him', what now follows will by and large eschew the strictly biographical except where it is different from, or not found in, earlier and more detailed accounts.

Orwell was able to live cheaply in Paris. He had relatives there: his favourite Aunt Nellie Limouzin (who may have helped him find his room at 6 Rue du Pot de Fer, Paris V)[10] and her husband, the Esperantist, Eugène Adam. He seems not to have sponged on them though he did visit them. Louis Bannier, who had (like Adam) been involved in the October Revolution in Petrograd in 1917, and who had founded with Adam the Workers' Esperanto Association of the World in Prague in 1922, met Orwell at the Adams's. Orwell argued 'seriously and noisily with his uncle'. Orwell praised the Revolution and the communist system, which Adam had abandoned several years earlier following a return visit he had made to the Soviet Union, finding, instead of socialism, 'a future prison. . . . So they were at each other's throats, despite the presence of the aunt.' Bannier's description of Orwell's support for communism in 1928 tallies with Jack Branthwaite's memories of Orwell in Spain in 1937. Although the one American in Orwell's group, Harry Milton (with whom Orwell 'spent hours discussing politics') thought Orwell was 'politically virginal', Branthwaite, a miner, described Orwell as 'leaning slightly towards the communists when I first met him'. Orwell 'had no respect for the Esperanto movement', according to Bannier.[11] Later, in 'New Words', Orwell seems to have shifted his attitude towards the creation of a new language. He there says that a 'thinking person' would argue that 'any *made-up* language must be characterless and lifeless' and would give Esperanto as an example. It would be maintained that 'The whole meaning of a word is in its slowly-acquired associations.' However, says Orwell, this is no more than a common response whenever it is suggested that anything be changed: it is 'a long-winded way of saying that what is must be'. He concludes: when 'our knowledge, the complication of our lives and therefore . . . our minds, develop so fast' it is curious that language 'should scarcely stir. For this reason I think that the deliberate invention of words is at least worth thinking over' (CEJL, ii.22,27; probably written February–April 1940, see *605*). Shortly after his return from Paris, Orwell's fascination with words is perfectly characterised in Chapter XXXII of *Down and Out in Paris and London*. There, Orwell steps aside from the autobiographical and fictional modes he has been adopting and lectures the reader: 'I want to put in some notes' – itself, in this context, a curious form of expression – 'as short as possible on London slang and swearing' (I.176).

Orwell's tailor's records show that he went to Paris well dressed, and there are little hints that he lived pleasantly, at least until his savings ran out (or were stolen) and he took on work as a *plongeur*. The enforced nature of this plunge into the lower depths for the last ten weeks of his stay of some 21 months in Paris suggests that Orwell had not planned such an experience. There is no doubt he was sometimes famished. Chapter VII of *Down and Out* was annotated by Orwell in the copy he gave Brenda Salkeld, 'This all happened': I.36 and 51–3 give a vivid impression of the pangs of hunger he experienced and their effects. In *Down and Out*, Orwell describes how his Russian friend, Boris, liked the Closerie des Lilas café in Montparnasse – not then an expensive restaurant – 'simply because the statue of Marshal Ney stands outside it' and he liked anything to do with soldiers (I.20). Writing from Hairmyres Hospital, Glasgow, on 24 March 1948, to Celia Kirwan who was then in Paris (3370), Orwell asked if Ney's statute was 'back outside the Closerie des Lilas – but I dare say the Germans melted him down to get the bronze'. Was this not so much Boris's as Orwell's favourite restaurant? And is it the origin of the Chestnut Tree Café of *Nineteen Eighty-Four*? The Closerie des Lilas in and before Orwell's time was much frequented by writers and artists – Mallarmé, Valéry, Gide, Sartre, Braque, Modigliani, Hemingway – and thus a place Orwell might have enjoyed. It also provides a direct link with *Nineteen Eighty-Four*. At the Chestnut Tree, the former revolutionaries, Jones, Aaronson, and Rutherford, while away the time before they will be arrested for the last time, drinking gin and with a chessboard in front of them 'but no game started' (IX.80). It was at the Closerie des Lilas that Lenin and Trotsky had played chess together.

Most of what Orwell wrote in Paris has not survived and what is left is not particularly distinguished. Curiously, however, it provides an epitome of much that was to concern him for the rest of his life. In his Introduction to *La Vache Enragée* (1935), the French translation of *Down and Out*, Orwell says, 'In the spring of 1928 I set off for Paris so as to live cheaply while writing two novels' (CEJL, i.137), and in his introduction to the Ukrainian edition of *Animal Farm* he says he 'wrote short stories and novels that nobody would print (I have since destroyed them all)' (VIII.110). There may have been only one novel; writing to Michael Meyer, 12 March 1949 (CEJL, iv.541), he said, 'I simply destroyed my first novel after unsuccessfully submitting it to one publisher for which I am rather sorry now.'

One story, inexpertly typed in the manner of a tyro, but showing Orwell's typewriting characteristics, survives, seemingly from this period. It is simply headed 'Short Story' (78). It tells of a young man who contrives to win the affection of a woman of 'astounding ugliness' – Orwell first wrote 'complete absence of charm' – telling her, 'with perfect truth', that he 'worshipped the very ground she walked on and the very jewels she wore'. The story tells how he disentangles himself from a mistress, who lives in poor and squalid surroundings (perhaps a precursor to 'the woman in the basement kitchen' of *Nineteen Eighty-Four*, IX.67–8), before he can marry the rich but ugly woman. He goes to break with his mistress but as he leaves her house, he runs into his brother-in-law-to-be, who sees the mistress. The story, and the 'moral', turn on the fact that his future relative believes him to have been visiting a prostitute in a brothel, not a mistress. He happily accepts that liaison: a prostitute is acceptable, but not a mistress and therefore the marriage can go ahead. The final twist to what is not a very well-told tale, is given in the painfully ironic last sentence: 'So [my brother-in-law's] good opinion of me was restored, and I was married, and (my wife dying early) lived happily ever afterwards.' What points to Orwell's fiction writing is not the story itself but a curious parenthetical note beneath the title: 'This never happened to me, but it would have if I had had the chance.' This seems to point to Orwell's capacity for writing on that narrow edge that separates fact and fiction, the edge which would distinguish elements of his first book, *Down and Out in Paris and London*.

When in Paris, Orwell wrote a number of stories. These were commented upon shortly after Orwell left the Hôpital Cochin by an American literary agent, L. I. Bailey of the McClure Newspaper Syndicate (77). The stories were, 'The Sea God', 'The Petition Crown', and 'The Man in Kid Gloves'. Bailey thought the first two had too much sex in them; the second showed 'very good powers of description', but there was too much of it; and the third was 'an extremely clever story ... and strikes a crisp note'. He tried, without success, to place it. All have disappeared.

Orwell wrote a number of items for minor, left-wing, journals. Some, such as a 'ballade' which the editor found 'extrêmement amusante,' and an article on 'les tendances du roman Anglais contemporain', do not seem to have been published, but he was more successful with two articles for *Monde* (edited by Henri Barbusse, a Communist, the author of an important Great War book

Under Fire, whom Orwell in a 1936 review of *The Novel Today* (CEJL, i.289) castigated for maintaining that a novel about bourgeois characters cannot for that reason be a good novel), and four for *Le Progrès Civique*. All were translated into French on Orwell's behalf and the English versions, printed for the first time in the *Complete Works*, have had to be cast back from the French. Those for *Monde* (not related to *Le Monde*) were 'Censorship in England', 6 October 1928 (*79*), and 'John Galsworthy', 23 March 1929 (*85*). It is not known if he was paid for these articles. For *Le Progrès Civique*, Orwell wrote a series of three articles on the plight of British workers; these were published on 29 December 1928, 5 and 12 January 1929 (*82, 83,* and *84*). The English titles supplied for the articles in the new edition are 'Unemployment'; 'A Day in the Life of a Tramp' (in effect, a version of his essay, 'The Spike', CEJL, i.58–65); and 'Beggars in London'. They are based on Orwell's experiences tramping in the months between his return from Burma and his departure for Paris. The articles are factual and direct, though the practice of breaking up the text into a multitude of short paragraphs in *Le Progrès Civique* is contrary to Orwell's style. So marked is the contrast between his long paragraphs when writing newsletters for the BBC during the war and the ultra-short paragraphs of his colleagues, that it can be a useful tool when distinguishing his work from that of others. *Le Progrès Civique* then published on 4 May 1929, 'How a Nation is Exploited: The British Empire in Burma' (*86*). Orwell was paid the regular rate of 75 francs per page for his articles and for each he earned 225 francs, a total of about £7.5s. in the English money of that time. Alok Rai has remarked that these Paris articles 'are characterised by a kind of brash and uncomplicated socialism which is not normally associated with Orwell. Thus we are informed that "Unemployment is a sub-product of capitalism" and that the worker must continue to "suffer until there is a radical change in the actual economic situation. . . . a revolution is not far distant".' Rai is correct, I think, in suggesting that this 'unfamiliar rhetoric' is, as much as anything, an indicator of the left-wing circles in which Orwell moved in Paris (though he does not mention Adam and Bannier).[12]

Orwell's association with France and her literature went beyond the time he spent in France. In *Keep the Aspidistra Flying*, Orwell mentions Villon on pp. 21 and 31 and quotes, slightly inaccurately, from Villon's *Le Testament* (line 1263) on p. 187. He evidently possessed a copy of Villon's poetry (and its associations with poverty doubtless appealed to him). This was an edition that included

'Poésies attribuées à Villon', possibly that edited by Pierre Jannet, with an introduction by Gautier, many times reprinted in the nineteenth century. This is the source of the rondel Gordon Comstock quotes to Rosemary in *Keep the Aspidistra Flying* when he is trying to persuade her to have intercourse (IV.123). The poem is, presumably, intended to suggest, rather than state openly, what Gordon has in mind. The passage given in the novel does not, as it happens, make this at all clear but the full poem is more explicit. It looks as if the poem was cut in the course of the novel's internal 'house censorship' (see below, pp. 58–60).[13]

One of Orwell's earliest reviews, published in December 1930, was of a book on the French penal settlement at Cayenne (*101*). This started a life-long interest in prison literature that bore curious fruit. When organising broadcasts to India during the war, he included programmes on prison literature at the very time the British had imprisoned India's future leaders. This was a very strange exercise in war propaganda, especially as Orwell told the broadcaster he had engaged, Reg Reynolds, that this was something he was 'particularly anxious to put across in India so far as it is possible' (*1136*). In May 1932, he reviewed Curtius's *The Civilization of France* (*125*) and reviews of Baudelaire (whom he quotes twice, in French, without mentioning his name, in *Keep the Aspidistra Flying*, IV.21 and 115), Mallarmé, Stendhal, and Balzac, followed. He wrote about French politicians – twice about De Gaulle and, in sharp contrast, on Henri Béraud and the Fascist weekly, *Gringoire*. A major influence on *Nineteen Eighty-Four* was his reading of the French version of Zamyatin's *We (Nous Autres)*, which he reviewed at length early in 1946 (CEJL, iv.95–9). Before and after the war he corresponded, usually in French, with Yvonne Davet, André Gide's secretary, and they exchanged left-wing journals. It was she who translated *Homage to Catalonia* into French. Orwell also translated Anatole France's *Crainquebille*, and turned it into a radio play which the BBC broadcast to India in 1943 (*2230*). Finally, among Orwell's five-hundred-or-so books at his death were some three dozen in French.

While in Paris, Orwell had one success in England. *G.K.'s Weekly* (G. K. being G. K. Chesterton) published 'A Farthing Newspaper' on 29 December 1928. The newspaper in question was *L'Ami du Peuple*, a nationalist, anti-left journal published by the wealthy industrialist, François Coty, better known for the perfumery business to which he gave his name. Orwell does not mention the irony implicit in the paper's title. The original *L'Ami du Peuple* was an inflammatory radical paper edited by Jean-Paul Marat at the time of the French Revolution. In August 1929, just before he started his stint as a dishwasher, he sent an article to Middleton Murry's *The New Adelphi* which was almost certainly the original of 'The Spike'.[14] Encouragement by *The Adelphi* after his return to England, especially in the persons of Max Plowman and Sir Richard Rees, enabled him to develop the fledgling talent revealed in his Paris articles. What is remarkable about those articles is that they encapsulate the interests that were to make Orwell famous as an essayist and journalist: his concern with those of the underclass, his brand of independent socialism, his literary and social criticism, his anti-imperialism, and his interest in popular culture.

DOWN AND OUT: FINANCIAL RETURNS

In the three years after Orwell returned from Paris just before Christmas 1929, he went tramping and lived with down-and-outs; wrote reviews for *The Adelphi*; his first important articles were published: 'The Spike', April 1931 (CEJL, i.58–66), 'A Hanging', August 1931 (CEJL, i.66–71), 'Hop-Picking', 17 October 1931 (*116*), and 'Common Lodging Houses', 3 September 1932 (CEJL, i.121–4); taught at The Hawthorns, a fourth-rate private school; wrote and rewrote what was to be published as *Down and Out in Paris and London*; and, in the autumn of 1931, made a start on *Burmese Days*. For part of the time he lived with his parents at Southwold. His new course of life perplexed and distressed them, especially his father. His experiences in Burma, tramping, and hop-picking, provided material for his articles; his hop-picking, teaching, and a failed attempt 'to know about prison from the inside' – he spent no more than a night in police cells after deliberately getting himself arrested for being drunk and disorderly[15] – were worked into *A Clergyman's Daughter* and *Keep the Aspidistra Flying*. The night in the cells was written up as 'Clink', August 1932 (CEJL, i.109–19), but this was not published in his lifetime. In *A Clergyman's Daughter*, Dorothy suffers torments making armour with glue and brown paper (III.84, 296–7) for the production of her play, *Charles I*. This is based on Orwell's experience in producing the school play he wrote at The Hawthorns, *Charles II* (see below, pp. 63–4). In a typically self-deprecatory style he wrote to his agent, Leonard Moore on 23 December 1932 (CEJL, i.134), 'The miserable school play over which

I had wasted so much time went off not badly.' Despite himself, Orwell may have enjoyed writing and producing his little play. Most of the reviews were on literary subjects, but there were pointers to his other concerns, such as the review of Karl Bartz's *The Horrors of Cayenne* (see above, p. 29). Lionel Britton's *Hunger and Love* (105) he described as 'a kind of monologue on poverty', a description that might be applied to *Keep the Aspidistra Flying*. He took up the subject of hanging again in *The English People* (CEJL, iii.24) and in 'As I Please', 15 November 1946 (CEJL, iv.278–9). It is difficult to work out precisely what Orwell earned in this period but estimates are given in Table 2.1.[16]

What might be described as the completion of Orwell's apprenticeship as a writer was marked by the publication of *Down and Out in Paris and London*. Orwell had completed his first version of the book by about October 1930. It was then in the form of a diary. Orwell kept diaries throughout his life, sometimes more than one at a time, one devoted, say, to political events, and another to domestic affairs (especially gardening and the progress of his livestock). The book was then some 35 000 words in length (about half the length of this study) and was called 'Days in London and Paris'. Like the title *Burmese Days*, this glances ironically at the travellers' and colonialists' memoirs of the period. The book was rejected by Jonathan Cape who found it too short and fragmentary. He restored some of the material he had cut out and sent it back to Cape, who again rejected it. Then, in mid-December 1931, he sent the manuscript, now titled 'A Scullion's Diary', to Faber & Faber; T. S. Eliot read it but, on 25 February 1932, rejected it. Orwell gave up but a friend, Mabel Fierz, sent the manuscript to a literary agent, Leonard Moore, and he passed it to Victor Gollancz, who accepted it; Moore became Orwell's literary agent and Gollancz his first publisher.[17]

Gollancz asked Orwell to make changes to avoid legal action and to ensure that the book would not be refused by the circulating libraries: 'Names are to be changed, swearwords etc. cut out,[18] and there is one passage which is either to be changed or cut out – a pity, as it is about the only good bit of writing in the book', another instance of Orwell's self-deprecation (CEJL, i.107–8; 132). This was Charlie's story, Chapter II; it was not cut out but modified. The French edition of 1935 restored some of the cuts and the *Complete Works* edition of 1986 makes such restorations as are practicable. This was to be Orwell's first experience of the subject of his first

Table 2.1   Orwell's earnings, 1922–35 (estimated)

	1922–27	1928–29	1930	1931	1932	1933	1934	1935
Regular employ-ment	£3000 +bonuses over 5 yrs					Apr↔Jly H'thrns @ £2? £60?	Sp↔De Frays @ £4? £50+£48?	
Occasional employ-ment		Tutor £15? *Plongeur* £15	Tutor Sch hol £20? £10←odd	Tutor Sch hol £25? jobs→£10			Oct—Booklvrs Cnr @15/-pw £10	£40
Books [Advances] Calculated as 1937 Contract less 12⅛%						D&O £140 [£40] US D&O £95	BD(US) £166 [£50]	BD £119 CD £74 D&O Fr £5
Sub-Total (Books)						£235	£166	£198
Articles e.g. @: Adph £2 Trb to £5 NEW nil		Monde 2 PrCiv 4 GK's 1		Adph 2 NS&N 1	NS&N 1			
Reviews e.g. @: Adph £2 NEW nil			Adph 4	Adph 3	Adph 4 NEW 1	Adph 3	Adph 6	Adph 3 NEW 3
Other p = poem £2						Adph 3p	Adph 1p	Adph 1p
Sub-total (Jnls)		£14	£8	£12	£10	£12	£14	£8
TOTAL (est.)	over 5 yrs £3000 + bonuses	over 2 yrs £44	£38	£47	£70	£345	£190	£246

Source for Tables 2.1 and 5.1: Reproduced from P. Davison, 'Orwell: Balancing the Books', *The Library*, VI, 16 (1994), pp. 96 and 97, by kind permission of the Bibliographical Society.

commercially published article, 'Censorship in England' (79). On 6 July 1932, Orwell told Moore that he proposed to call the book 'The Lady Poverty' or 'Lady Poverty' from Alice Meynell's verse, 'The Lady Poverty was fair, / But she hath lost her looks of late' (CEJL, i.108). In the same letter he said he wanted the book published pseudonymously. On 15 November, he naively asked Moore, 'do you think that 'X' is a good pseudonym?' (CEJL, i.129), but later, and famously, chose George Orwell (CEJL, i.131). Adrian Fierz believes that this pen-name was suggested by his father when he and Orwell were walking in Suffolk by the River Orwell.[19] Gollancz proposed that the book should now be called 'Confessions of a Down and Out in London and Paris' (the London events having chronologically preceded those in Paris), and page proofs survive with this title and the pseudonym, 'X'. Orwell preferred 'Dishwasher' to 'Down and Out'. He told Eleanor Jaques that he was particularly against 'Down and Out' as he did not answer to that name (CEJL, i.130) and to his agent he wrote, 'I would *rather* answer to "dishwasher" than "down & out", but if you and Mr G. think the present title best for selling purposes, then it is better to stick to it' (CEJL, i.132). Eventually, between page-proof and publication, 'Confession of a' was dropped from the title.

Although the final title is more striking, it is unfortunate in one important sense. Orwell has since been burdened with the charge that he claimed to be down and out when, as students especially are quick to point out, 'he could borrow £5 when he needed it to get back to London' (I.113, 116), and he could always go home to his parents and he did do so. Orwell was only too well aware that he was not a down-and-out but Gollancz's fictional description has stuck, as has the idea, as Edwin Muir claimed in 1952, that Orwell longed to be the 'working man' he never could become. Michael Meyer (who knew Orwell) responded saying that 'Orwell never sought to identify himself with the working classes'. He wrote about them from intimate knowledge but from a detached viewpoint – 'his great virtue as a social analyst'. Orwell, wrote Meyer, lived among miners and worked as a scullion 'to find out at first-hand how poverty and near-starvation conditioned people's outlook. He felt that there had been too much theorising about the feelings of the poor'.[20]

Experience was not the only source of *Down and Out*. In Chapter IX of *The Road to Wigan Pier* he confesses that while at Eton he could agonise over the sufferings of the working class through the medium of books, yet simultaneously hate and despise them. As an example of the sort of book that he then knew he mentions Jack London's *People of the Abyss* (1903), which describes its author's adventures in the world of the labouring poor of the East End of London in 1902. David Smith and Michael Mosher in their *Orwell for Beginners* (a more sophisticated study than it sounds), provide graphic comparisons between *Down and Out, The People of the Abyss,* and Friedrich Engels's *The Condition of the Working-Class in England in 1844*.[21] It is conceivable that Orwell knew the work of Egon Kisch, the Czech-German author of *Der Rasende Reporter* (1925). This is a series of documentary-style short pieces the first of which gives an account of a night spent among the homeless in a Salvation Army hostel in Whitechapel.[22] Another possible influence is a little-known book by David Christie Murray, *A Novelist's Note Book* (1887). Chapters that might have interested Orwell for *Down and Out,* his essay, 'A Hanging', and *The Road to Wigan Pier,* are 'The Hangman', 'The Miner', 'Among the Miners on Strike at Durham', 'Histrionics of the Street' (on the techniques of beggars), 'An Artist on Stone', and 'The Street Acrobat'. The last three have parallels in *Down and Out* on pp. 174–5, 172 (where the work of 'screevers' is described), and 171: 'The most prosperous beggars are street acrobats and street photographers. On a good pitch – a theatre queue, for instance – a street acrobat will often earn five pounds a week' (rather more than the average weekly wage at that time). These parallels may, of course, do no more than point to the persistence of the conditions they describe.

There is one 'source' that demands identification. In what hotel was Orwell a scullion? M. Possenti of the Hotel Splendide, Piccadilly, London, angrily attacked the truthfulness of Orwell's account. Orwell replied on 11 February 1933 (CEJL, i.139–40); he said he was not talking about hotels in general but a particular hotel in Paris. Among those suggested have been the Ritz, Crillon, Lotti, and the George V. Sonia Orwell believed it was the Crillon. The Lotti can stake a literary claim. It was to the Lotti that Ashenden was summoned in Ch. 7 of Somerset Maugham's novel of that name, published in 1928 (while Orwell was in Paris), and recommended by him to Brenda Salkeld (*166*). (Recent holiday guides give all these hotels the highest recommendations. The Hotel Splendide was until recently the headquarters of the Arts Council of Great Britain.) 'Blair' made a curious reappearance in an advertisement for Le Grand Hotel, Paris (opposite the Opéra) in August 1988. Inserted into a drawing of the hotel were the words, 'Blair: Comeback planned', but there was no evidence to support this seeming claim to this being the hotel in which Orwell worked.

The records of Victor Gollancz Ltd show that initially 1500 copies of *Down and Out* were printed. Later in its month of publication, a further 500 copies were printed and a third impression of 1000 copies was printed at an unknown date. No copies were remaindered. The type was distributed on 13 February 1934. Harper & Brothers, New York, published 1750 copies in June or July 1933, of which 383 copies were remaindered; Willison records that, coincidentally, that type was also distributed on 13 February 1934. The French translation, which Orwell greatly admired (in contrast to that of *Burmese Days*), was published in May 1935; 5000 copies were printed but by the mid-fifties they had not all been sold. Its title, *La Vache Enragée*, is idiomatic for 'to rough it' in Orwell's context; it was also the title of a satirical monthly journal published in Paris in 1896 for which Toulouse-Lautrec designed a poster. *La Vache Enragée* had an introduction by the Romanian writer, Panaït Istrati, who unfortunately died three weeks before the French edition appeared. In his introduction he makes a number of comparisons between Gorki and Orwell and concludes that Orwell makes one think and meditate on life's griefs, just as does a novel by Balzac – but without having to endure Balzac's tedious detail. In 1940, Penguin Books published an edition of 55 000 copies. Orwell's estimated earnings are given in Tables 2.1 and 5.1.

Orwell gave his friend, Brenda Salkeld, a gym-mistress at St Felix School for Girls, Southwold, a copy of *Down and Out* on 28 December 1932, and this he annotated, marking in sixteen places what was factual, what autobiographical, and what fictitious.[23] Virtually all the annotations point to the truthfulness of the book, allowing for certain rearrangements and occasional exaggerations. The three elements that are incorrect are of very little significance: Charlie's story (p. 7 ff.) is marked '*Not* autobiography. The fellow really did talk like this, tho'; Bouillon Zip was an invented name for Bouillon Kub, a soup cube (p. 24); and the former public schoolboy was not an Old Etonian but from some other school, the name of which Orwell had forgotten (p. 160).[24]

An examination of the figures given in *Down and Out* throws light on the factual accuracy of the book and on Orwell's degree of poverty at the end of his time in Paris. The rates of exchange he quotes show that the book is based on the notes – the diary? – written at the time he was in Paris. 'Six francs is a shilling', he says (p. 13), almost exactly the rate of exchange (124 fr to the £) until 1930, when the first version of the book was completed; by 1933, when it was published, the rate was 86 fr to the £. In Ch. IV Orwell says he received 'exactly 200 fr due to me for a newspaper article' (pp. 19–20). This ought to have been a little before he became a *plongeur*, 'towards the end of the autumn of 1929', as he told his French readers (*211*). However, the articles we know he wrote in Paris appeared between October 1928 and May 1929. For each of those in *Le Progrès Civique* he was paid 225 fr. It could be that 200 fr was a very belated payment by *Monde* – *Le Progrès Civique* paid very promptly – or it may be a fiction. It would be strange at this point in the book, when the author is so poverty-stricken, to invent a windfall that would enable him to live, according to his calculations, for three to four weeks. I am inclined to think, therefore, that there is another article by Orwell from this period that, despite a thorough search, has not been traced.

A measure of Orwell's contrasting financial states before going to Paris and by the end of his stay there is revealed by what he paid for his clothes and what he received when he pawned them. Stephen Wadhams uncovered the records of Orwell's tailor, Denny & Son, Southwold.[25] These show what Orwell bought in 1922 before going to Burma and, after his return, between September 1927 and January 1928. They reveal that he went to both places well dressed. Thus, in 1922 he bought flannel trousers at 32s. 6d.; the 'going rate for a normal flannel in those days was about six shillings and sixpence'. His riding breeches at 1984 prices would have cost from £160 to £180. In 1927–28 he bought an overcoat which at 1984 prices Mr Jack Wilkinson Denny calculated would cost £180–£200 and a three-piece suit that would be about £350. He must have been relatively well-off on his return from Burma and clearly he did not despise good-quality clothes then. When he says in *Down and Out* that the clothes and suitcase he was pawning (not including the overcoat) cost 'over twenty pounds' (p. 19) for which he received 70 fr (just over twelve shillings) he is doubtless recording actuality. When he came to pawn his and Boris's overcoats he describes them both as shabby but this is doubtless artistic licence so far as his coat was concerned. For those he was surprised to receive as much as 50 fr (p. 41). These little details point to the underlying accuracy of Orwell's narrative.

One of Mr Denny's remembrances graphically illustrates Orwell, his father, and his sister, Avril. Orwell's father, Denny recalled, would walk past him on Southwold promenade 'with no gesture of recognition' for Denny, though a high-class tailor, was, nevertheless, a tradesman. Denny went on:

Old man Blair was terribly autocratic. If anyone got in his way at the golf course they'd get it in no uncertain terms! He felt his weight very much; he was full of his own importance. A typical retired civil servant. Avril was a bit the same. It was a bit of an honour to be served cakes by her! They'd all got a bit of that. I didn't notice it with Eric [Orwell] so much, though.[26]

3

The Profession of Author

Reviewing Alex Comfort's *No Such Liberty* in October 1941 (*855*), Orwell commented, 'I think I am justified in assuming that it is autobiographical, not in the sense that the events described in it have actually happened, but in the sense that the author identifies himself with the hero, thinks him worthy of sympathy and agrees with the sentiments that he expresses.' This takes us back to the subtitle of 'Short Story', which Orwell wrote in Paris: 'This never happened to me, but it would have if I had had the chance' (p. 27 above), and forwards to his autobiographical fictions of the thirties, *Burmese Days*, *A Clergyman's Daughter*, *Keep the Aspidistra Flying*, and *Coming Up for Air*, and then to 'The Prevention of Literature', January 1946, in which he declares that the imaginative writer 'may distort and caricature reality in order to make his meaning clearer, but he cannot misrepresent the scenery of his own mind' (CEJL, iv.88). The degree to which he is in sympathy with his principal characters varies. There is, I think, a very close association between Orwell and Dorothy despite the gender difference, but an ironic detachment from Gordon Comstock. Studies such as Lynette Hunter's *George Orwell, The Search for a Voice* and her essay, 'Stories and Voices in Orwell's Early Narratives', both 1984, and more recently, Bernard Gensane's *George Orwell: Vie et écriture*, 1994, have considered Orwell's 'search for a voice'. Of *Down and Out in Paris and London*, Lynette Hunter justly remarks that it is 'not a "naïve" story, but a study of varied ways of telling and writing in the first person. The same experimentation with voice is found in *Burmese Days*.'[1] Gensane endeavours to tease out the distinctive characters that make up 'Orwell' and the voices that give expression to his biological self (Blair), and the various masks he adopted as a writer. Thus, in his headings, he subtly distinguishes between '"Je" ou "Moi"', 'Vous et moi', '"Je" et "je"', 'Blair, "Orwell", Orwell', 'Auteur/Narrateur', and there are headings such as 'Quel "je" fictif?' and 'Sur deux glissements'. The third and final part of his book is given the title, 'Voies d'une voix, voix d'une voie'.[2]

Much is often made of the twin personalities, Blair and Orwell, but, as Gensane demonstrates, this duality is an oversimplification: Orwell adopted several masks and, as he and Lynette Hunter show, these revealed themselves in different voices. That Orwell *did* present himself to friends and acquaintances as Eric Blair and George Orwell, depending on how they had first come to know him is well known; less well known is that, especially at the BBC, he did not rigidly keep these distinctions and would even sign one name over the typed form of the other. This determination to see Blair/Orwell as twin personalities is mistaken. Orwell adopted several roles and he had groups of friends associated with each role. Friends in one group could be unaware of his circle of acquaintances in another. There was nothing sinister or even odd about this: it grew out of Orwell's slow development as writer and personality. What is important is that he and his writing are not interpreted as if there were a sharp dichotomy between Blair and Orwell. The reality is much more subtle, varied, and interesting. Alok Rai has suggested that *Down and Out in Paris and London* contained 'exactly the kind of material which might have tempted into tirades a young socialist with half-baked ideas about capitalism. Instead, Orwell produced a book which might almost be a model of "objective" observation.'[3] Yet, as Rai notes in his Paris articles, Orwell adopts a rhetoric which owes much to the circles in which he was moving (see p. 28 above). These rhetorical stances (which occur before the Blair/Orwell name-shift) may reflect several things. They may show Orwell's development as political thinker and as writer; they may show how he adapted his attitude and what he said to circumstances; they may indicate different degrees of personal involvement.

Dennis Collings, who knew Orwell well at the time, acutely analysed Orwell's tramping. Orwell tried, he said, to identify himself with the lowest ranks of the working class; tramps 'were people who'd outcast themselves. After all, it wasn't as hard to get a job in those days as it's been made out' (a statement that could, surely, be challenged). Orwell, said Collings, 'was a masochist in a way', and he seemed to be 'trying to atone for something', having been 'caught up with a feeling of guilt when he came back from Burma'. Collings never took the tramping seriously: 'it was an anthropological experiment' by someone who 'had no anthropological outlook at all' (Collings was an anthropologist) which led to something that could be written about, but Collings never understood why Orwell put himself through such agony to write about 'that sort of thing . . . when there are so many other things he could have written about'. Collings pinpoints just what made Orwell tick as man and polemicist: 'I think he just wanted to see *change*. Even if he was in heaven he'd want to change the order of the angels.' It was not, he thought any deeper than that: a subconscious belief that 'Things must be *changed*.'[4] There is no doubt Orwell did develop as writer and man, but within that there was also, as Collings noted, an urge simply to see and effect change and change does not necessarily coincide with progressive development.

Related to change, but in this context differing from it, is another characteristic shown by Orwell: his many-sidedness, partly shown in the variety of his voices. The result can be, or can seem, contradictory. In *Down and Out in Paris and London*, Orwell speaks of the fear of the mob as 'superstitious': 'The educated man pictures a horde of submen, wanting only a day's liberty to loot his house, burn his books, and set him to work minding a machine or sweeping out a lavatory' (I.121). In his essay on Dickens, Orwell refers to Dickens's 'profound horror of mob violence', and his delight 'in describing scenes in which the "dregs" of the population behave with atrocious bestiality'. He quotes one of Dickens's descriptions in *Barnaby Rudge* in which the mob's maniacal behaviour might lead one to think 'Bedlam gates had been flung open wide'. He goes on,

> You might almost think you were reading a description of 'Red' Spain by a partisan of General Franco. One ought, of course, to remember that when Dickens was writing, the London 'mob' still existed. (Nowadays there is no mob, only a flock.) (CEJL, i.460–1)

By 'nowadays' Orwell meant the late thirties. To Dickens, the French peasantry of *A Tale of Two Cities* is 'sub-human', and the French Revolution inevitable as a direct result not of 'historic necessity' but because of centuries of oppression: 'The descriptions of the Paris mob . . . outdo anything in *Barnaby Rudge*' (CEJL, i.462–3).

However, Orwell's expression runs away with him in *Down and Out*. The mobs of *Barnaby Rudge*, *A Tale of Two Cities*, or, after Orwell's time, the submen of *A Clockwork Orange*, might loot, burn, and mug, but setting the victim to work at a machine would hardly occur to them. Nevertheless, the idea of fear of the mob as mere superstition did not hold good for Orwell himself. In the revealing eighth and ninth chapters of *The Road to Wigan Pier*, Orwell tells us a great deal about himself, often self-critically, but he also gives in graphic detail an unflattering picture of the working class of his youth. He describes how they became 'a race of enemies' who hated people of his class, and he actually describes them as 'almost sub-human'. He then describes 'A recurrent terror of my holidays . . . the gangs of "cads" who were liable to set upon you five or ten to one.' Then, referring to the fate of Oscar Wilde, he actually introduces the phrase, 'The London mob' when describing 'the strange, obscene bursts of popular fury' that followed the trial: 'The London mob had caught a member of the upper classes on the hop, and they took care to keep him hopping' (I.117–19).

It is important when discussing Orwell and class to bear in mind this early fear – no mere superstition but something deeply felt – but also always to take Orwell in the context of the moment. The man and the voice change and vary; in addition, there may also be concealed irony, even a comic sub-text. For example, when Orwell was required to change the advertising slogans in *Keep the Aspidistra Flying* (see below p. 58), the replacements provide a comic commentary on the originals (and perhaps allowed Orwell a modest measure of revenge). Thus, instead of the genuine slogan, 'Guinness is good for you' he invented, 'Get that waist-line back to normal'; in place of a night-starvation advertisement, 'Prompt relief for feeble kidneys', suggesting a different reason for nightly wakefulness; 'The Truth about Bad Legs' became 'New Hope for the Ruptured'; 'Drink Habit conquered in Days' became 'Earn Five Pounds a Week in Your Spare Time'; and, for 'Are you a Highbrow? Dandruff is the Reason', the flaky skin is suggested in the substitute, 'Kiddies clamour for their Breakfast Crisps' (IV. 57 and see notes to 55/8–9, 57/28–9 and 263/1–7). More deliberate humour, in that he initiated it himself, is concealed in 'As I Please', 4 February 1944 (2416). Orwell is commenting on the decline in comic verse brought about because middle-class life was no longer carefree and it was no longer possible to go 'from birth to death with a boyish outlook'. He quotes four lines but does not identify their source or author:

Once a happy child, I carolled
On green lawns the whole day through,

Not unpleasingly apparelled
In a tightish suit of blue.

A little digging shows how personal this was for Orwell and is
indicative of his peculiarly wry humour. The author was one of
Orwell's favourites, R. S. Calverley; the poem, 'On a Distant Prospect of Making a Fortune'. This title could easily apply to Orwell,
at least, before *Animal Farm* was published. But there is more.
Calverley's title parodies Gray's 'Ode On a Distant Prospect of Eton
College', which had an obvious significance for Orwell; and the
green lawns suggest the Sixth Form Lawn at Eton on which Orwell
was at one time privileged to walk.

Change, variety, wit, coupled with Orwell's development politically and artistically, lend a special interest to Orwell's writing.
His personal odyssey, his varied moods, voices, and roles, are all
reflected in what he wrote. These make even more complex the
relationship of fact to fiction, complicating the categorisation of his
writings. Publishers and librarians will categorise *Down and Out in
Paris and London* as fiction or autobiography; *A Clergyman's Daughter*
is obviously fiction – is it?; *The Road to Wigan Pier* is social reportage
– well, Part One – but Part Two?

Some of these moods, voices and roles are to be found in *Down
and Out in Paris and London*. Its genre is not easily defined. It is, as
the copy Orwell annotated for Brenda Salkeld shows (see p. 35
above), in large part autobiographical, modified a little by Orwell's
direct and covert censorship. Where he worked as a *plongeur* he
referred to simply as Hôtel X, yet he named the Closerie de Lilas.
He told Mabel Fierz that it was 'a little trollop he'd picked up in a
café' who had robbed him, not a young Italian. It was the English
publisher who censored swearwords and had Charlie's story toned
down (Chapter 2).[5] The fictionalising of his experience becomes
significant at the point Orwell sets about tramping in England. As
that had taken place before he went to Paris it was necessary to
invent a story to explain the chronological switch. Hence the unexpected departure abroad of the family of the 'tame imbecile' he was
to teach, leaving Orwell stranded in London with only 19s. 6d.
(perhaps £35–40 in today's money) to last the month until they
returned (I.127–8). This led to a sequence of fictions – that he had
not 'the slightest notion of how to get a cheap bed in London'; that,
although he had experience of making a little money go a long way
in Paris he had no idea how to do that in London; and despite

having read about doss-houses, he knew nothing about them (I.128, 129, 130). But again, as a letter Orwell wrote to Sir Sacheverell Sitwell in 1940 reveals, he had tutored a 'backward boy' at South-wold some ten years earlier (653). He could hardly have been one of the three sons of C. R. Peters (who was serving in the Indian Imperial Police), whom he also tutored in 1930 and 1931, one of whom became a senior civil servant and another (from whose memoir of Orwell Professer Crick quotes at length, pp. 219–20) a professor of philosophy.

Although in the context used here, 'fiction' means primarily a narrative in the form of novel or short story, the word carries many connotations. To tell a fiction, a story, a tale, to romance, to invent, to counterfeit, may have dishonest implications: to lie, to forge (which also can imply honest or dishonest labour). Fact as opposed to fiction in certain contexts is the distinction between truth and lies, hence the dubious nature of the genre of 'faction'. Orwell's fiction-alising at the start of his English adventures is acceptable because the 'truth' being offered is independent of the artistic reorganisa-tion. In this case the rearrangement of the material seems to have stemmed from the attempts to lengthen the book, to assist in con-verting it from its original diary format, and to satisfy the publish-ers to whom the manuscript was at various times submitted. What was to concern Orwell deeply was the rearrangement of events in order to falsify history. Orwell could, if pressed, claim he was not, through such distortion, 'misrepresenting the scenery of his mind'.

Orwell adopts various techniques to depict reality in *Down and Out in Paris and London*. The opening 'street scene' is a dramatic sketch (note Orwell's, 'I sketch this scene, just to convey something of the spirit of the Rue du Coq d'Or', the name he gave the Rue du Pot de Fer, I.1). The opening of the second chapter is reportage but Charlie's story is, as he told Brenda Salkeld, 'Not autobiography' but 'The fellow really did talk like this.' This is, presumably, to some degree fictional: 'creative writing'. If this is so, his comment to his agent that 'it is about the only good bit of writing in the book', as it was originally submitted to Gollancz, takes on a par-ticular significance (CEJL, i.108). The chapter ends lamely with one of those apologetic statements that Orwell makes from time to time in *Down and Out*: 'He was a curious specimen, Charlie. I describe him, just to show what diverse characters could be found flourishing in the Coq d'Or quarter' (I.11). It is as if he is uncertain of the tone, or voice, he should be adopting. Similar uncertainties are to be found at the end of Chapter XXI: 'These are only my own ideas about the basic facts of a *plongeur's* life ... I present them as a sample of the thoughts that are put into one's head by working in a hotel' (I.122); and the openings of Chapters XXXVI, 'I want to set down some general remarks about tramps'; and XXXVII, 'A word about the sleeping accommodation open to a homeless person in London' (I.203, 210). Chapters XXXVI and XXXVII are prototypes of the social surveys Orwell was to develop in Part One of *The Road to Wigan Pier*, and the 'political circumstance' chapters of *Homage to Catalonia*. In terms of genre they sit strangely in a work of fiction or even in autobiography. This Orwell recognised in *Homage to Catalonia*; he later decided that Chapters V and XI of that book as originally published should be turned into appendixes (as they were, belatedly, in 1986).

Perhaps the most telling passage in *Down and Out in Paris and London* is Orwell's account of the occasion when 'quite a hundred men ... dirty types' waited outside a church, 'like kites round a dead buffalo'. They had come for a pound jam-jar of tea and six slices of bread and margarine. The 'price' to be paid for this sustenance was attendance at an evangelical service. This tramps treated it as 'a purely comic spectacle', and Orwell admits it was 'sufficiently ludicrous'. However, to Orwell, the behaviour of the tramps 'passed all bounds' and he describes the 'queer, rather disgusting scene' he witnessed, contrasting the 'handful of simple, well-meaning people, trying hard to worship' with the 'hundred men whom they had fed, deliberately making worship impossible'. He asks, 'What could a few women and old men do against a hundred hostile tramps?' This is the same Orwell who, sixty pages earlier, had decried the superstitious fear of the mob, but now: 'They were afraid of us, and we were frankly bullying them.' Then, percipiently, he remarks, 'It was our revenge upon them' (and he does not shy away from including himself in the mob's response) 'for having humiliated us by feeding us.' Having described so feelingly this 'disgusting scene', Orwell stands back and coolly remarks, in the role of social commentator, 'The scene had interested me' because it was so different from the way tramps normally behaved. The recipient of charity 'practically always hates his benefactor' and, with 'fifty or a hundred others to back him, he will show it' (I.184–6). The combination of sensibility and objectivity here makes this one of the most telling moments in *Down and Out in Paris and London*; it gets to the heart of social problems that are still with us in our dependency culture, and yet reveals something of the heart of tramp and observer.

In another moment of disgust in which Orwell shocks the reader, Orwell, simultaneously, touches a chord of sympathy. Although he had difficulty coming to terms with the working-class people he met (and this will be considered later), the problem seemed resolved so far as outcasts – tramps – were concerned. He obviously got on well with Bozo, but it is a moment at the end of Chapter XXXV that is so telling. Little Scotty, the Glasgow tramp, insists on repaying Orwell with that most precious of commodities, cigarettes: 'he put four sodden, debauched, loathly cigarette-ends into my hand' (I.202). There is no more perfect conjunction of the loathsome, the sensitive, and the affectionate in Orwell. This, surely, is autobiography.

Down and Out in Paris and London is not only Orwell's first book, but, a meeting point of what he would write about Burma and Wigan. He describes the *plongeur*, though 'a king compared with a rickshaw puller or a gharry pony', as nevertheless a slave whose slavery is 'more or less useless' (I.119). Earlier he describes the experience deep below the hotel's public rooms in terms that will become familiar in his description of the pits below Wigan: the stifling heat, the stuffiness, the shafts, and the dark labyrinthine passages, 'so low that I had to stoop in places' (I.54–5, 60–1). Here, coincidentally, Orwell's past and future meet.

BURMESE DAYS

Maung Htin Aung, who had, while a student, met Orwell in Rangoon and who later became that University's Professor of English (see p. 15 above), concluded his article, 'Orwell of the Burma Police' with a remarkable tribute: 'Orwell's rejection of imperialism was plausible, significant and impressive because Blair was an Assistant Superintendent of rich promise when he decided to resign.'[6] That rich promise was to take many years to come to fruition in Orwell's chosen field, but Burma was the inspiration for two of Orwell's finest essays, 'A Hanging' and 'Shooting an Elephant', and a novel that, despite weaknesses, can stand alongside the work of Kipling and Forster in its understanding of the Raj, its peoples and servants. Orwell managed to get inside the minds and attitudes of ruled and rulers, if not quite as well as did Kipling, rather more perceptively than Forster.

If the two essays are taken simply as essays, it matters little whether Orwell witnessed a hanging or shot an elephant,[7] but in a literary biography this must be touched upon. His statement that he once watched a man hang (which must serve as the foundation for 'A Hanging') has already been mentioned (on p. 16). Maung Htin Aung states that Orwell not only saw a hanging but shot an elephant. He relates the 'rogue elephant, which had ceased to belong to its herd', to Orwell, likewise 'utterly alone . . . in killing the elephant he felt he was killing a part of himself'.[8] The tape-recorded reminiscences of one of Orwell's colleagues in Burma, George Stuart, also provide evidence that the shooting *did* take place. He records that when news was brought to the club in Moulmein that an elephant was ravaging a bazaar and thought to be a danger to life, Orwell set off in his old Ford, picked up a rifle, and went in search of the elephant. He shot the creature but then was in considerable trouble because the elephant, which was valuable, belonged to one of the influential European timber companies. The author of the essay claims to be a poor shot, but this was a fiction: Orwell was as good a shot as Flory. Orwell's superior, Colonel Welbourne, deliberately set out to denigrate Orwell, describing him as a disgrace to Eton. According to Stuart, 'Everyone was disgusted with the way he ran Blair down.'[9] Orwell was transferred to Katha – Kyauktada, where the events of *Burmese Days* take place.

Orwell makes much more of the incident than the telling of an adventure of the kind appropriate to the genre of 'colonial reminiscences' (a style Orwell glances at ironically in the title, *Burmese Days*). It *is* 'a good yarn', but it is much more. Just as 'A Hanging' touches on the sanctity of human life, highlighted by the stray dog and the wonderful moment when the condemned man steps aside so as not to walk through a puddle of water in order not to get his feet wet, even though in a few moments he will be dead, so Orwell combines his unwillingness to shoot the elephant, his realisation that 'every white man's life in the East, was one long struggle not to be laughed at', with an epitome of the position of those who ruled the Raj. Thus the master becomes the servant as, fearing he might be laughed at, he feels constrained to shoot the elephant. The account of the great beast's slow, agonising end, protracted over a half-hour, is much more than belle-lettrist description. At the first shot, the elephant 'looked suddenly stricken, shrunken, immensely old. . . . An enormous senility seemed to have settled upon him. One could have imagined him a thousand years old'; this is wonderfully sensitive but also a perfect anticipation of the last throes of the Raj itself. The elephant's eventual collapse is like a natural disaster, an earthquake: 'down he came . . . with a crash that seemed to shake the ground even where he lay'. By the afternoon, the Burmans had stripped the elephant's body almost to the bones, a foretaste of the future for many of the former European colonies. The essay's final sentence is perfect Orwell (and in the style of the last sentence of his Parisian 'Short Story', p. 27 above): 'I often wondered whether any of the others grasped that I had done it solely to avoid looking a fool.'

As with so many of Orwell's books (and, indeed, later editions of his works), *Burmese Days* suffered a chequered publishing history. The novel was first rejected by Gollancz for fear of giving offence in Burma and India. Orwell later told Henry Miller that he believed the India Office 'might take steps to have it suppressed' (27 August 1936; CEJL, i.258; *323*), although there are no grounds for believing that the India Office was interested enough to do that. The novel was published in the United States by Harper & Brothers on 25 October 1934. It was more successful than has been suggested.[10] A second impression was published on 11 December. The first impression is marked I–1 and the second K–1. These were almost certainly from the same setting of type; there are no variants but one word shows type damage in the second impression (p. 87, line 18) and the same misprint appears in both versions (p. 102, line 27). There were 2000 copies of the first impression; no records survive to show how many copies were printed for the second, but as nearly a thousand copies were remaindered, it is likely that a second 2000 copies were run off. This was not a great sale but it was respectable. There is no record of what royalties Orwell earned.

Burmese Days was sufficiently successful to persuade Victor Gollancz to publish the book in England provided he could be sure that no legal action for libel or defamation would ensue. Gollancz sent Orwell a telegram on 19 February 1935 asking him to come to his office to discuss *Burmese Days* at 2.30 p.m. on the 22nd. Orwell wrote to his agent, Leonard Moore, later in the afternoon of the 22nd (*238*), to tell him that he had had a long talk with Gollancz and his solicitor, Harold Rubinstein. (Rubinstein was a distinguished libel lawyer, a perspicacious literary critic and the author of several plays; he gave his hobby as 'Work'.) Stansky and Abrahams, on the basis of information provided by Norman Collins, then Deputy Chairman of Victor Gollancz Ltd, state that Orwell's meeting was with Collins.[11] (During the war, Collins was one of Orwell's superiors at the BBC and was later instrumental in setting up the independent television service.) Orwell does not mention that Collins was present at the meeting with Gollancz and Rubinstein. However, Collins, recalling events many years later, gave Stansky and Abrahams a detailed report of 'his' conversation with Orwell. Orwell, said Collins, maintained that the novel was entirely based on fact and that all the characters had been given their real-life names. 'Eventually, however – if not that afternoon – he accepted the seriousness of the problem' and agreed to make changes. As Stansky and Abrahams point out, in the light of Orwell's 'sweeping claims to Collins, it comes as something of an anti-climax to discover that the changes were only three in number': Dr Veraswami became Dr Murkhaswami, U Po Kyin became U Po Sing; and (though not listed by Stansky and Abrahams), the third change referred to was probably Latimer for Lackersteen. (Further name changes are noted below.) It is just possible that Collins met Orwell at a preliminary meeting, but given the extent of the changes made, and the principle upon which they were based, it is probable that Collins cast himself in a more significant role in this little drama than he played. However, he may well be right in reporting Orwell's assertions that the novel was based on fact and that some of the names were of real-life characters. We know, for example, that the name U Po Kyin was that of a Burmese Police colleague of Orwell's.[12]

Shortly before the meeting with Gollancz and Rubinstein, Orwell had received a letter dated 5 February 1935 from John R. Hall, Book Editor of the Democrat-News Printing Company of Marshall, Missouri, expressing his admiration of the novel. From the notes Orwell wrote on the back of this letter, he evidently took it along to the meeting, presumably to help him persuade Gollancz to publish *Burmese Days* in England. Orwell noted a number of page references which refer to 'Topog[raphical] changes' and certain other notes, one about Dr Veeraswami. Even more important is a sketch-map of Kyauktada, drawn by Orwell. A reproduction of Orwell's drawing and notes is the frontispiece to the Secker & Warburg edition of *Burmese Days* (1986), and a key to the sketch-map is reproduced in that edition, p. 392 (with identifications of its features, pp. 305–8); the key to the sketch-map serves as the frontispiece to the Penguin reprint. Clearly, what occurred was that Orwell was asked to delocalise the novel so that it would make it much more difficult to identify Kyauktada with Katha. In the course of this the three names already mentioned were changed, Pereira (II.23; and see p. 23 above) became Walters, and Macdougal's name was omitted (II.296); and a number of topographical details were modified (e.g. Upper Burma became Burmese and Kyauktada was made a railway junction instead of a terminus, p. 15, lines 5 and 9). Orwell made some changes that were not required by Gollancz. He corrected the direction of the monsoon wind at 66/11 and changed the date 1910 at 15/6 to 'the Second Burma War'. That war took place in 1852 and it points more correctly than does 1910 to the changes made in Upper Burma. These unforced changes point to problems an editor faces in realising Orwell's intentions in *Burmese Days*: distinguishing between forced and voluntary modifications.[13]

Orwell was later to resent the fact that these changes were required and he used his strongest term to condemn what had happened: the edition was, he said, 'garbled'. At the time, he told Moore that Gollancz would publish the book 'subject to a few trifling alterations which will not take more than a week' (*238*). On 28 February, Orwell sent Gollancz the 'changes specifically asked for by Mr Rubinstein' (*239*), and to the accompanying letter he added a postscript thanking Gollancz for six complimetary copies of *A Clergyman's Daughter*. The typescript of *Burmese Days* was sent for a printer's estimate five days later. On 8 March, the order to print the book was given and proofs were received a mere eight days after that. Such expedition for what was, so far as the publishers were concerned, merely one of many books they were getting out, was then the norm, but would today, despite all the electronic aids now available, be quite astonishing. Gollancz ordered 2500 copies to be printed on 3 April and a further 500 copies were ordered on 23 July. As there were some overs, 3180 copies were printed. The type was distributed on 5 May 1936 and on 21 April 1943, the rights reverted to Orwell.[14] No copies were remaindered and 50 copies were sent to Canada for sale there.

In May 1944, Penguin Books published *Burmese Days* at 9d. They printed 60 000 copies, all of which were sold. In Orwell's lifetime there were French and Italian editions (August 1946 and November 1948), a new edition in the Secker & Warburg 'Uniform' series (3000 copies in January 1949 and a further 3000 copies in February 1951), and, two days before he died, a second American edition was published (3000 copies with a second impression of 2000 copies on 5 April 1951). A French edition, *Tragédie Birmane*, was published by Nagel, Paris, on 31 August 1946 (7800 copies), and an Italian edition,

Giorni in Birmania, by Longanesi, Milan, on 18 November 1948 (3012 copies).[15] This record indicates a modest success in Orwell's lifetime and the novel has rightly gained in popularity and esteem over the past half-century.

Authorial changes to the Penguin edition tell us something about Orwell's character. When this was in proof, Orwell wrote in his *Tribune* column, 'As I Please', 10 December 1943 (*2391*), on 'the horrors of the colour war'. There was, he said, one small thing that could be done and that was to avoid using insulting nicknames: 'It is an astonishing thing that few journalists, even in the Left wing press, bother to find out which names are and which are not resented by members of other races.' Negro (in those days acceptable) was 'habitually printed with a small "n" '. The Indian writer, Cedric Dover, who was broadcasting for Orwell at the time at the BBC, pointed out to him the importance of the capital 'N'. The word 'native', which made 'any Asiatic boil with rage' had been dropped even by British officials in India for a decade, yet it continued to be used in England. He noted that 'Mahomedan' was becoming resented and one should say 'Moslem'; and he had been going through *Burmese Days* cutting out 'Chinamen', which was becoming 'a deadly insult', and substituting 'Chinese'.

A second change, already referred to (p. 10), points to contrasting characteristics of Orwell's memory. In 1945 he asked that 'sat' (p. 282, line 22), an error which, he said, had been introduced by the American compositor, be corrected to 'knelt' (*2648*). This shows both how retentive was Orwell's memory (as in his ability to quote both verse and prose without recourse to a text), but also points to the way he put out of mind that 'garbled' edition of *Burmese Days* of 1935, in which he had already had that error corrected.[16]

One aspect of the editing of *Burmese Days* has implications for a critical understanding of the novel and shows how even typographical niceties can prove significant. The various editions of *Burmese Days* pursue different practices when marking alien words but these are not pursued systematically. Thus, *weiksa*, Burmese for a conjuror, appeared in the pre-1986 Secker Uniform Edition in italic, in roman, and in roman within quotation marks. In order to rationalise these different practices (prompted by Orwell's wish that the Spanish of *Homage to Catalonia* should be corrected in any new edition), I distinguished between words that are still alien to English, such as *thakin* and *thugyi-min*, and these have been systematically italicised, and words which have been assimilated, such as anna, pukka, rupee, sahib, and taboo, which are printed in roman.[17] Because Orwell uses many non-assimilated words, there is a fair amount of italicisation. The effect is to remind the reader throughout the novel that, although the story is told from a British point of view, and must, of necessity, be written in English, it is the British who are alien to this society. This subtly reinforces the implications of imperialism. Orwell is able to use alien words so effectively and so confidently that his reader will understand his meaning, that, at a crucial moment in the novel, when it is driven home to Flory that he has lost Elizabeth, the language used is Hindi. As Elizabeth and Verrall are emerging together from the jungle, Orwell writes: ' "Dekho!" said the mali in his plum-in-the-mouth voice' (II.229). Orwell has earlier established that the mali is the gardener, and the Indian Army slang form, as in 'Take a dekko' ('take a look'), has entered the English language. The effect is doubly to isolate Flory, first from Elizabeth; secondly, through his familiarity with Hindi and Burmese from the English establishment.

Orwell's use of personal names can also be significant, though that significance is not always directly related to the fictional world. Verrall suggests the virility that Flory ('flowery'?) lacks and, as occurs elsewhere in Orwell, he shows his delight in teasing the Scotch (see p. 59 below) and Welsh by giving unpleasant characters Celtic names: Ellis and Macdougall, the dull lout, of Burmese Days; Jones, the farmer, of Animal Farm; and Gordon of Keep the Aspidistra Flying.

Macgregor may also fall into this category but Orwell much more subtly undermines him by a brilliant stroke of hidden wit. Orwell writes that 'His bulky shoulders, and a trick he had of thrusting his head forward, reminded one curiously of a turtle', but then modifies that by giving him the nickname by which he was known to the Burmese: 'the tortoise' (II.25). Why this shift? To understand Orwell's point demands a knowledge of Burmese. Maung Htin Aung explains that Orwell arrived at a time of political tension. A monk had recently assaulted an Imperial policeman and cut off his nose and 'the lovely Burmese girls' were shouting slogans against the British Government and 'throwing away their tortoiseshell combs with contemptuous gestures, for the Burmese word for "tortoise" was similar to the Burmese word for "English". . . . Blair must have recoiled from Burma and the Burmese in horror and disgust.'[18]

Orwell is so often described as a writer of 'window-pane' prose that it is easy to forget to look at the medium through which the eye must pass. Orwell will tease the reader, challenging him or her to recognise allusions. Thus when, with delightful irony, Orwell has Dr Veeraswami defend the British Empire, Flory complains that the British creep round the world building prisons. Then he adds, 'rather regretfully' because the doctor 'would not recognise the allusion': 'They build a prison and call it progress' (II.41). Veeraswami leaps in, defending the British because they do so much more than build prisons. They construct roads, and, in case the reader as well as the good doctor has not picked up the allusion, Orwell gives a clue to the hidden meaning by having him add, 'they irrigate deserts'. Orwell's reference (and it will be recalled that his best mark in the examination to join the Indian Imperial Police was in Latin, p. 15 above), is to Tacitus, the *Agricola*. The British leader before the battle of Mons Graupius declares of Imperial Rome, then subjugating the British, that those who have created the Roman Empire, 'ubi solitudinum faciunt, pacem appellant' – 'when they make a desert they call it peace'.[19]

Flory is an outcast in two senses. In a manner akin to the way Dennis Collings described tramps (see above, p. 39), he had 'outcast himself' from his colleagues because they and what they stood for disgusted him. But he also felt an outcast on the grounds of 'colour'. He was, of course, a white man, but the first thing one noticed about him 'was a hideous birthmark stretching in a ragged crescent down his left cheek, from the eye to the corner of the mouth. . . . He was quite aware of its hideousness. . . . he manoeuvred constantly to keep the birthmark out of sight' (II.14). Two pages later he is described as turning sideways so that the birthmark was away from Westfield. When Elizabeth, so much taken up with Verrall that she had almost forgotten Flory, did think of him, 'it was for some reason always his birthmark that she remembered' (II.222). It is only at the church service, just before Ma Hla May's irruption to denounce Flory, that he risks sitting with his birthmark towards Elizabeth (II.282). After the dreadful scene in the church, Flory shoots himself (and his pet dog), 'With death, the birthmark had faded immediately, so that it was no more than a faint grey stain' (II.294). Two paragraphs later, the official verdict declares Flory died accidentally and Orwell comments ironically, 'All Englishmen are virtuous when they are dead'; he might have added in Flory's case, 'and now white'.

It is easy to see the colonialism of *Burmese Days* depicted through the vile Ellis, the contemptible Verrall, the superficial Elizabeth, and the tedious whites-only club, and this is correct, but it is not all.

Orwell also provides a running commentary through his use of Burmese and Hindi and, especially, through Flory's 'colour'. This is particularly effective because Flory is far from being a wholly sympathetic character: he is weak and the secrecy of his revolt against the system has poisoned him 'like a secret disease' (II.69). He is to some extent destroyed because the country which he hated had become 'his native country, his home' (II.72). He has become, as he describes himself, a 'Sneaking, idling, boozing, fornicating, soul-examining, self-pitying cur' (II.62). Although very different from Orwell himself, just as is Gordon Comstock, there are traits of Orwell in both characters. Orwell describes Flory's bursts of anger directed at his mistress and Ko S'la, his servant. In *The Road to Wigan Pier* Orwell describes how he had bullied subordinates, snubbed aged peasants, and hit servants and coolies with his fist in moments of rage (adding, in parenthesis, 'nearly everyone does these things in the East, at any rate occasionally: orientals can be very provoking', V.138).

Orwell provides a counterpart to Flory: U Po Kyin, the magistrate who is always a step ahead of those he so obsequiously serves. U Po Kyin is as malicious, adept and 'brilliantly successful' (II.1) as Flory is well-meaning, ineffective and a failure. Orwell's description of the way U Po Kyin rose from nothing to be honoured by the Indian Government at the durbar that concludes the novel is particularly well-drawn, especially the witty way in which Orwell characterises how he wins the confidence of the British in the novel's first three pages. He first failed to win a Government appointment 'being poor and friendless'; 'a lucky stroke of blackmail' enabled him to buy a Government clerkship; then, by denouncing the peculation of his fellow clerks (to which he was party), he was made an Assistant Township Officer 'as the reward of his honesty'. As a magistrate he took care to accept bribes from both parties and then decide cases on strictly legal grounds, winning 'a useful reputation for impartiality'. Although all Burmans knew of his private taxation of villagers, there was no point in denouncing him because 'no British officer will ever believe anything against his own men'. These repeated ironies are typical of Orwell's Trollopian technique. Orwell does not make the mistake of idealising the Burmans. U Po Kyin is as vile as Ellis; the constable's wife misappropriates money intended to buy food for the prisoners (II.76); and when Ellis strikes the schoolboy, although the boy is badly hurt, it is the Burmese doctor, who, 'by applying some poisonous concoction of crushed leaves to his left eye, succeeded in blinding him' (II.254) – again, the irony, 'succeeded' in blinding him. As in Tourneur's *The Revenger's Tragedy*, there is no good; there are only shades of evil and degrees of weakness. The imperialist system allows – virtually encourages – the different vices of Ellis and U Po Kyin. Without such a system, Orwell implies, there would be less scope for corruption. Despite the beauty of the jungle, to which Orwell could respond, especially, even in the most oppressive heat, the flaming Pieris (II.116), it was insufficient compensation for his being part of 'man's dominion over man', as he puts it in *The Road to Wigan Pier* (V.138).

THE REJECTED 'POT-BOILERS'

A Clergyman's Daughter and *Keep the Aspidistra Flying* ran into censorship troubles and Orwell came to reject both novels. When he sent the manuscript of *A Clergyman's Daughter* to his agent, Leonard Moore, on 2 October 1934, he described the novel as having 'a good idea, but I am afraid I have made a muck of it . . . there are bits of it that I don't dislike' (typical of Orwell's self-deprecatory manner), 'but I am afraid it is very disconnected as a whole, and rather unreal' (CEJL, i.165). Writing to Brenda Salkeld on 16 February 1935, he said he wanted *Keep the Aspidistra Flying* 'to be a work of art', but 'that can't be done without much bloody sweat' (CEJL, i.172). Later he saw both books as 'silly pot-boilers which I ought not to have published in the first place' but that was perhaps in part influenced by the degree to which he was forcing himself to get out a novel every year – *Burmese Days* in 1934 and then these two books in 1935 and 1936; and secondly because they were, to use his description, 'garbled' owing to the changes forced upon him.

The clergyman's daughter is Dorothy Hare; she devotes herself with unremitting care to assisting her mean-spirited father, the Rector of St Athelstan's, Knype Hill, Suffolk, as an unofficial 'curate'. Whereas she is unworldly and has a sweet and gentle disposition, her father is described by Orwell as 'a "difficult" kind of man' of 'almost unfailing ill-humour' (III.17). Mr Warburton (he is given no first name), a rakish neighbour whom the local girls rightly fear, part-genuinely and part-teasingly befriends a reluctant Dorothy. Their 'sort of friendship' had begun inauspiciously two years earlier by his 'making love to her violently, outrageously, even brutally. It was practically an assault' (III.41). In the original manuscript

Warburton had been said to attempt to rape Dorothy, but that had to be cut out. When the novel opens he again presses his attentions on Dorothy and she leaves him, late at night, very upset. By the time she has returned to the Rectory, most of her agitation has disappeared but she then faces a mountain of work that she is far too tired to tackle (83–4). She has a complete mental breakdown and awakes in the New Kent Road, London, not knowing who she is. As we have the novel, this transition is without proper explanation but whether this is entirely due to what Orwell described as the story's disconnectedness, or whether that has been aggravated by the censorship we know took place, and perhaps by cuts about which there is no information, it is impossible to tell. If the transition was as drastic in the original manuscript, it seems very unlikely that it would have been accepted. Dorothy then begins a series of degrading and humiliating experiences, living in abject poverty, tramping, working in a hop-field, ten nightmarish nights among down-and-outs in Trafalgar Square, and teaching in an appalling private school. Warburton finally rescues her and she returns to Knype Hill only to resume her bleak life, her faith shattered, but determined to stiffen her courage to 'remake the whole structure of her mind' (292).

Gordon Comstock of *Keep the Aspidistra Flying* is as ungracious and opinionated as Dorothy Hare is charming and uncertain. He has a gift for words as an advertising copy-writer, but despises commerce and is anxious to achieve success as an author. He determines to abandon the 'money-god' and seeks a life of virtuous poverty. He takes work as a bookshop assistant (based on Orwell's own experiences) but having received a modest cheque from an American journal for a poem, he squanders it on a vulgarly ostentatious celebratory dinner at which he entertains his girlfriend, Rosemary Waterlow, and his benefactor, Philip Ravelston (based lightly on Sir Richard Rees, a close friend and Orwell's literary executor), the editor of *Antichrist*, a 'middle- to highbrow monthly, Socialist in a vehement but ill-defined way' (IV.88, and based on *The Adelphi*). His behaviour at the dinner is embarrassingly atrocious and, after a drunken fracas, he ends up in a magistrate's court. He is sacked from the bookshop but eventually finds work running a tenth-rate lending library in the Waterloo Road and lives in 'a filthy kip' (231) in a nearby slum. Ravelston and Dorothy, with remarkable generosity of spirit, stand by him. Dorothy, like Rosemary Hare, is drawn with a certain over-simplified, even schoolboyish, idealism. She suffers an inept attempt at lovemaking at Burnham Beeches (where Orwell took Eleanor Jaques), and finally conceives in Orwell's disgusting bed-sit. Her pregnancy leads Gordon to realise that 'You don't escape [the money-god] merely by taking refuge in dirt and misery' (245). He returns to the world of advertising, stuffs the manuscript of his masterwork down a drain-hole, marries Rosemary, and joyfully sets up home in a flat off the Edgware Road, complete with that symbol of middle-class respectability, an aspidistra.

Orwell told his literary executor that he did not want these two novels reprinted but he did 'not object to cheap editions of any book which may bring in a few pounds for my heirs' (2648). The Complete Works editions of these two novels published in 1986 and 1987 have tried to restore what can be restored and to make plain what cannot be recovered. It is too easy to criticise Victor Gollancz for what, today, seems undue caution in what he allowed to appear in print, but circumstances were very different in the 1930s. Gollancz had to tread warily. An easy way to halt a left-wing or avant-garde publisher was simply for wealthier parties to take the publisher to court. The expense and delay of repeated lawsuits, even if the plaintiffs lost, could soon put a smallish publisher out of business. Ironically, one of the things then actionable was saying anything that could be construed as critical about a patent medicine. The manufacturers were wealthy and powerful and could more readily afford to take Gollancz to court than he could afford to defend himself. Nowadays, false claims made for such medicines would land manufacturers in court. Belatedly, Orwell has won the argument. Gollancz had suffered from actions for damages arising from criticism of a private school and he would also have had in mind a prosecution of an earlier publisher that had had the most serious consequences.

In 1889 (and the years when these two books were published were much closer in time to 1889 than we are to the mid-thirties), Henry Vizetelly, publisher of Tolstoi, Dostoievsky, and the Mermaid Series of Elizabethan Dramatists, was, despite his age (he was 69) and ill-health, gaoled for publishing Zola, even though he had taken the precaution of 'garbling' the text of one of the novels, *La Terre*. The experience permanently damaged Vizetelly's health.[20] In 1931, Gollancz published Rosalind Wade's novel, *Children Be Happy*. This was based on her experience as a teacher at a school in Kensington. A flood of libel actions followed.[21] It was hardly surprising, therefore, that Gollancz was cautious. What *is* surprising is that he allowed Orwell as much leeway as he did, though Orwell certainly did not see it in those terms. Part of the problem was the way in which the changes were required, especially the timing of those for *Keep the Aspidistra Flying*. After the text had been accepted, it seems that the printer got cold feet and alerted the publishers to what might be defamatory. Orwell had by then left for Wigan where he received several letters from Norman Collins requesting (quite tactfully) 'in the light of the extraordinary laws of this peculiar country' that Orwell make substitutions. As Collins put it, 'you may have noticed that no fewer than four books have been withdrawn during the past week or so as a result of actions for libel' (267). What made it so much worse for Orwell was that these changes struck him as singularly trivial in comparison with the appalling conditions he saw in the north, and the painful experience he had just suffered walking miles underground (see p. 61 below).

A *Clergyman's Daughter* was the worse affected and has proved the harder to restore. The 1986 hardback, and the 1990 Penguin editions give details, fully and in summary respectively, of what was censored and what it has been possible to restore. Some of the changes required are slight. Thus, a reference to Lambeth Public Library (145/13) had to have 'Lambeth' omitted and the errant bank manager (45/26 and 269/23) could not be identified as being in charge of a branch of Barclay's Bank. However, some twenty pages of text about Mrs Creevy's School based on Orwell's experience teaching at The Hawthorns, Hayes, Middlesex, and Dickens's Salem House in *David Copperfield* (itself based on a real school, Wellington House Academy, to which Orwell refers in his essay on Dickens, CEJL, i.467) had to be modified extensively. Orwell explained 'that throughout 'this school part I have toned down, but not cut out altogether, the suggestion that private schools of this type are apt to be more or less a swindle'. The most serious change has already been referred to: Warburton's attempted rape. This, it was feared, might lead to a charge of obscenity. Its suppression was presumably linked with Warburton's repeated love-making and the two, one imagines, were meant to 'explain' Dorothy's amnesia. Orwell felt his work had been garbled and, as it stands, the narrative line is broken-backed, but whether to the extent Orwell originally intended is surely unlikely.

The manuscript of *A Clergyman's Daughter* was sent for estimate on 12 January 1935; 2000 copies were ordered and the first 1500 were bound on 28 February, just over six weeks after the estimate was ordered. The remaining five hundred copies were bound in two batches on 6 and 27 March and 500 copies were reprinted and end-papered (but not bound) for Harper's in New York on 6 January 1936. Harper's records state that the edition consisted of 1000 copies of which 256 were remaindered. The type was distributed on 20 March 1936 and the rights reverted to Orwell's estate on 3 July 1950, six months after his death.[22]

In comparison, the changes required to *Keep the Aspidistra Flying*, although they infuriated Orwell, were, in the main, relatively unimportant. Orwell's use of genuine advertising slogans could not be permitted and he had to invent spurious ones (see p. 41). One genuine slogan was allowed to stand, 'Have a Camel', for an American cigarette. Presumably it was thought that it was not only used inoffensively but that the Americans would not prosecute. A genuine advertising 'character', 'Roland Butta', had to be changed. Because he appeared frequently and the type was set (in those days in hot metal, a form that did not, as does a modern word processor, permit instant relineation), Orwell had to produce a name with precisely the same number of letters. In the circumstances his solution was ingenious: 'Corner Table'. The imaginary trade-name, 'Bovex' was treated with great suspicion because it might suggest Bovril, Oxo, Beefex, Exox, etc. Orwell pleaded for its retention on the ground that he had had to cut out the word 'garbage' so that there was now 'no comment on the quality of the things'. Though further doubts were expressed, the name was allowed to stand. References to two furniture stores, Drage's and Times, and a business college, Clark's, had to be omitted (and these cannot be restored); the name of a real newspaper, the *Hampstead and Camden Town Messenger*, had to be changed to the innocuous 'a bi-weekly paper' (IV.211). As with *Burmese Days*, there was some delocalisation. Thus on p. 222, a reference to the Waterloo Road had to be altered to a 'desolate stretch of road south of Waterloo Bridge'. Even the epitaph on the tombstone (IV.40) was challenged and Orwell had to give an assurance that it was 'quite imaginary'. It was feared that Orwell's use of 'sod' might 'chop off a sale of several hundreds' of copies and Collins suggested 'swine', except where 'devil' was proposed. Orwell refused point-blank on the grounds that Robert Graves had used it frequently in *Good-bye to All That*, which had proved a bestseller. It was allowed to stand.

The libel lawyer was much exercised about the possible likeness of the bookshop-owner in the novel, McKechnie, to Orwell's employer at Booklovers' Corner, Francis Westrope. Was Westrope a 'secret drinker', as Comstock in the novel thought McKechnie might be (212/11)? In fact, Orwell had anticipated the objection that Westrope might be identified with McKechnie. He told Norman Collins on 18 February 1936 that he had suggested that Mr Westrope OK the passages referring to the bookshop. He would, if necessary 'get him to furnish a written undertaking not to bring a libel action'. It did not come to that, perhaps because Orwell assured Collins that whereas McKechnie was described as 'an old man with white hair & beard who is a teetotaller & takes snuff', Mr Westrope 'is a middle-aged clean-shaven man who is not a teetotaller & never takes snuff'. Other personal names queried, in case they referred to actual people, were Flaxman, Lorenheim, Wisbeach, Hermione Slater, Cheeseman, and Meakin. Orwell's assurances that these did not refer to real people were accepted. Orwell never lost the habit of using the names of real people. His friend, the bookseller Louis Simmonds, found his surname used on the side of the van that carried poor Boxer away (VIII.82). Far from being upset, he was one of a group of booksellers who wished to raise money in 1949 to enable Orwell to recuperate in Switzerland.

Surnames that did not attract the libel lawyer's attention were Gordon's and Dorothy's. The miserable Comstock's first name, Gordon, may have been selected for its Scotch associations. Writing to Anthony Powell on 8 June 1936, Orwell said he was glad Powell used 'Scotchmen', not 'Scotsmen': 'I find this a good easy way of annoying them' (CEJL, i.252). He was later to come to love his time on Jura: it would become his personal 'Golden Country'. Comstock and Waterlow may be examples of Orwell's subversive humour. Anthony Comstock (1844–1915) was the organiser of the New York Society for the Suppresion of Vice and a keen advocate of censorship. Waterlow's are printers of paper money – ironic in that Gordon loved Dorothy but loathed the 'money-god'.

Two good examples of what Orwell wanted to say being subverted by in-house censorship are provided by the adjective he used to describe Player's Weights cigarettes and the use of the word 'garbage'. He described the taste of these cheap cigarettes as 'papery'. The libel lawyer wasn't sure what was meant but was certain it was defamatory. Orwell explained that one tasted more paper than tobacco but changed the adjective to 'acrid'. That also implied criticism and in the first edition the cigarettes were described as

'soothing'. As with every change the position of which can be identified, the original has been restored in the 1987 and 1989 editions.
'Garbage' presents a more serious problem. Orwell wished to link
his description of 'patent foods and patent medicines' as 'synthetic
garbage' (IV.4/1–2) with the 'garbage' written by such authors as
Ethel M. Dell and Warwick Deeping (IV.7/34). Both words were
cut out in 1936. Orwell bitterly resented these forced changes. (As
the 1987 Secker & Warburg edition shows, the passage on p. 7
cannot be reconstructed and so 'garbage' is still omitted; with an
element of conjecture, 'garbage' has been restored to p. 4.)

Orwell sent his last batch of changes to Gollancz on 24 February
(these included the slogan and 'Roland Butta' substitutions, *283*)
and the same day he wrote to Leonard Moore expressing his anger
at what he had been forced to do and its timing. He pointed out
that after the manuscript had been approved by the solicitor he had
had to make changes requiring him entirely to rewrite the first
chapter and modify several others. 'They asked me to make the
alterations when the book was in type and asked me to equalise the
letters, which of course could not be done without spoiling whole
passages and in one case a whole chapter' (*284*). Orwell may have
exaggerated what had to be done but there is no doubting the depths
of his feelings and why, quite apart from the pot-boilerish nature of
these two books, he wished they had not been published. His final
point was more significant, however, and gives some indication of
the care Orwell took in the construction – the subtext – of what he
wrote. He asked Moore to arrange with Gollancz that in future all
alterations should be requested while the book was still in typescript, because 'In general a passage of prose or even a whole chapter revolves round one or two key phrases, and to remove these, as
was done in this case, knocks the whole thing to pieces.' Orwell
almost certainly has in mind here the use of the word 'garbage' to
link patent foods and medicines and what he regarded as third-rate
fiction. On 26 February, Moore passed to Collins what Orwell had
said, adding, 'As you will see, he is by no means unreasonable and
I hope next time you will not send the book to press until everything that needs to be done has been done to the typescript.' To his
credit, Collins ensured that Moore's letter was passed on to
Gollancz.[23]

When one reads this interchange of letters in the context of
Orwell's 'Wigan Diary', the enormity of what was being asked of
Orwell is brought home. In particular, the answer to Collins and

the letter to Moore written on the evening of the 24th, are seen to have followed Orwell's descent into the Crippen Pit. He walked, half crouching, some two miles and what he saw, and the pain he felt, put into sharp relief what must have seemed to him the petty nature of the changes required. His Diary entry for 24 February indicates what he, so tall a man, went through as he made his way through the mine's tunnels:

> After a few hundred yards of walking doubled up and once or twice having to crawl, I began to feel the effect in a violent pain all down my thighs. . . . On the way back my exhaustion grew so great that I could hardly keep going at all, and towards the end I had to stop and rest every fifty yards. The periodical effort of bending and raising oneself at each successive beam was fearful, and the relief when one could stand upright, usually owing to a hole in the roof, was enormous. At times my knees simply refused to lift me after I had knelt down. (CEJL, i.211–12)

It must have been singularly dispiriting to come back to Collins's letter asking him to find another name for Roland Butta – with the same number of letters. For the publishers, the issues were serious enough; the absurdity was rooted in the conventions and law of the time, but inevitably Orwell's anger was directed at his publishers and especially Norman Collins. This had a long-term effect, for Collins was to be in a superior position to Orwell at the BBC and they were to cross swords again. It is hard not to feel a certain sympathy for Collins, but even more for Orwell. In her history of Gollancz, Sheila Hodges wrote that 'Libel was generally something of a nightmare with Orwell's books. It was not that he was deliberately difficult – on the contrary; but he seems to have had great difficulty in grasping either what constitutes libel in this country . . . or the very real dangers involved.'[24]

One last proposed alteration is worth mentioning because it may indicate Orwell's knowledge of sexual behaviour. Collins questioned 'Come here. Not a bad mouth. Come here' at 197/6–7. He added a handwritten suggestion that the words should be excised (presumably because he did not want his typist to see what he was pointing out): 'for reasons wh. it wd. be easier to explain in conversation than in writing!' Collins presumably thought this was a reference to oral sex. Orwell annotated the letter, 'Not altered. Cannot see any dirty meaning here.' In a covering letter he wrote, 'I can't see any harm in this. Of course, if the public read dirty meanings into it, so much the worse, but you can read dirty meanings into anything.' The passage was allowed to stand. The meaning implied by Collins (which he was anxious not to expose to his secretary) may either have been lost on Orwell, or he may have found nothing unusual in such sexual activity. Had it been possible to show in a law court that this did refer to oral sex, the passage would have been regarded as obscene and so it is likely that Orwell simply hadn't made the connection.

Printing of *Keep the Aspidistra Flying* started on 30 January 1936, the day before Orwell left for the north of England. Three thousand copies were printed and the first 2000 were bound on 7 April. Later small batches of sheets were bound up, bringing the total to 2500. The rest of the sheets were destroyed when the binder, Leighton's, was bombed; 463 bound copies were salvaged after the bombing. However, the records state that 484 stock copies were sold as a cheap edition at 3s. 6d., without dust-jackets, but with sticky labels pasted on the bindings, on 16 March 1942. It looks as if a maximum of 2500 copies was sold, but the figures are not clear. Type was distributed on 1 May 1936 and the rights reverted to Orwell on 26 May 1944. No American edition was published until 1956.[25]

Critics tended to pounce on the way in which it was thought Orwell had too slavishly imitated Joyce's Nighttown sequence of *Ulysses* in the Trafalgar Square section of *A Clergyman's Daughter*. Certainly Orwell admired *Ulysses* enormously, as is shown by his long letter to Brenda Salkeld, 10 December 1933 (CEJL, i.150–54), but whether the influence, or imitation, amounts to plagiarism is doubtful. Of all the criticism of *A Clergyman's Daughter*, perhaps the most interesting comment was that made by Orwell's flatmate, Michael Sayers, in *The Adelphi*, August 1935. He quotes 171/16–23 and 177/14–18; these passages, he says, are 'a fair specimen of Mr Orwell's style. The lucidity – so to speak, the *transparence* – of his prose is a necessary quality of the realistic novel, which aims at exhibiting action rather than significant language.'[26] This seems to anticipate Orwell's statement that 'Good prose is like a window pane' in 'Why I Write', 1946 (CEJL, i.30). The likeness may be co-incidental but possibly Sayers knew a dozen years before 'Why I Write' that this was Orwell's aim.

A Clergyman's Daughter can be read in the tradition of the nineteenth-century novels of the loss of faith. Orwell was certainly aware of this tradition though it is impossible to say whether or not that awareness came before his writing of *A Clergyman's Daughter*. He refers to *The Way of All Flesh* in 'As I Please', 21 July 1944 (CEJL, iii.220) but the copy among his books at his death was his wife's, Eileen's, and although she did not die until 1945 it is likely that the book had been in her possession well before that. Possibly the 'spiritual autobiographies' closest to *A Clergyman's Daughter* are *The Autobiography of Mark Rutherford, Dissenting Minister* (1881) and *Mark Rutherford's Deliverance* (1885) by William Hale White, 1831–1913). Basil Willey says Rutherford (to use his pen-name by which, as Orwell for Blair, he is best known),

> merely records, in accents whose low pitch and austere restraint only just conceal the underlying passion, some incidents of his own passage through the Slough of Despond and the Valley of Humiliation. His books belong to the confessional tradition; far from being manufactured for literary effect, they have been forced from him by 'bitter constraint and sad occasion dear'. There is nothing in them that has not been felt, pondered and proved upon the pulses.[27]

Orwell does write for literary effect, although his technique is usually covert (the Trafalgar Square chapter is exceptional), but in other respects Willey's comments on Rutherford might be applied to Orwell in *A Clergyman's Daughter*. Orwell knew Rutherford's work and discusses Rutherford in his first 'As I Please Column', 3 December 1943 (CEJL, iii.75–6). Rutherford was a radical, remarkably objective (two characteristics Orwell notes), and Orwell describes *Deliverance* in terms that might be applied to *A Clergyman's Daughter*, as 'pseudo-autobiography'. Like Rutherford, Orwell had a 'natural tendency to believe the worst' and a 'perpetual undying faith in principles'.[28] It would be wrong to make too much of this relationship, or indeed of the direct identification, despite the gender difference, of Dorothy and Orwell,[29] but Dorothy's experiences are obviously very closely patterned on Orwell's – teaching (and Orwell told Gollancz that when he referred to Southbridge, III.197, he had 'vaguely in mind' Hayes, Middlesex, where he had taught), hop-picking, and tramping. The association with Orwell's first school is very close. It was for The Hawthorns that he wrote his play, *Charles II* (154; as *Charles I* of the novel) and he produced it at Christmas 1932. He told Eleanor Jaques on 18 November 1932 that he was making armour for the school play and 'I have been

suffering untold agonies with glue and brown paper etc. Also paint-
ing a cigarette box for the Church Bazaar, which I very rashly
undertook to gild' (CEJL, i.130–1). Dorothy went through the same
agonies with glue and brown paper before her amnesia (III.58–9
and 84) and again following her return (III.293–7). And, of course,
it was while Orwell was at Hayes that he made friends with the
curate, attended church, and reluctantly took Communion (CEJL,
i.128, and see pp. 132–3 below).

Much more significant than this recruitment of experience for the
novel is the way the novel ends. Patrick Reilly, in an excellent
analysis of the novel, describes Dorothy's odyssey as concluding
with her return to her father, the Rector, but not to her Father in
Heaven.[30] It is worth pondering on the novel's last few pages, particularly for the way Dorothy considers the relationship of faith to
life. 'Faith vanishes, but the need for faith remains the same as
before' (III.292) is quintessentially Orwell. Then, as the glue starts
to boil, 'The smell of the glue was the answer to her prayer. She did
not know this. . . . the solution to her difficulty lay in accepting the
fact that there was no solution' (III.295). And finally, in the last two
sentences of the book there comes Dorothy's (and, I think, Orwell's)
solution. The problem of faith and no faith has vanished and 'with
pious concentration' she works at her task. The word 'pious' and
the implicit likening of the smell of the glue to the burning of in-
cense are telling. Where shall she (and Orwell) go? As Basil Willey
puts it in his introduction to Rutherford, 'in the direction, perhaps,
of what is now (since Bonhoeffer) called "religionless Christianity"
– and this is the second phase of Mark Rutherford's deliverance'.[31]

This is the Orwell who, though he would constantly attack the
weakness of the church and its representatives (especially Roman
Catholics), and deny belief in an afterlife, yet sees a ghost (CEJL,
i.71–3), suspects a poltergeist at work (653), writes on the day he
marries that he has one eye on the clock and one on the Prayer
Book (CEJL, i.253), has his adopted son christened, and asks to be
buried according to the rites of the Church of England. He is, too,
the man who wrote the poem, 'A happy vicar I might have been'
(CEJL, i.27), who seems to have a understood 'the special Christian
vision of the necessity and sadness of death', which he finds in
Hopkins's 'Felix Randal' (CEJL, ii.160), and who could write in *The
Left News*, April 1941, that he did not believe 'that Western society,
during recorded time, had made any real advance except in the

adoption of Christianity' (782). Orwell's 'religionless Christianity' might be summed up in that quality, 'decency', to which he so often appealed. As he put it at the end of the first section of his essay on Dickens, ' "If men would behave decently the world would be decent" is not such a platitude as it sounds' (CEJL, i.469). Later he remarks that Dickens found science uninteresting, machinery cruel and ugly, business fit only for ruffians, and politics for the Tite Barnacles: 'In the last resort there is nothing [Dickens] admires except common decency' (489). And again, he maintains that Dickens's 'radicalism is of the vaguest kind', and that he has 'no constructive suggestions, not even a clear grasp of the nature of the society he is attacking, only an emotional perception that something is wrong. All he can finally say is, "Behave decently", which . . . is not necessarily so shallow as it sounds' (501–2). Wigan and Spain would form Orwell's radicalism (though it would remain idiosyncratic), but, like Dickens, he pinned his faith on that precept, 'Behave decently'.

A Clergyman's Daughter is by no means a great novel. It is flawed in execution and through censorship, but it is more moving than is sometimes claimed; it is, perhaps, one of those 'good bad books', as Orwell classed them. I, for one, cannot see a pitiful bundle of blankets in a shop doorway in the West End of London, nor bear to pick up a coin in the street, for thought of 'the clergyman's daughter'.

In 1956, Louis Simpson claimed that *Keep the Aspidistra Flying* 'may be the best book Orwell wrote',[32] but that its persistent pessimism, its desperate search for integrity which, in the end, is contrivedly given up for middle-class gentility (represented by the aspidistra that, like a flag of a sinking ship, is kept flying), and the unpleasant Gordon Comstock, make the novel unsympathetic. Although the bookshop experiences, jail, and the attempt to be a poet, are close to Orwell's experiences, Comstock is a failed Orwell and Orwell is always ironically detached from him. This is what Orwell might have been but, fortunately, was not. Its best virtue is one that Simpson picks out in his review: 'the vision of lower depths which pervades *Down and Out in Paris and London*, is put to use. The nightmare terrors of *Nineteen Eighty-Four* are made relevant to our everyday lives.'[33]

What these two novels attempt, and in part achieve, is a relationship between fact and fiction summed up to perfection by Robert Browning in *The Ring and the Book*:

It is the glory and good of Art,
That Art remains the one way possible,
Of speaking truths.

Book 12, lines 842–4

Orwell's task would next become a way of speaking truth directly,
'to make political writing into an art', as he put it in 'Why I Write'
(CEJL, i.28).

4

The Turning-Point:
Wigan and Spain

THE ROAD TO WIGAN PIER

Two months in the north of England and six in Spain proved the turning-point in Orwell's political education, his development as a writer, and his health. Two myths about *The Road to Wigan Pier* must first be dealt with: that it was commissioned by the Left Book Club, and that he went to Wigan 'armed with a large advance from Victor Gollancz', sometimes specified as £500, based on information from Geoffrey Gorer.[1] As £500 would, in today's money, be about £20 000, it would have been a huge advance; £500 was more than twice the average annual wage in the mid-thirties, so in terms of average wages today it would be equivalent to about £32 000. Whichever way one looks at it, £500 would have been a great deal of money in 1936 and, had Orwell received that, there might be some justification for those who see him as being richly paid to poke into the affairs of those living in poverty. The confusion over who commissioned Orwell is well demonstrated by the current Penguin Twentieth-Century Classics edition (1993). This states, correctly, in its description of the book in its preliminaries, that Orwell was 'commissioned by Victor Gollancz to visit areas of mass unemployment in Lancashire and Yorkshire', but on its back cover states that the book was 'Commissioned by the Left Book Club in 1936'. The first Penguin edition (1962) did not make that error. It did suggest, however, that Orwell's 'comments on Socialism in the second part of the book could still serve to educate an opposition'.

The Left Book Club could not have commissioned Orwell because it had not been formed when he left for Wigan on 31 January 1936. On his way back from the north, he stayed at his sister's house in Leeds for a day or two and left for Hertfordshire on 26 March. The first advertisement announcing that a Left Book Club was being formed for those 'who desire to play an intelligent part in the struggle for World Peace, and a better social and economic order, and *against* Fascism' appeared in *The New Statesman and Nation* on 29 February 1936. Its first books were published in May 1936. When Orwell posted the manuscript of *The Road to Wigan Pier* to his agent on 15 December 1936, he told Moore that he thought the chances of the book being made a Left Book Club selection were slim. Typesetting of the edition was ordered on Christmas Eve 1936, and still a decision had not been taken to make the book a Club selection. It was not until Orwell was in Spain that it was decided to publish Left Book Club and trade editions; *The Road to Wigan Pier* became the Club's twenty-second book.[2]

None of the eight surviving letters that Orwell wrote to Geoffrey Gorer between May 1936 and January 1946 mentions the advance he received from Gollancz. Gollancz thought it foolish to set advances at more than was likely to be earned.[3] As *The Road to Wigan Pier*, when commissioned, was only considered for publication in a trade edition – the Left Book Club not having been formed – calculations as to the probable return from sales must be related to what a trade edition might bring in. Of the initial printing, 1650 copies were in cloth for the trade; at 10s. 6d. each they would, if all sold (which Gollancz could not guarantee when he planned what advance he would give Orwell), bring in £866 5s. A further 500 copies were cloth-bound and so the total return from the trade edition was £1128 15s. At least one-third of this would be paid to booksellers, leaving Gollancz £752 10s. Now, in addition to this supposed £500, Orwell *was* paid an advance of £100, so described in a letter from Gollancz to Orwell's agent of 24 December 1936. Thus, out of total possible receipts of £752 10s., Gollancz, if he had paid Orwell £500 + £100, would have been left with £152 10s. to print, bind, and market a book of 264 pages with 32 pages of half-tone plates – and make a profit. Gollancz was far too sensible a man to make such a foolish bargain. Indeed, even after the sale of all the hardback copies and some 44 000 copies of the full edition to members of the Left Book Club, Orwell's receipt from royalties was just under £600 after paying his agent's commission.

Another way of looking at the size of the initial advance is by considering Orwell's financial state before and after his journey north. The first few days of the Wigan Diary show that Orwell was so short of money, having 'only 3d. in hand', that he had to pawn his scarf for 1s. 11d. on 4 February (CEJL, i.197). He was then able to cash a cheque. This might have been a cheque of his own or one from Gollancz. He paid £1 5s. a week for his board and lodgings in

Wigan and, obviously, had other expenses. On his return to his cottage in Hertfordshire in April he set up shop. About 16 April he wrote to Jack Common to ask whether, if he put down a deposit of £5, wholesalers would advance him credit of £15 to enable him to stock his shelves (*300*). This is hardly a man who had an advance of £500 ten weeks earlier. On 12 October 1938, Orwell wrote to Common recalling that when he and Eileen married (9 June 1936), and he was writing *The Road to Wigan Pier*, 'we had so little money that sometimes we hardly knew where the next meal was coming from, but we found we could rub along in a remarkable manner with spuds and so forth' (*498*). Orwell was generous but not profligate and £500, twice what he earned in 1935 and two-and-a-half times his earnings in 1936, would surely have lasted him from February until June. Had he been advanced £50, however, that would have given him about £6 a week for the time he was up north. That would have enabled him to pay his board and lodging, travel about, and meet other expenses, but would leave little over when he got back to 'The Stores'. It is not possible to be sure just what Orwell received in the way of an advance, but pretty certainly it was not £500.

Orwell sent Leonard Moore his manuscript on 15 December 1936. On 19 Saturday, Gollancz telegraphed Orwell in Hertfordshire (Orwell had no telephone) saying it was exceedingly important that they meet on 21 December because 'I think we can make [the book] a Left Book Club Choice' (*341*). By Monday he and his libel lawyer had read the book. Clough Williams Ellis, the founder of Portmeirion, was present at their meeting and it was decided to illustrate the book. The little piece of blotting paper on which Gollancz wrote the names of those who might provide photographs has survived (illustrated at I.xxxiii) and Norman Collins was instructed to follow up these suggestions. Two days later Orwell left for Spain.

Gollancz intended to have the production of *The Road to Wigan Pier* 'rushed through', as Eileen put it in a letter to Gollancz's secretary, Miss Perriam of 17 January 1937 (*356*). It had been arranged that Eileen should have the proofs for 24 hours but it seems that not even that proved possible. She took that to mean 'that no alterations have been necessary to the text to conform with any laws and conventions' and she hoped that 'the proof-correctors have not made too many emendations'. The letter also reveals one change Gollancz had asked Orwell to make: 'rooks *courting*' for 'rooks *copulating*' (V.16/16). Eileen asked for the offending word to be changed to *treading* because Orwell had 'seen rooks courting hundreds of times'.

However, if Gollancz had 'changed his mind and left *copulating*, that would be better still, but I expect there is no hope of that'. The change was made to 'treading' and, in 1986, Orwell's preferred reading was introduced, fifty years after he wrote his book. At first, as Professor Crick explains, Gollancz tried to persuade Moore and Eileen to allow him to produce a small trade edition of both parts of the book and to issue to members of the Left Book Club only Part I.[4] They refused. Gollancz could not bear to reject the book, despite what seemed to him its repugnant second half and, as Ruth Dudley Evans puts it, Gollancz 'albeit nervously, did overrule C[ommunist] P[arty] objections in favour of his publishing instinct. His compromise was to publish the book with what . . . Bernard Crick rightly calls "an extraordinary introduction", full of good criticism, unfair criticism and half-truths.'[5] In fact, a relatively small number of copies of Part One only were issued at 1s. 0d., compared to 2s. 6d. for the full LBC edition. It is, perhaps, significant that, despite Gollancz's qualms (not wholly unjustified given the specialised nature of the LBC readership and Orwell's often cruel jibes at what he saw as trendy socialists who did more harm than good to the cause), only 890 copies of Part One were called for. A second issue of 2000 copies was printed on 21 April 1937. In all, 44 150 copies of the full LBC edition were sold; 2150 copies of the trade edition; 890 copies of Part One; and 150 sets were lost through enemy action, a total of 47 340 copies. The type was distributed on 14 June 1937 and the rights reverted to Orwell's estate on 8 July 1950. No American edition was published until after Orwell's death; it was the only edition after the first to include the illustrations until 1986.[6] Secker & Warburg issued the book in its Uniform Edition in 1959 and Penguin Books published it in 1962; both omit Orwell's third example on p. 48, the Penguin edition renumbering the items that follow. From this error, and others it reproduces, it is plain that that Penguin edition took the Uniform Edition as its copy.

On 11 February 1937 (*361*), Eileen asked for copies of the book to be sent to Sir Richard Rees, Henry Miller (the American novelist whom Orwell visited in Paris on the way to Spain), Mabel Fierz, Eleanor Jaques, Geoffrey Gorer, Nellie Limouzin (who was staying at the Orwell's cottage), his parents, and his brother-in-law, Laurence O'Shaughnessy. Whether between them Orwell and Eileen (who was rushing to get to Spain) forgot people in the north, or whether Eileen had no addresses for them, the failure to send copies to people Orwell had met there was a regrettable oversight.

Orwell saw his book in its published form at the very end of April, or in the first days of May 1937. Only then did he see how it was illustrated. Writing to Gollancz from the Hotel Continental, Barcelona, on 9 May, the day after the internecine fighting in the streets of Barcelona concluded, he said, 'I liked the introduction very much, though of course I could have answered some of the criticism you have made. It was the kind of discussion of what one is really talking about that one always wants & never seems to get from the professional reviewers' (368). Orwell never shrank from directness and although Sonia Orwell said that later he reacted differently, he may not have had his tongue in his cheek. Orwell *did* like discussion. He probably saw Gollancz's argument no differently than he did the objections of the students who crowded into his railway carriage after he had struck a schoolboy (p. 16). Contrast his immediate reaction at having to make 'a few trifling alterations' to *Burmese Days* with his later resentment at the way the text had been 'garbled' (p. 49).

Orwell's account of what he saw in the north of England was supported by a considerable amount of research. He visited libraries in the north, collected a mass of newspaper cuttings, wrote to local government officials, read books, and visited the British Museum Library. Some of this material has survived. A selection reprinted in the *Complete Works* edition takes up the last fifty pages of Volume 10. Orwell's arithmetic was often faulty and a recalculation of the payments in the miners' slips he collected shows that he slightly exaggerated the amounts received by the miners (if anything, to the detriment of his case). The corrected figures are given in the 1986 and 1989 editions, p. 38.

Just after Orwell left to fight in Spain, Gollancz sent Eileen a draft contract setting out terms for publishing his next three novels. The royalties were set at 10 per cent for the first thousand copies, $12\frac{1}{2}$ per cent for the second thousand, and 15 per cent for the next three thousand, and 20 per cent thereafter. He was to receive 10 per cent for cheap editions sold at between 2s. 0d. and 3s. 6d. and $7\frac{1}{2}$ per cent for editions selling at less than 2s. 0d. There were a number of other conditions, including arrangements for royalties. The final contract has not survived; it was signed by Eileen on her husband's behalf on 31 January 1937. When she returned the contract she told Leonard Moore that she was delighted by it and knew Orwell would be: 'I had not fully realised before how satisfactory it was' (358).[7]

Orwell's motivation to travel north was clearly Gollancz's commission, but did anything specific, other than the general concern for the distress of the unemployed, prompt Gollancz? It is possible that the documentary film, *Housing Problems* (1935) made by Arthur Elton and Edgar Anstey for the British Commercial Gas Association, put the idea into Gollancz's mind. The illustrations to *The Road to Wigan Pier*, though an afterthought, show a remarkable similarity to what Elton and Anstey revealed. Certainly, there is no better introduction than this film to an understanding of those times and of Orwell's book.

Stephen Wadhams, in *Remembering Orwell*, remarks correctly that not everyone in Wigan thanked Orwell for 'making the name Wigan synonymous with poverty and degradation'.[8] On the other hand, several of the interviews he prints praise Orwell for showing up the conditions for what they were and one concluded: 'He was always a man for decency in that way. He was a noble character in many respects.' One of the earlier analyses of the book is still worth reading: Chapter 8 of Laurence Brander's *George Orwell*. Orwell, Brander says, was politically naive at the time (as Part II exemplifies), yet Orwell's attempt to face up to the issues posed by Wigan, the need for socialism, and the weakness, as he saw it, of its advocates, though it must infuriate the faithful, shows the peculiar virtue of a deeply troubled man's personal struggle. No understanding of Orwell is possible without a careful reading of Chapters 8 and 9. Brander frequently likens Orwell to a preacher. For all the book's virtues, to Brander it was a failure and he concludes his chapter with a vivid picture of Orwell (whom he knew well, of course), as a 'simple, single-minded zealot' calling out to the people:

> It was a curious sermon to deliver from the end of a non-existent pier. We wonder at his simplicity, but we are bound to admire the courage of the preacher as well as the odd shafts of both common sense and prescience that light up the chaotic murk of his most disappointing performance.[9]

Perhaps 'erratic' might be more accurate than 'disappointing' because, despite its faults, like *Homage to Catalonia*, it still speaks to us a half-century later on in ways that do few, if any, other books on its subject. It can still infuriate, especially when it is misread (sometimes perversely). People still will imagine that Orwell said that the working class smelt. What he said was that in childhood 'we were taught – *the lower classes smell'* (V.119; Orwell's italics). Unfortunately it is only too true that not only the working class of that time, but most English people had a reputation for washing infrequently. Australians, as late as the 1960s, made that gibe, and not without foundation. Anyone who, forty and more years ago, went into a large class of children in a state school on a rainy day would not doubt that people smelt. Once again, Orwell's essay on Dickens provides a useful point of reference. Discussing the 'class-sex theme' as it arises in Thackeray, Trollope and Meredith, he notes that Trollope, in *The Three Clerks*, 'even gives the typical class-reaction by noting that the girl "smells"' (CEJL, i.479). Orwell himself encloses 'smells' in quotation marks, so marking his anomalous use of the word. No one puts this question of smell (a sense acute in Orwell) into better perspective than Richard Hoggart, who, in his childhood, knew conditions like those Orwell described in Wigan. Orwell, he says, 'knew that not everyone was filthy, but the filth was the true indication of the cost of capitalist industrialisation in one of its worst forms'. Gollancz, writes Hoggart, couldn't accept Orwell's 'directness about a class he only knew through his intellect. He would have been less shocked if Orwell had said that the Hampstead intelligentsia smell.'[10] This puts it in a nutshell.

A frequent complaint about *A Road to Wigan Pier* is that Orwell pays little attention to working women. To Beatrix Cambell, Orwell had a 'toxic scorn' toward women and working-class socialists. In 'Orwell – Paterfamilias or Big Brother?', she argues that Orwell's choice of miners for study 'is significant. As the mysogynist (*sic*) he is, it is not surprising that he has chosen the most masculinised profession.'[11] This would be more compelling were miners not then invested with mythic stature as a result of their industrial battles (and not only the General Strike of 1926), but also as typified in such films as *Coal Face* (1935). This idealisation was encouraged by documentary films throughout the forties, for example, in the re-creation of the Czech mining village of Lidice through the people of Cwmgiedd in *The Silent Village* (1943). If miners, the heroes of industry, could be so humiliated, what chance had the rest of the working class? That said, there is no doubt that a more balanced picture of men and women at work, or laid off, would have been possible in, say, Preston.

It is, of course, correct, that women are described as adjuncts, housewives making do as best they can in appalling circumstances, yet the most vivid picture in *The Road to Wigan Pier*, perhaps in all

Orwell, is of a woman, exhausted, trying to clear a blocked drain, with 'the most desolate, hopeless expression I have ever seen', facing 'how dreadful a destiny' (V.15). The passage is often picked out and compared with its source in the Diary for 15 February 1936 (CEJL, i.203). Although Part One is factual, often providing pages of details that can be backed up, word for word, from Orwell's source material, Orwell's creative imagination has been at work on the material. He is here, as he puts it in 'The Prevention of Literature', modifying – distorting – what he sees so that he can make his meaning clearer. This is justifiable because he does not, as he puts it, 'misrepresent the scenery of his own mind' (CEJL, iv.88). In the Diary, Orwell records direct contact – the woman looks up and catches Orwell's eye; in the book, Orwell is safely ensconced in a train, moving away from the horrors of Wigan, he is only 'almost near enough to catch her eye': he is insulated from her dreadful condition as, in truth, he and so many middle-class people then were. That is Orwell's point, that is the distortion demanded to accord with 'the scenery of his mind'. As he says in the 1946 essay, and as he demonstrates through the recasting and expansion of this fleeting moment, this epiphany, 'there is no such thing as genuinely non-political literature'.

What must be borne in mind in considering the relative non-appearance of women in *The Road to Wigan Pier* is that this is absolutely typical of such studies, even those written by women, in the first fifty years of the twentieth century. Orwell (relatively rarely in his day, especially in a working-class family) was not the kind of man who would not wash up; he willingly changed young Richard's nappies at a time when few men did such things. But he was writing about a society which was dependent on the man working and, in working-class society, orientated to that end far more than was the world of the middle-class. Examination of a number of books of the first half of the twentieth century that have obvious parallels with *The Road to Wigan Pier* reveals few working women. Maud Pember Reeves, *Round About a Pound a Week* (1913); Margery Spring Rice, *Working-Class Wives* (1939); Ellen Wilkinson, *The Town That Was Murdered: The Life-Story of Jarrow* (1939); Wal Hannington, *The Problem of the Distressed Areas* (1937); and F. Zweig, *Labour, Life and Poverty* (1948) (the last three all Left Book Club publications) pay working women scant attention, yet the authors of three of these five books (selected simply because they are on my shelves) are women. Occasionally a woman will be described as taking in washing, or doing office-cleaning (as in case-studies 6 and 16 in *Working-Class Wives*), but only because their husbands are unemployed, but none considers the working woman as such. Zweig offers no fewer than 75 case-studies, many very interesting and some relevant to Orwell – for example, 25 is a pavement artist (see *Down and Out in Paris and London*, I.172); 37 a kitchen-hand; 65 and 74 are vagrants – but not one is a woman. Hannington's book (published seven months after Orwell's) also has 32 plates; only one shows would-be wage-earning women: women queuing to apply for a job as a librarian (plate 8). No study brings out the dependence on male earnings better than Maud Pember Reeves's book. She maintains that a man earning £1 a week or less in 1913 should not marry (this was a time when marriage was a norm, of course); at 25s. a week, he could marry but the couple should have no children; at £1 10s., marriage with one or two children was possible (p. 219).

Before leaving *The Road to Wigan Pier* something should be said about Orwell's attitude to class. On p. 106 he asks (from a middle-class point of view), 'is it ever possible to be really intimate with the working class?' and he devotes Chapter X to considering this problem. At the start, he poses another question: 'why is it so easy to be on equal terms with social outcasts' (V.143) and one's mind goes back to Scotty's soggy, loathsome dog-ends (p. 45 above), and to his compelling descriptions of his fear at being asked to drink from a bottle passed round from one lower-class mouth to another, and then his willingness to drink tea out of the same snuff-tin as a tramp when 'you have seen the worst and the worst has no terrors for you' (V.122). There is no short-cut (V.144); whichever way you turn,

> this curse of class-difference confronts you like a wall of stone. Or rather it is not so much like a stone wall as the plate-glass pane of an aquarium; it is so easy to pretend that it isn't there, and so impossible to get through it.
>
> Unfortunately it is nowadays the fashion to pretend that the glass is penetrable. . . . (V.145).

There is no future in 'merely wishing class-distinctions away' (V.149). Things may have changed a little in the past sixty years but such changes that have taken place have, I think, been superficial.[12]

The problem was not peculiar to Orwell. In his essay on Dickens, Orwell picks out the passage in which David Copperfield says his

conduct and manners ensured that, though he was 'perfectly familiar' with the other boys at the blacking warehouse, they were
'different enough from theirs to place a space between us'. Orwell
notes:

> It was as well that there should be 'a space between us', you see.
> However much Dickens may admire the working classes, he does
> not wish to resemble them. Given his origins, and the time he
> lived in, it could hardly be otherwise. . . . Dickens is quite genu-
> inely on the side of the poor against the rich, but it would be next
> door to impossible for him not to think of a working-class exte-
> rior as a stigma. (CEJL, i.478)

Except for his not thinking of 'a working-class exterior as a stigma'
(and in that respect, perhaps the working and middle classes had
come a little nearer since Dickens's day), Orwell and Dickens are
very close here. In Orwell's own time, George Woodcock, anarchist
colleague of Orwell on the Freedom Defence Committee, makes
pertinent points about Arthur Koestler and the working class.
Koestler, he said,

> tended at first to have bourgeois illusions about workers, rather
> than a deep and intimate knowledge such as Silone shows for his
> poor Italian peasants and labourers. When Koestler did come
> into a close and prolonged contact with real workers in large
> numbers, it was in the French concentration camp of Le Vernet,
> and he found it the disillusioning experience which comes sooner
> or later to any intellectual who has idealised the working class,
> unless he remains insulated from real contact with them all his
> life.[13]

At Le Vernet, Koestler learnt the bitter lesson that 'the workers
whom he had previously tended somewhat naïvely to idealise, could
be as despicable and as treacherous as any other class'. No progress
was possible, argued Woodcock, until 'the masses had become
awakened and educated to their responsibilities' and that required
'a certain degree of material social progress' to remove the 'numb-
ing influence of want and suffering'; only then could they 'discover
their moral responsibilities to society'.[14] This is as tough as anything
Orwell has to say, and it is written by someone with a deep concern

for the social well-being of the masses. It illuminates the dilemma in which Orwell and Koestler (who were close friends) found themselves. Woodcock, like Orwell, shows sentiment (feeling) but no sentimentality, a distinction many people find hard to make.

The difference between the classes, as Orwell sees it, is well revealed in the important essay, 'Looking Back on the Spanish War' (written autumn 1942, published mid-1943, CEJL, ii.286–306). In this he contrasts the working class as 'the most reliable enemy of Fascism' because 'it can't be permanently bribed', with the intelligentsia, 'who squeal loudest against Fascism, and yet a respectable proportion of them collapse into defeatism when the pinch comes . . . and moreover they can be bribed'. (Notice, incidentally, the wry humour of 'respectable'.) Orwell goes out of his way here to assert (though one can ask, how convincingly) that 'this is not to idealize the working class'; he points out that in the long struggle following the Russian Revolution, it was the working class which had been defeated, and comments, quite unsentimentally, 'it is impossible not to feel that it was their own fault' (CEJL, ii.298–9). Orwell developed this self-defeat in *Animal Farm* in what might be termed 'the Kronstadt incident' (see below, pp. 127–8). This comparison is made the more telling because Orwell had earlier in the essay dramatically illustrated a contrast in working- and middle-class values, at a time when, in the trenches, 'the effects of safe and civilized life' were overridden and primary emotions of gratitude and generosity were easier than they ordinarily were. Orwell described the false accusation made against the 'wild-looking boy from the back streets of Barcelona' who was believed to have stolen a bundle of cheap cigars from Orwell's bunk, an accusation Orwell had half-believed. The boy was cleared and Orwell's description of how he tried to make amends he himself describes as 'horrible'. Yet the boy showed later, in his vehement loyalty to Orwell, a natural generosity that Orwell found profoundly touching (CEJL, ii.292–3).

It is sometimes suggested that Orwell condescended to working-class people.[15] I doubt whether Orwell intended to condescend in the sense that that word is usually, and pejoratively, used. He may, of course, have given that impression: his accent alone might have caused that. But 'condescension' is, or was, not quite as simple, or as inevitably wicked, as is normally implied. When Orwell was at St Cyprian's and at Eton he would frequently have heard at church services on the second Sunday after the Epiphany, the Epistle set down for that day, St Paul's Epistle to the Romans, 12: 6–16.[16] (In those days there was no great range of alternatives as there is nowadays.) Orwell knew the Book of Common Prayer extremely well. Mulk Raj Anand, who broadcast to India for Orwell during the war, said Orwell could quote from memory lengthy passages from the Prayer Book, and often did so.[17] It is worth reading that passage in full, if only for the light it casts on Orwell. Its precepts are those one can see him carrying into practice: the exhortations to love without dissimulation, not to be slothful, to be patient in tribulation, given to hospitality. The final words of the lesson are especially relevant to Orwell: 'Be of the same mind one to another. Mind not high things, but condescend to men of low estate'. An alternative translation of this passage brings home the point without the use of that troublesome word for us, 'condescend': 'Do not be haughty but go about with humble folk.'

Did Orwell take that lesson against pride to heart? Perhaps the answer is to be found in the extraordinary success of *The Road to Wigan Pier*, and not only in its own day. Who nowadays reads what is, in many respects, an excellent book, Wal Hannington's *The Problem of the Distressed Areas*, similar in date and production, even to its illustrations? That Orwell can still speak to us through his description of conditions sixty years ago, and through his wrestling with problems of class, socialism, and personal integrity, however irritating and (to our superior frame of mind) naive he may at times be, suggests that he did succeed in the very best sense in conveying something of what the humble folk with whom he went about suffered, and continue to suffer.

Orwell began life experiencing the 'recurrent terror' of gangs of working-class boys (V.118); when he was 17 or 18, having read Jack London's *The People of the Abyss*, he 'could agonise over their sufferings, but I still hated them and despised them when I came anywhere near them' (V.131); he came to accept and be accepted by outcasts and he developed an emotional sympathy for the sufferings of the unemployed; his experience in the north of England developed that, but he still found it difficult to be 'really intimate' with members of the working class, as is well illustrated by Orwell's slightly sticky relationship with Jack Common; it was only his experience in Spain, in the trenches, almost entirely with working-class men, Spanish and British, that enabled him to win the complete confidence of working-class men and women, some of whom remained his friends for life and even now still remember him with deep affection.[18]

HOMAGE TO CATALONIA

When Orwell's friend (and later, his literary executor), Sir Richard Rees passed through Barcelona in April 1937, just before the fighting began which led to the liquidation of the Partido Obrero de Unificación Marxista (the anti-Stalinist Workers' Party of Marxist Unification, usually referred to as 'the POUM'),[19] he called on Orwell's wife, Eileen, who was working in the POUM office. She struck him as being in a very strange mental state.

> She seemed absent-minded, preoccupied, and dazed. As Orwell was at the front I assumed that it was worry about him that was responsible for her curious manner. But when she began talking about the risk, for me, of being seen in the street with her, that explanation no longer seemed to fit. In reality, of course, as I realised afterwards, she was the first person in whom I had witnessed the effects of living under a political terror.[20]

It was this 'Living under a Terror' that Orwell, Eileen, and others, experienced in Spain. In time, that shaped *Animal Farm* and inspired *Nineteen Eighty-Four*. But it had all begun so hopefully: *Homage to Catalonia* is a personal odyssey from hope to its betrayal.

At the beginning of *Homage to Catalonia*, Orwell explains that he went out to Spain 'with some notion of writing newspaper articles, but I had joined the militia almost immediately, because at that time and in that atmosphere it seemed the only conceivable thing to do' (VI.2).[21] The front to which Orwell was assigned was relatively quiet. For that reason he decided to transfer to the International Brigade although Bob Edwards, the leader of the ILP contingent, tried to dissuade him. The internecine conflict between the Nationalist factions in Barcelona in May 1937 (described by Orwell in Chapter IX) convinced him that the Communist Party's attitude to the POUM demanded that he remain with the ILP/POUM contingent. This was fortunate for he would almost certainly have been liquidated had he transferred to the International Brigade. Although the front was quiet, Orwell did see some action and his surviving comrades have made it plain that he did not hesitate to put his life at risk, especially on night patrol. Douglas Moyle describes how he admired Orwell's 'leadership and decisiveness' when he accompanied him on patrol. The attack Orwell records in Chapter VI of *Homage to Catalonia* was described more pungently by his American colleague, Harry Milton, as 'a hellish business; the whole thing was botched up' (though that was not Orwell's fault). Moyle recalls Orwell throwing a grenade 'and there was a scream from a person being wounded, or perhaps even killed by it'.[22] The incident was written up as 'Night Attack on the Aragon Front' in the ILP's journal, *New Leader*, 30 April 1937. Moyle told Ian Angus in a letter of 9 April 1965 that Orwell was 'quite cross with how the ILP handled the story'. He thought that they had blown it up into 'a sort of 1914–18 battle . . . George never felt quite the same about the ILP after that & did not encourage them to use him for propaganda purposes when he came back to England' (*366*).

Perhaps the most notable 'engagement' was one Orwell described five years later in 'Looking Back on the Spanish War'; in this he deliberately did not shoot a Fascist soldier. The trenches were about 300 yards apart. Orwell worked himself across no-man's land to within 100 yards of the Fascist trenches to snipe. A man appeared suddenly, 'presumably carrying a message . . . and ran along the top of the parapet in full view. He was half-dressed and was hold- ing up his trousers with both hands as he ran. I refrained from shooting . . . partly because of that detail about the trousers. I had come there to shoot at "Fascists"; but a man who is holding up his trousers isn't a "Fascist", he is visibly a fellow creature, similar to yourself, and you don't feel like shooting him' (CEJL, ii.291–2). In this account Orwell says he was a poor shot (as does the nar- rator in 'Shooting an Elephant', see above, p. 46) and would prob- ably have missed a moving target. As his time in Burma showed, this was not true; it may be another instance of Orwell's self- deprecation, or artistic licence.

Edwards, in a BBC broadcast made in April 1960, described Orwell's hatred of the rats that abounded in the trenches: 'He had a phobia about rats.' On one occasion a 'particularly adventurous rat had annoyed George for some time and he got out his gun and shot it'. The noise in the confines of the dug-out was such that 'the whole front and both sides went into action', with, for the ILP/ POUM soldiers, the destruction by artillery-fire of their cookhouse and two buses that had brought up reserves.[23]

Jon Kimche, who had worked with Orwell at Booklover's Corner and on *Tribune*, said Orwell 'always *reacted* to situations, to people, to individuals. He had certain basic gut attitudes. Very decent but not attuned . . . to complicated political or military situations. . . . He was never very analytical, never theoretically searching out how to deal with a situation . . . That's why he wrote so very clearly and very simply.'[24] As Orwell shows in *Homage to Catalonia* (as he had in *The Road to Wigan Pier*) he was ill-prepared politically and socially for what he was to be faced with. Both books reveal a learning process presented in such a way that the reader is taken through the experiences described. It is that personal exploration and the expression of those gut-reactions, the appeal to 'decency' (so important a concept for Orwell) that lifts these books out of their time. It was this impulse to respond immediately to situations, to people – to use an out-dated phrase that would have been less strange to Orwell than it is to us today, 'to do the decent thing' (compare below, what was 'not done', p. 106) – that led him, unthinkingly, and unaware of the political implications, to join the POUM militia. This reaction to the needs of people is perfectly, but, I suspect, unconsciously expressed in his account of his meeting with the Italian militiaman with which *Homage to Catalonia* starts and the poem with which 'Looking Back on the Spanish War' concludes. Orwell's Spanish experience is epitomised in his meeting when he first arrived in Spain with this militiaman, whose name he never learned, and, towards the end of his time there, through Bob Smillie, whose 'death is not a thing I can easily forgive' (VI.1 and 134–5, 171). Orwell believed that the Spanish revolution had been self-betrayed by the Communists. Before showing how this was so from Orwell's point of view (and going on to suggest, following the release of documents from Spanish archives a few years ago, that it was a deliberate betrayal) it would be fair to note here that Jon Kimche disagreed:

> I don't think the Spanish revolution was betrayed, as Orwell says, by the communists, because if the communists hadn't taken over the others wouldn't have been able to hold out as long as they did. Only the anarchists possibly could have done something of their own against Franco, but even they would have had to do it with the communists. At the time I took the same view of it as Orwell, but looking back on it now [1983], it was inevitable that the communists wouldn't tolerate other groups.[25]

In Appendix I (Chapter V of the earlier editions), Orwell gives a clear account of the opposing strategies adopted by the heterogeneous forces which opposed the Army and the Roman Catholic Church led by Franco. On the one hand were the Anarchists, the POUM (with whom Orwell fought), and a section of the Socialists who stood for revolution first, that is, for workers' control, on the basis that unless the workers controlled the army, the army would control and defeat the workers; on the other hand were right-wing Socialists, Liberals, and Communists, who stood for 'centralised government and a militarised army' (VI.205). Initially, Orwell 'preferred the Communist viewpoint to that of the POUM'. The Communists had 'a definite practical policy' whereas 'the day-to-day policy of the POUM, their propaganda and so forth, was unspeakably bad'; the 'revolutionary purism of the POUM . . . seemed to me rather futile. After all, the one thing that mattered was to win the war' (VI.205–6).[26] It was only when the POUM came under attack from their alleged allies and were described as 'traitors in the pay of the enemy [Franco]' (VI.207) that Orwell became disenchanted with the Communists and their allies and defended the POUM. Orwell was quickly appointed *cabo* (corporal) and was reasonably successful in bringing some sort of order and discipline into his little group. When Bob Edwards returned to England, Orwell was *elected* as the ILP contingent's representative;[27] just before he was wounded he had been recommended for promotion to lieutenant. One thing that Orwell does not represent in *Homage to Catalonia* is his personal bravery and the high regard in which he was held by his colleagues.

If the unknown Italian militiaman and Bob Smillie represent respectively the high hopes and the betrayal of the cause which had led him to tell Cyril Connolly, 'I have seen wonderful things and at last really believe in Socialism' (CEJL, i.301), the three visits he paid to Barcelona mark his initial excitement, his sense of dismay, and his awareness of self-inflicted tragedy that was the Spanish War as he saw and experienced it. On returning on leave for his second visit to Barcelona, he discovered 'by innumberable signs that my first impression was wrong. A deep change had come over the town' (VI.89–90). A single cameo highlights what disturbed him:

> Now things were returning back to normal. The smart restaurants and hotels were full of rich people wolfing expensive meals, while for the working-class population food-prices had jumped enormously without any corresponding rise in wages. . . . The restaurants and hotels seemed to have little difficulty in getting whatever they wanted, but in the working-class quarters the queues for bread, olive oil, and other necessaries were hundreds of yards

long. . . . A fat man eating quails while children are begging for bread is a disgusting sight. . . . (VI.93, 95)

Orwell's third visit followed his being wounded in the throat and it was to end with his fleeing the country. Chapter XI opens in a way reminiscent of Orwell's favourite play by Shakespeare, *Macbeth*, a play redolent with the spreading miasma of fear and terror:

> In Barcelona, during all those last weeks I spent there, there was a peculiar evil feeling in the air – an atmosphere of suspicion, fear, uncertainty, and veiled hatred. . . . there was a perpetual vague sense of danger, a consciousness of some evil thing that was impending. However little you were conspiring, the atmosphere forced you to feel like a conspirator. (VI.148)

It was this experience and what caused it, that formed the basis for *Animal Farm* and *Nineteen Eighty-Four*, though not even Orwell knew (however much he suspected) just how much he and his wife were in danger. Bill Alexander, a Communist, a commander of the British Battalion of the International Brigade, and one of its Political Commissars, wrote disparagingly that after the Barcelona Events of May, and the suppression of the POUM, 'Orwell, his wife, McNair and Cottman decided they *might* be arrested and left Spain' (my italics); David Corkhill and Stewart Rawnsley talk of Orwell joining 'the rest of the ILPers in beating a hasty retreat to the safety of the French border'.[28] What Orwell sensed, what Sir Richard Rees saw in Eileen's eyes, but what Alexander, Corkhill and Rawnsley dismiss, was only too accurate. Fenner Brockway, General Secretary of the ILP at the time (later Lord Brockway), met Orwell and Stafford Cottman in Perpignan just after they had crossed into France. Orwell, he said, was 'terribly thin' and hoarse-voiced. He was 'absolutely shocked by the Stalinist actions of the communists in Barcelona. It was about the only time I saw him really angry.'[29]

The sacrifices made by Spaniards and foreign volunteers on behalf of the Left were enormous and must not, in what follows, be overlooked. Alexander lists 526 killed of some 2050 brigaders, a death rate of over 25 per cent; this is higher than that of the Battle of the Somme. Some national brigades suffered even higher casualty rates. Eight of 22 British Political Commissars were killed: 36 per cent.[30] An even more horrific record is that of the number of brigaders executed by their comrades. Recently, attention has been drawn to the execution of 307 British soldiers for offences such as cowardice and desertion (both often a direct result of shell-shock) in the First World War. Yet this terrible indictment of authority pales almost into insignificance when compared with the record of the International Brigades. André Marty, a Communist Deputy in the French Parliament, 'placed in direct control of the International Brigades by the comintern', admitted – boasted of – executing some 500 brigaders of a total enrolment of slightly under 60 000, so justifying his soubriquet, Le Boucher d'Albacete (the Brigade Headquarters where an NKVD-like prison operated by the SIM, the political police, was situated). And these were not the only men executed. Among the 'crimes' for which men could be executed were political deviance or even criticism of the communist leadership. Walter Tapsell, communist commissar of the British Battalion and an outspoken critic of communist policy in Spain, is recorded as having been killed near Belchite but he and Arnold Reid, onetime editor of the US Communist Party's journal, *New Masses*, were probably victims of their communist colleagues.[31] The ILP was, because of its association with the POUM, regarded as a deviant organisation. Thus, when in Moscow in December 1936, the order was given to destroy the POUM, before Orwell had even left for Spain,[32] the fate of the 'ILPers' was already sealed. Whether Bob Smillie really died of appendicitis in prison, or whether he was a victim of 'the Terror', cannot now be ascertained. Orwell certainly had his doubts for when he feared that Andrés Nin, the POUM leader, had been killed, he wrote to Charles Doran on 2 August 1937, 'I suppose it will be "suicide" or perhaps appendicitis again' (*386*). Nin was murdered by the communists.

It was only recently that a deposition was discovered by Karen Hatherley in the National Historical Archive in Madrid charging Orwell and his wife with espionage and high treason. The document is dated 13 July, three weeks after the Orwells got across the border into France. The ground for this charge was simply that they were members of the ILP. That was crime enough. Further, copies of the document were sent to Albacete and Moscow (*374A*). On the basis of this charge Eileen and Orwell could – would – have been thrown into prison. They might not have been executed, but given the state of Orwell's health he would have been lucky to survive, especially given the appalling conditions (outlined by his commandant, George Kopp, in a letter of 7 July 1937, *378A*). A full account of this document and its implications will be found in the *Complete Works*, but two aspects are worth mentioning here. The first is that if a copy of the document had to be sent to Moscow, that may be where Orwell's diary, seized from his hotel room in Barcelona, may still be kept. Secondly, the copy for Albacete was sent to a David Wickes. It has been possible to discover quite a lot about Wickes, except his fate. He enlisted as an ambulanceman but when he arrived in Spain it was decided he had no appropriate experience (had Rees or many another the appropriate skills?) but as he could speak French and German he was made a translator at the Political Commisariat Headquarters. However, he was an ILPer. What must have been his reaction on seeing the charges laid against the Orwells? What is certain is that there is no record of David Wickes in the published lists of those who served in the International Brigade, nor is his fate recorded in the Archive of the British Battalion at the Marx Memorial Library, despite his being at Brigade Head-quarters. Why, one wonders? Did he attract the attention of the Servicio Investigaciòn Militar – the SIM – at Albacete, where he was based?

Despite the immediate experience, and 'memories that are mostly evil', despite the 'appalling disaster . . . slaughter and physical suffering' of the Spanish people, the result for Orwell was neither cynicism nor disillusion: 'Curiously enough the whole experience has left me with not less but more belief in the decency of human beings' (VI.185–6): decency, again. Orwell's belief, expressed in *Nineteen Eighty-Four* that 'If there was hope, it *must* lie in the proles' (IX.72) stemmed from this 'decency of human beings'; so did his understanding of the power of propaganda to lie and distort; and so, too, his awareness of the havoc that any 'violent conspiratorial revolution, led by unconsciously power-hungry people' (3128) could wreak. This last he would first confront in *Animal Farm*; all three would be his concern in *Nineteen Eighty-Four*. Laurence Brander concluded that *Homage to Catalonia* was

> built of generous incidents, so that while it exposes Communism it also suggests the answer. . . . Communism, which at many stages seems to be generous and friendly, always seems to get to a stage where generosity and that welling up of human feeling, which is the prime mordant of all human society, completely disappears. So the answer to Communism is unselfishness and generosity of mind.[33]

How *Homage to Catalonia* came to be rejected by Gollancz and published by Fredric Warburg is an oft-told story. Suffice here to say that Gollancz would not touch the book, although Orwell called at the publisher's offices to try to persuade Norman Collins to do so.[34] Gollancz did, however, pass on to Harry Pollitt at the *Daily Worker*, Orwell's bitter letter of complaint about attacks made on him because he had fought with the POUM; these repeated lies that Orwell had said the working class smelt and included a libellous campaign against those who had fought with the POUM. Orwell referred particularly to the expulsion of 'a boy of eighteen' (Stafford Cottman) from the Young Communist League for his association with the POUM. Although there were the usual denials, the attacks stopped.[35]

Orwell had one more novel published by Gollancz. *Coming Up for Air* in 1939, the first of three he was contracted for, and *Inside the Whale*, a book of essays, in 1940 (see pp. 108–9), but the refusal to publish *Homage to Catalonia*, and later *Animal Farm*, brought to an end Victor Gollancz Ltd as Orwell's publishers. After *Animal Farm*, Secker & Warburg became Orwell's publishers and it was they who reaped the benefit of all that Gollancz had invested in Orwell when he was struggling to establish himself. Although Gollancz deserved to benefit, Fredric Warburg twice came to Orwell's rescue when important books, especially *Animal Farm*, looked like being unable to find a publisher. In fact, relationships between Gollancz and Orwell improved during the war and they collaborated happily on *Betrayal of the Left: An Examination and Refutation of Communist Policy*, March 1941 (see p. 109). The subtitle clearly indicates how Gollancz, after the Soviets and Nazis became allies, came round to Orwell's position *vis-à-vis* communism as practised in the Soviet Union.

As a book, *Homage to Catalonia* proved a bad risk. In April 1938, 1500 copies were printed. Copies were lost in an air-raid, and even the type was destroyed by bombing. Some copies were sold off cheaply, and it has been said that when the Uniform Edition was published in February 1951, the last copies of the first edition had only recently been sold. Warburg paid Orwell an advance of £150 but his royalties probably did not exceed £130. In Warburg's words, it 'caused barely a ripple on the political pond. It was ignored or hectored into failure'. An Italian translation was published by Mondadori in December 1948 (2060 copies) and an American edition of 4000 copies was published by Harcourt Brace on 15 May 1952 at $3.50, with a second impression of 3000 copies on 3 July 1952.[36]

Orwell was very keen to have changes made to *Homage to Catalonia* if the book were reprinted or translated. He had been in correspondence before and after the war with Yvonne Davet, his French translator, about many of the changes planned for a French translation, though that was not to appear until 1955.[37] When Secker & Warburg decided to reprint the book in its Uniform Edition, Orwell typed up a list of the changes he required and asked that various items should be checked. He particularly wanted the two 'descriptive political chapters' of the first edition, V and XI, made into appendixes. In addition to a typed list, on his deathbed he marked up a copy of *Homage to Catalonia* indicating what he wanted. The way Orwell's request for alterations was dealt with by Roger Senhouse (the director responsible for Orwell's work), was shameful. Senhouse ignored all Orwell's wishes and Orwell's marked-up copy of *Homage to Catalonia* was sold (probably with Senhouse's effects after his death). The Uniform Edition appeared in February 1951, just over a year after Orwell's death. Not only were none of Orwell's requests met, but errors in the 1938 edition were reproduced and the Uniform edition added its own. Madame Davet and the French publishers behaved very differently. They took account of what Orwell was thought to have wanted even though he was five years dead and could not answer queries which arise for any editor in the light of Orwell's requests. English readers had to wait until 1986 and even then the corrected edition, which came out with *Down and Out in Paris and London* and *A Clergyman's Daughter*, suffered yet another malign stroke of fate. The printers substituted the uncorrected material for that which had been proof-corrected and the complete editions had to be pulped, but not, alas, before copies had been sent for review. It is a mark of the perspicacity of English reviewers that only one noticed anything amiss: D. J. Enright. The 1986 and 1989 editions give an account of the changes made, one of which, unlike much bibliographical apparatus, has the additional merit of being comic. Thomas Parker was shot through the top of the thigh; that was 'nearer to being a DSO than he cared about' (VI.58). The French translator asked what this meant and Orwell explained that it parodied Distinguished Service Order and meant 'Dickie Shot Off'.[38]

5

Orwell as Reviewer and Essayist

Spain, with its twin inheritance of 'memories that are mostly evil' and 'more belief in the decency of human beings', was to haunt Orwell for several years. His letters and reviews on his return are full of the agony of Spain, its sufferings, and those of his colleagues in filthy gaols facing an uncertain future. If (and the conditional mood is important), if *Down and Out in Paris and London* was in part an exorcism of his experience of and contribution to imperialism, *Animal Farm, Nineteen Eighty-Four,* his post-1937 essays and reviews, and his practical political work, especially with the Freedom Defence Committee, helped to justify that Spanish experience. Nothing better exemplifies the bitterness Orwell felt in the months after his return than a letter that has recently come to light. Andy Croft, working on a critical biography of Randall Swingler, discovered in Swingler's papers Orwell's reply to Nancy Cunard requesting him to contribute to *Authors Take Sides on the Spanish War,* published by *Left Review* in 1937.[1] The pamphlet published statements by 148 writers, mostly supporting the Government. Orwell's reply is angry, even intemperate. It starts, 'Will you please stop sending me this bloody rubbish', and includes offensive personal abuse of Stephen Spender. Croft remarks, 'it is worth remembering just what a bad-tempered and offensive writer [Orwell] could be, and just how awkward his anti-communism once made everyone feel'.

There is not much 'decency' about this letter, taken in isolation. But it was not written in isolation. Orwell was particularly aware when he received the request to write half-a-dozen lines declaring himself 'for democracy and against Fascism' that, to invert the precept in his Dickens essay (p. 65 above), the world was not decent and men were not behaving decently. Having fought Fascism and been wounded doing so, he and his colleagues had been branded Fascists. Further, the request came at a particularly unhappy time. He replied to Nancy Cunard on 6 August 1937; on 29 July he had heard from his commandant in Spain, George Kopp, who was languishing in gaol, in appalling conditions, on hunger-strike, facing the possibility of execution (*378A*). He wrote to Amy Charlesworth on 1 August that he feared some of his friends were to be shot 'for opposition to the Communist Party' (*384*); on the following day he told Charlie Doran, who had served in Spain, that Stafford Cottmann was being victimised by Communists, that he feared, correctly, that the leader of the POUM, Andrés Nin, would be murdered (see p. 84 above), and that his review of *The Spanish Cockpit* by Franz Borkenau had been rejected by the *New Statesman* (ironically, the journal that published Croft's article), because it controverted its political policy (in 1938, he received an apology from Raymond Mortimer, the literary editor of the *New Statesman*, for this unwarranted rejection, *424*). Although the abuse of Spender was uncalled for (and later they became friends), the bitterness and frustration of the letter is wholly explicable in the circumstances in which it was written. To Orwell, the people making up manifestoes and signing petitions (then, as now, too often a conscience-saving proxy gesture) were those who had fulminated in the comfort and safety of London publishers' offices and were the very people who had turned on him and his colleagues in the POUM, that is, on those actually serving and dying at the front. The letter is important because it shows how deep was Orwell's depression at this time and how impotent he felt. His last two novels spring from this mood.

In all probability it was the Spanish War that started Orwell off in a direction that was to have an important influence on his writing that has yet to be thoroughly explored: his pamphlet collection. In his review of pamphlet literature, 9 January 1943 (CEJL, ii.326), Orwell says he had been collecting pamphlets for six years and had now 'several hundreds'. That would indicate that he began collecting at the time he went to Spain. However, he may have started a little earlier, for in his Notes for his Literary Executor, 1949 (*2648*), he writes of having between 1200 and 2000 pamphlets 'collected between 1935 and 1945', and he asks that they be given to the British Museum Library, where they are now to be found. It is, of course, very easy, looking back, to be uncertain about dates. Orwell had no need to state one date rather than another and so this is no more than simple confusion. He certainly collected some pamphlets (though not the same proportion as for earlier years) after 1945. The implications are important, however.

Many of the pamphlets are political. If Orwell began collecting in 1935, it might explain how it was that everyone was astonished 'including Marxist theoreticians, by his interventions in discussions' about Marxism at *The Adelphi* Summer School at Langham, Essex, in August 1936. 'Without any parade of learning he produced breathtaking Marxist paradoxes and epigrams, in such a way as to make the sacred mysteries seem almost too obvious and simple.'[2] Professor Crick, understandably, thought that a reading of the second half of *The Road to Wigan Pier* indicated that Orwell could not have 'studied the classic texts of Marxism closely; and there is no evidence . . . that his knowledge of Marxism was anything but secondary'.[3] Had Orwell begun collecting pamphlets in 1935, that might explain not only what knowledge he had, but the way he displayed it. Had Orwell by then any of his Socialist Party of Great Britain pamphlets? Or Litvinoff's *The Bolshevik Revolution* (1918; which he described as 'rare'), or the Communist Party's *Where is Trotsky Going?*, or G. A. Aldred's *For Communism* (1935; his friend, Charlie Doran was a member of Aldred's Anti-Parliamentary Federation in Glasgow)? Non-political pamphlets include a number on cremation, which Orwell rejected, stipulating he should be buried. W. J. West has pointed to the influence of J. Middleton Murry's *The Brotherhood of Peace* on *Nineteen Eighty-Four*,[4] and the pamphlets provide clues to Orwell's thinking from *Homage to Catalonia* to the writing of his last novel.[5] One of the 'finds' in this mass of pamphlets, election paraphernalia, and newspaper cuttings, is a newspaper illustration of a group of men practising throwing hand grenades. They are in civilian clothes and from details on the verso, this was printed about the end of August 1940. It shows early Home Guard volunteers and one of them is George Orwell.

On his return home, Orwell's main concern was to write a book about his experience in Spain, but he continued to write articles and reviews. Table 5.1 shows how rapidly after 1937 Orwell's contributions to journals increased. When he was in Paris, Orwell had six articles published in French and one in England on a French subject. Between then and his going to Spain he published eight articles, 47 reviews and six poems. In 1937 he had three articles and ten reviews published. In this nine-year period, therefore, he published 18 articles, 57 reviews and 6 poems – 81 items. In the next six years, that is until five months after he had joined the BBC when most of his journalistic work ceased, he produced 42 articles, 149 reviews (52 of which were of plays and films), two Forewords to books, and five broadcasts written before joining the BBC – a further 198 items; 279 items from his time in Paris until the end of 1943. The financial returns were meagre. *The Adelphi* paid £2.00 for articles and reviews. This was generous in itself at a time when the average wage for a working man was a little under £5.00 a week; the problem was that Orwell simply didn't get enough books to review and not many articles were accepted. After 1940, when he wrote for *Tribune*, he was paid more for articles but often less for reviews. (Details of the amounts paid by the various journals are given in Table 5.1.) However, the *New English Weekly*, for which he wrote four articles (two in 1937) and 27 reviews (two in 1937) paid nothing, nor did some of the low-circulation, left-wing journals. In 1937, therefore, his 13 articles and reviews brought him only about £20 – about a month's pay for a working man.

Writing reviews can be an excellent training in concise and objective writing. It was for Orwell a training in technique and in social and political thinking. One of Orwell's characteristics is his ability to engage the reader's attention at the start of review, article or book, and to re-activate interest later on in a longer work. The opening of a review from this period, so far not republished, is a good example of Orwell's technique. On 15 August 1936, Orwell reviewed three travel books, including Peter Fleming's *News from Tartary* (322A). It begins:

A journey by train or car or aeroplane is not an event but an interregnum between events, and the swifter the vehicle the more boring the journey becomes. The nomad of the steppe or the desert may have to put up with every kind of discomfort, but at any rate he is living while he is travelling, and not, like the passengers in a luxury liner, merely suffering a temporary death. Mr Peter Fleming, who set out . . .

It is useful to bear in mind when reading this that Orwell had never flown in an aeroplane and never would, but anyone who has, say, flown from San Francisco to London overnight will know what he means by that 'temporary death'. Dozens of examples could be cited to illustrate Orwell's ability to catch the reader's attention. *Coming Up for Air* starts off engagingly innocuously with a single, short sentence as its first paragraph: 'The idea really came to me the day I got my new false teeth'; *Nineteen Eighty-Four*, famously, with, 'It was a bright cold day in April, and the clocks were striking

Table 5.1 Orwell's earnings, 1936–45 (estimated)

	1936	1937	1938	1939	1940	1941	1942	1943	1944	1945
Regular emplmt		Jan–Jun Spain	Sep↔Mar Marrakesh £300 loan			Aug←BBC→ £267	£640	Nov Dec←LitEd Trb→Feb £580 [cf. Connolly Hor = £400]	£400?	£66
Occasl emplmt	Bk's Cnr Wgn; Jan £3; £15	£50?; –£12 (Shop)						£33?		Feb–May (Jn); Obs £500; + MEN £42?
Books (advances) calculated as 1937 contract by $12\frac{1}{8}\%$	CD(US) £33; KTAF £65 [£75]; D&O Fr; £5 ······· £5	RWP £594 [£100]; £5 ······· £5	HtC Adv £150 [Ear'd] c£130]; £5 ······· £5	CUFA £100? [stock bombed]; £5	D&O (Pgn) £91; I. Whale £30? [£20]; [stk b'd]	Lion&Uni say £150 ?B'tyl of Left nil?	KTAF (chp iss) £6.49		BD (Pgn) £148; AF(Adv) £90	AF £88; Eng Ppl £20; Tlk/India £16
Sub-total (Books)	£103	£599	£155	£105	£121	£150+?	£6.49		£238	£124
Articles e.g. @ Adph £2 Trb to £5 NEW nil	NEW 2; NWtg 1; Ftny 1	NEW 2; C'try 1	Adph 1; NLdr 1	H'way 1; NWtg 1; LftF 1	FNWtg 1 +Rpt; T&T 2; Hor 1; Trb 1; NS&N 1	PartR 3 (@ £2.50); LftNs 3; DExpr 2; Hor 2; E.Std 1; PixPt 1; NRep 1; NDir 1	PartR 4; Trb 2; Hor 1; Obs 3; FabS 1	PartR 1; Trb 3; Obs 1; NRoad 1	LISTED IN PAYMENTS BOOK (totals below)	

Reviews e.g. @ Adph £2 Trb 10s–£2 Hor £2 NS&N £2 NEW nil									
Adph 2 NEW 9 T&T 7 List 2 (1–1½gn) NS&N 1	NEW 2 T&T 7 NS&N 1	Adph 1 NEW 7 T&T 2 List 2 NLdr 1 NS&N 1	Adph 5 NEW 3 T&T 3 List 1 PceN 1	Adph 3 NEW 2 T&T 10 List 4 (1–2½gn) NS&N 9 Hor 5 Trb 10 L&L 2 LabS 1	Adph 1 T&T 1 List 1 (1 gn) NS&N 6 Hor 2	List 1 Obs 3 NS&N 1 Hor 1 Trb 1	T&T 1 List 1 NS&N 1 Hor 1 Trb 2		
Other P-poem £2 Th/Film £1									
Adph 1p			T&T	ThR 14 FlmR 7 B'ct 1	ThR 11 FlmR 20 B'ct 4 BkFwd 2		+ Payt Bk £154 ...... £541 .... £782		
£35	£20	£20	£25	£159	£156	£60	£40		
£206 (inc exp)	£631	£175+loan+£130	£280	£573	£706	£807		£1179	£1514

1939←Eileen employed as Civil Servant→1944

thirteen'. We now have a 24-hour clock, but clocks still do not strike thirteen, so there is still, nearly fifty years on, an element of surprise here. This page of typescript of the surviving manuscript probably dates from 1946.[6] Orwell first typed, 'It was a cold, blowy day in early April, and a million radios were striking thirteen.' Later he changed 'a million radios' to 'innumerable clocks' and then to 'the clocks', and he added 'bright' and crossed out 'blowy'. This final and much more effective result was not achieved without careful revision. The typescript and manuscript of the draft show what a great deal of rewriting was involved in producing the final version of *Nineteen Eighty-Four*, even though for much of the time Orwell was ill, in pain, and conscious of racing the clock.

Two examples in which Orwell uses similar material are instructive. Part II of *The Road to Wigan Pier* begins, 'The road from Mandalay to Wigan is a long one and the reasons for taking it are not immediately clear.' Certainly, the relationship of Mandalay and Wigan is not obvious but Orwell goes further by drawing attention to the incongruity of what he has written (a self-conscious technique with which we are now much more familiar); only then does he go on to describe his upbringing. In *Homage to Catalonia*, Orwell extends this device. When he returns to Barcelona on leave, after three-and-a-half months at the front, he begins a new chapter with 'From Mandalay, in Upper Burma, you can travel by train to Maymyo. . . . Suddenly you are breathing cool sweet air that might be that of England. . . . Getting back to Barcelona . . .' (VI.87). What in the earlier book was a striking juxtaposition that enables Orwell to launch into a personal odyssey, in *Homage to Catalonia* becomes in itself a miniature odyssey. But the purpose is the same: to attract attention – a verbal 'standing on his head' of the kind that first drew Jacintha Buddicom's attention to him (see p. ix above). Orwell developed this technique in his reviews and articles. Chapter IX of *The Road to Wigan Pier* provides another fine example of a striking opening: 'When I was fourteen or fifteen I was an odious little snob.'

Orwell can reasonably be credited with revivifying the art of the essay. With him it had a purpose; it was no bland causerie, certainly not an elegant space-filler, no decadent relic of the art of the belle-lettrist. Even though, working against the clock, he made slips, he was nevertheless a highly skilled artist. His essays, time after time, are purposeful, vigorous, often polemical, and a real attempt (the proper use of 'essay') to see things afresh. The style is always

said to be plain, to eschew ornateness, but though he avoids superficial 'literariness', he is often a cunning artificer. He does not set
out to shock for the sake of shocking, but he is never afraid to be
unpopular and has, when necessary, that tough, fiery indignation
he so admired in Swift. His column in *Tribune*, 'As I Please',[7] though
informal, was given point and purpose, yet he took time out (sometimes to the annoyance of the po-faced Labour Party stalwarts who
made up most of his readership), to delight in such everyday matters as the blooming of the Albertine rose he had bought at Wool-
worths for sixpence ($2\frac{1}{2}$p) and which, certainly until recently, was
still going strong outside the cottage he had lived in at Wallington
before the war.

The essays reveal much about Orwell and the concerns of his
times. The many references to Orwell's long essay on Charles Dickens given earlier will have shown how often what Orwell says
about Dickens illuminates his own character. Sometimes Orwell's
deepest wishes and elements of his novels were prompted by what
he reviewed. A good example is to be found in his review of *Priest
Island* by E. L. Grant Wilson, *Tribune*, 21 June 1940 (*640*). Orwell did
not think much of this novel, about a man exiled for sheep-stealing
in the early nineteenth century to a small Hebridean Island, but
in his diary for 20 June (by when he would have submitted the
review, of course), he notes:

> Thinking always of my island in the Hebrides, which I suppose
> I shall never possess nor even see. Compton Mackenzie says that
> even now most of the islands are uninhabited (there are 500 of
> them, only 10 per cent inhabited at normal times), and most have
> water and a little cultivable land, and goats will live on them.
> According to R[ayner] H[eppenstall], a woman who rented an
> island in the Hebrides in order to avoid air raids was the first air
> raid casualty of the war, the R.A.F. dropping a bomb there by
> mistake. Good if true.
>   The first air raid of any consequence on Great Britain the night
> before last. (CEJL, ii.400)

Evidently Orwell had done some elementary research and the entry
also shows, besides his keen wish for such an island, other typical
characteristics, such as his wry humour and his love of goats, which
he kept with some success.[8] Orwell would see, if not possess, 'his'
Inner Hebridean island, Jura, first visiting it in September 1945,

after Eileen's death. From 1946 he rented Barnhill on Jura and tried to realise the idyll of which he had dreamed. This, too, is one origin of the idea, if not the place, of the Golden Country in *Nineteen Eighty-Four*. Another source is almost certainly also literary: the natural habitat beyond the Green Wall that bounds the totalitarian regime in which Yevgeny Zamyatin's *We* is set (a book reviewed by Orwell in its French-language version in *Tribune*, 4 January 1946, CRJL, iv.95–9). That 1940 diary-entry, and the review that prompted it,. are the first indication we have of Orwell's wish to live on a remote island. Here, literature and life conspired one with another.

Although there are many more significant essays, none is perhaps more effective, or more skilfully crafted than one of his shortest, 'Some Thoughts on the Common Toad'. The essay, published in *Tribune* on 12 April 1946 (CEJL, iv.171–5) has only eight paragraphs, yet it combines Orwell's love of nature with political purpose. In this it exemplies his wish (expressed in 'Why I Write', CEJL, i.28) that from 1936 what he had most wanted to do was 'make political writing into an art'.

The topic is, at least initially, a strange one for a political journal that, like all periodicals at that time, was struggling to fit too much copy into too few strictly-rationed pages. The first three paragraphs might come from a nature broadcast for schools. The opening words win immediate attention: 'Before the swallow, before the daffodil, and not much later than the snowdrop, the common toad salutes the coming of spring after his own fashion . . .'. This simple but subtle device of altering the natural order of events – it should be snowdrop–toad–daffodil–swallow – focuses attention on the least attractive representative of spring and early summer that Orwell selects, and somehow elevates the toad, despite the superstitious fear it can generate, and its being so off-putting to the touch, to the beauty of the other three. The 'shudder' that can be the reaction of some to the toad is cunningly transferred to 'some kind of shudder in the earth' which Orwell surmises might be one reason for the toad being awoken from its winter sleep. That shuddering of the earth suggests that it is Mother Earth herself who spawns the toad. The first paragraph concludes with Orwell's engaging admission that, in truth, his own knowledge of toads is limited. Toads sometimes 'appear to sleep the clock round and miss out a year from time to time': at any rate, he has dug them up in mid-summer, alive and apparently well. This gesture to his lack of knowledge paradoxically inspires in us confidence in what Orwell has to say about the toad that will carry through to the 'political' part of the essay.

In 'Politics and the English Language', published in the same month as 'Some Thoughts on the Common Toad', Orwell had castigated the use of 'dying metaphors' by those who would not take the trouble to invent phrases for themselves. However, 'A newly invented metaphor assists thought by evoking a visual image' (CEJL, iv.159). His next paragraph introduces a striking metaphor and a truly imaginative simile: 'after his long fast, the toad has a very spiritual look, like a strict Anglo-Catholic towards the end of Lent'. There is a hidden resonance here, often lost on modern readers but not, surely, on Orwell. 'Lent' is not only a period for fasting but, in Anglo-Saxon, 'Spring' (*lencten*). Orwell's humour surfaces more obviously in the fourth paragraph. The spawning of toads, he says, is one of the phenomena of spring that most deeply appeals to him, 'and because the toad, unlike the skylark and the primrose, has never had much of a boost from poets'. That serves as the launching point for the main thrust of the essay: the pleasures of spring are available to everyone and cost nothing. Had Orwell left it at that, this would be no more than a cliché, but Orwell expands his delight in spring to encompass the way it touches even the most dismal parts of the city, again with humour: 'I have heard a first-rate performance by a blackbird in the Euston Road.'

The second half of the essay is concerned with the 'miracle' (and Orwell puts the word in quotation marks as if to draw attention to the cliché) that is spring. Here he brilliantly contrasts this dying metaphor, this 'worn-out figure of speech', with a simile that a Metaphysical Poet would have been proud to own. Spring comes 'seeping in everywhere, like one of those new poison gases which pass through all filters'. This yoking together of opposites – spring and poison gas – makes the worn-out metaphor come as a welcome return to normality, to what we know only too well. But, of course, Orwell is keen that the reader should understand that miracle afresh. Orwell now invokes Persephone, who, like the toad, 'always rises from the dead'. Persephone fulfils a double function here, as a goddess of Hades but also as goddess of the germination of the seed, a conjunction of death and life as remarkable as spring and poison gas.

Paragraph six opens with the question that transforms what has so far been an essay on the joy of returning spring to a political challenge; 'Is it wicked to take pleasure in spring and other seasonal

changes? To put it more precisely, is it politically reprehensible . . . ?'
(or, as we might now put it, 'is it politically incorrect?'). Does spring
lack a class angle, so preventing its being exploited by editors of
left-wing journals? This brings together two aspects of socialism (or
rather, perhaps, socialists) that perplexed Orwell. He mentions one
here, that whenever he makes 'a favourable reference to "Nature"'
in an article it brings him abusive letters. According to the hard-line
socialist, people should be discontented, not enjoy what is natural
and free; it is the socialists' task 'to multiply our wants' rather than
increase enjoyment of what we already have. What Orwell is ques-
tioning here is the basis of that kind of socialism that can only
thrive if people are unhappy. To Orwell (surely correctly?) that was
not true socialism but merely a basis upon which a totalitarian
regime might be established.

The second aspect is explored in an article he wrote for *Tribune*
under the pseudonym, John Freeman, called 'Can Socialists Be
Happy?' (*2397*). In this he argues ('at the risk of saying something
that the editors of *Tribune* may not endorse') that the 'real objective
of Socialism is not happiness'; happiness is a by-product; the real
objective is human brotherhood. Unfortunately, nearly all creators
of Utopias, who by implication include socialists, resemble a man
with toothache who thinks that 'happiness consists in not having
toothache' – that is, being rid of discontent. 'Some Thoughts on the
Common Toad' argues that 'retaining one's childhood love' of nature (including toads) 'makes a peaceful and decent future a little
more probable' and helps ensure that human beings will not instead resort to 'hatred and leader worship'. The last paragraph light-
ens the tone. Spring is here, even in London, N1, 'and they can't
stop you enjoying it'; for 'neither the dictators nor the bureaucrats,
deeply as they disapprove of the process, are able to prevent' the
coming of spring.

In 'Why I Write' Orwell gives four reasons for writing: sheer
egoism, aesthetic enthusiasm, historical impulse (the desire to see
things as they truly are), and political purpose (to nudge the world
in a certain direction). This short essay fulfils the second, third, and
fourth of these aims (and, perhaps the first, but only Orwell could
show that). That brings me back to the title: 'Some Thoughts . . .'.
Why not 'The Common Toad'? No, here 'Some' does not imply
mere random reflections; this is no belle-lettrist causerie. The point
is, of course, that only *some* of the thoughts expressed refer to the
toad and these are not the only thoughts in this essay.

The range and variety of Orwell's essays and broadcasts (especially if one takes into account his column, 'As I Please' and his London Letters for *Partisan Review*) is extraordinary. They also range greatly in length, from short, independent subsections of 'As I Please' to the book-length, *The Lion and the Unicorn: Socialism and the English Genius*. Many stem directly from his own experience: 'The Spike', 'A Hanging', 'Shooting an Elephant', 'Bookshop Memories', 'Marrakech', 'Confessions of a Book Reviewer', 'How the Poor Die', and 'Such, Such Were the Joys'; there are essays on literature – on Dickens, Kipling, Yeats, Gissing, Reade, Smollett, Thackeray, Twain, 'Poetry and the Microphone', 'The Rediscovery of Europe', 'The Frontiers of Art and Propaganda', Swift, Jack London, Shaw, Koestler, Wodehouse, 'Lear, Tolstoy, and the Fool', and on individual works, 'Felix Randal', *Macbeth*, *Lady Windermere's Fan*; he virtually inaugurated in England the study of popular culture through such essays as 'Boys' Weeklies', 'The Art of Donald McGill', 'Pamphlet Literature', 'Good Bad Books', 'Nonsense Poetry', 'Grandeur et décadence du roman policier anglais' ('The Detective Story', 2357), and 'Riding Down from Bangor'; there are political essays on the Spanish War, 'My Country Right or Left', antisemitism, Nationalism, 'Pacifism and the War', 'The Politics of Starvation', 'The Prevention of Literature', 'Propaganda and Demotic Speech', 'Politics and Literature', 'Writers and Leviathan', and 'Reflections on Gandhi'; and there are essays that analyse cultural characteristics such as 'Benefit of Clergy: Some Notes on Salvador Dali', 'The Sporting Spirit', 'Raffles and Miss Blandish' (which could as well be included under the head of popular culture), 'Decline of the English Murder', 'Revenge is Sour', 'Books v. Cigarettes', and, perhaps, his defence of English cooking and 'A Good Word for the Vicar of Bray'. And these are but a selection of the more obvious titles.

Often, Orwell's enthusiasm and his range of interest and reference leads him to relate diverse elements, and there are many personal touches. For example, when writing about the Vicar of Bray, who, for all his faults had, by planting what grew into a magnificent yew tree, proved in the end a public benefactor, he remarks that he regrets never having planted a walnut tree. He hopes to remedy this 'some time'. The article was written in April 1946 and a few months later, Orwell sketched out a number of layouts showing his Jura garden in 1946 and how he intended to develop it in 1947 and 1948 (3089). He notes where he will plant cherry trees but there is no sign of a walnut. Perhaps he thought it would not flourish on Jura. From external evidence we can probably guess why he chose 'Felix Randal' for his broadcast on 14 May 1941 on 'The Meaning of a Poem' (CEJL, ii.157–61). Writing to Stephen Spender from Aylesford Sanatorium in Kent on 2 April 1938 (less than a year after he had so abused him in his letter to Nancy Cunard, see above, pp. 88–9), he told him that when he was on sentry-go in the trenches near Alcubierre, he used to say this poem over and over to himself 'to pass the time away in that bloody cold'. That, he adds, 'was about the last occasion when I had any feeling for poetry' (CEJL, i.346). His analysis of 'Felix Randal' seems to suggest that already in 1941 he had Boxer of *Animal Farm* in mind. Orwell argues (in the best tradition of close reading), that 'sandal' in the poem's last line, 'Didst fettle for the great grey drayhorse his bright and battering sandal', is the poem's best, 'one might say the especial touch'. 'Sandal' pins the whole poem together, gives it an air of majesty, 'a feeling of being tragic instead of merely pathetic'. Having explained this, he suggests that the cart-horse is suddenly converted into 'a magnificent mythical beast, something like a heraldic animal'.

Orwell recovered his feel for poetry sufficiently to write one or two more poems, notably 'The Italian soldier shook my hand' in 1939, and 'Memories of the Blitz', published in *Tribune*, 21 January 1944, his last published poem, for which he was paid 10s. 6d. (52½p). He never lost his love of reading poetry, even attempting Dante in Italian with the aid of an Italian–English dictionary when he was ill in bed in 1949, and, almost at the last, reading *The Divine Comedy* in a bilingual edition.[9] Among his papers at his death was an incomplete draft of a poem (3724). This starts,

> Joseph Higgs, late of this parish,
> Exists no longer as the memory of a memory.
> His wooden graveboard vanished in a cold winter,
> A mishap with the inkpot blotted him from the register . . .

it then becomes disjointed but concludes,

> I see no justification
> For Joseph Biggs, late of this parish.

One isolated line is particularly interesting given the circumstances of the poem's composition. It is taken from the *Dies irae*: 'Ne me

perdas illa die' (Do not destroy me on that day), the plea to Christ
for salvation on Judgement Day (see above, pp. 62–5).

Orwell, understandably, made errors in his essays. Apart from
that being a common human characteristic, the pressure under which
he wrote gave him little time for the kind of meticulous checking
that is ideal but rarely now to be found even in the Groves of
Academe. It should be borne in mind that checking simple facts
was often, in Orwell's time, much harder than it is nowadays. For
example, he had great difficulty getting details of the circulations of
boys' weeklies. One serious error he made was his belief that the
stories that appeared in *The Magnet* and *The Gem* under the names
Frank Richards and Martin Clifford were written by several different writers. At the end of January 1940 he was asked by Gollancz's
libel lawyer whether he was sure they were by a number of authors.
He replied that it could be 'safely assumed' so, though he did slightly
modify the way he expressed this 'fact' (*588*). It transpired that this
could not be safely assumed and Frank Richards, the sole author of
the stories under those names and several others (including female
names) responded. Orwell told Geoffrey Gorer on 3 April 1940 that
he looked forward to Richards's reply 'with some uneasiness, as
I've no doubt made many mistakes, but what he'll probably pick on
is my suggestion that those papers try to inculcate snobbishness'
(CEJL, i.579), which Richards did (CEJL, i.535). He corrected Orwell
with a nice degree of amusement appropriate to an old hand commenting on a newcomer to the field. A nice touch is Richards's
expectation of a telegram from Orwell 'worded like that of the in-
vader of Sind'.[10] It has been customary always to publish Richard's
response after Orwell's essay. Orwell's list of national stereotypes
in this essay may have been suggested by a similar list in Book XI,
Chapter X of Tolstoy's *War and Peace* (to which Orwell refers in his
Dickens essay, which appeared in the same collection of essays; see
579 n. 52). Both share the same description of Italians (not, in itself,
an unlikely coincidence).

What may be a slight error, though based on information given
Orwell, appears in 'The Sporting Spirit'. This essay accurately fore-
casts the violence, ill-will and national hatreds that have come to be
associated with international sport. In the second paragraph Orwell
says he had been told that the match between Moscow Dynamos
and Glasgow Rangers towards the end of 1945 'was simply a free-
for-all from the start'. Memory plays one tricks, but I saw the match
and that is not how I recall it. But these are what one might call

'natural errors'. More significant are contrived departures from actuality. Two essays merit particular attention, 'How the Poor Die' (CEJL, iv.261–72) and 'Such, Such Were the Joys' (CEJL, iv.379–422).

'How the Poor Die' presents many problems. It is likely that a draft was written between 1931 and 1936 and that it was considerably longer than what we now have. In notes for his literary executor signed 31 March 1945 (*2648*), he says that the article was intended for *Horizon* but rejected. He goes on to say that it is 'a truthful account of some experiences in the Hopital (*sic*) Cochin in Paris in 1929, and the bit marked between brackets is worth printing'. The next year, at short notice, he provided George Woodcock with what is assumed to be 'the bit marked between brackets' and it was published in *Now* in November 1946. But when was it to have been published in *Horizon*? I can only guess, but I think it may have been intended for the December 1940 issue where there will be found a piece by Orwell on 'The Ruling Class' excerpted from *The Lion and the Unicorn*. In December 1940 no one needed gratuitous information on how the poor died: they (and others) were being killed rapidly enough as a result of the attentions of German bombers, especially in the East End of London. However, in 1946, when the NHS was mooted, 'How the Poor Die' must have seemed particularly timely.[11]

What can be stated for certain, however, is that Orwell did not stay in the Hôpital Cochin ('X' as he calls it) for several weeks, nor did he have pneumonia. The Hospital records show that he was admitted for two weeks suffering from *une grippe*. He probably had a severe bout of influenza which, given the state of his lungs, was serious. I suspect also that the 'five inches' of bathwater may have been suggested by the regulatory maximum of five inches of water that good citizens were asked not to exceed in wartime in order to conserve energy. Orwell is, presumably, endeavouring to put himself, and the reader, in the position of those who are treated, as medical argot still has it, like 'meat'. He needs to justify why he – and therefore the really sick patients – are treated like cattle, 'humiliated, disgusted and frightened', the doctors seeming to lack 'any perception that the patients were human beings'.

Orwell cleverly postpones telling us why, when he entered the grim ward at the Cochin, he was 'conscious of a strange feeling of familiarity'.[12] Many readers at first imagine (as I did) that he has in mind St Cyprian's, but the memory he reveals is of a poem he had read as a child, Tennyson's 'The Children's Hospital'. No reading of 'How the Poor Die' is complete without a reading of this poem. To adapt Orwell, it is a 'good bad poem'. The innocence of childhood, the image of 'the dear Lord Jesus with children about his knees', the simple faith that the Lord will come to Emmie's rescue and take her to heaven, and that he will recognise her if she stretches out her arms over the bedcover, have the hallmarks of Victorian sickly sentimentality. Yet – it is a harrowing poem. As the totally unfeeling doctor comes to her bedside, complete with his 'ghastly tools', 'The Lord of the children had heard her, and Emmie had past away'. Tennyson's poem tells us a great deal of what Orwell's socialism was about, especially a 'decency' towards one another foreign to the Cochin, and unknown to Tennyson's doctor, 'Fresh from the surgery-schools of France'. It also points to the need to read Orwell's essays in the context he brought to them if their full worth is to be appreciated.

The agonies of 'Such, Such Were the Joys' have been read in parallel to those of *Nineteen Eighty-Four*. Some years ago, Professor Crick believed the essay truthful 'if not literally accurate' but that the depiction of the school was 'either semi-fictional or heavily overdrawn'. Orwell's rage could be put down to 'a puritanical feeling of time so badly wasted'.[13] Recently Robert Pearce, in an excellent article, has shown more fully, and in specific detail, the extent to which Orwell distorted his experiences at St Cyprian's.[14] Orwell, he says, 'seems to have treated St Cyprian's with decidedly ungenerous anger and without his "common decency"'. Even as one prone to defend Orwell, I am inclined to agree. What is of importance, however, is *why* Orwell spent so much time on this essay when he was very ill, in great pain, and much concerned with other matters, including *Nineteen Eighty-Four* and the future of his son, Richard, especially as he knew that the essay could not be published in England in the lifetimes of those he chiefly attacked because of fear of actions for libel. One reason that has been suggested by several writers (including Pearce) was Orwell's animus against private schools. This is probable, but it is a more profound attack than has perhaps been fully appreciated.

In CEJL the completion of the essay is given as May 1947. Examination of the surviving typescript, identification of the typewriter faces, and knowledge of where the typewriters were (in London and Jura), enables the completion to be dated a year later, that is, after Orwell had completed *Nineteen Eighty-Four* and when he had entered Hairmyres Hospital very seriously ill.[15] He must have had something more than mere revenge (which was not Orwell's style in any case) driving him to write this article. The clue is, I think, to be found in his friend Tosco Fyvel's account of the first of a new series of 'As I Please' that Orwell started in May 1946. Fyvel was then the Literary Editor of *Tribune*. Orwell wanted to make a swinging attack on the Labour Government (then starting its second year of office), and he proposed to attack his friend Aneurin Bevan, one of the few politicans Orwell respected. Orwell wanted the government to give priority to three things: the abolition of public schools, titles, and the House of Lords. Bevan, Orwell argued, 'had let himself be diverted into enlarging the National Health Service and the public housing sector and into measures of nationalization' instead of 'tackling the basic inequalities of British society'. Fyvel laughed Orwell out of his making this attack and that instalment of 'As I Please' was never written.[16] Even though Orwell desperately needed health care (and the NHS as it then was could not provide him with the streptomycin that it was thought he needed),[17] he still thought the abolition of private schooling was paramount for the health of the country. In the January 1946 issue of *Polemic*, in one of his most famous essays, 'The Prevention of Literature', Orwell considered distortion in writing:

> The journalist is unfree, and is conscious of unfreedom, when he is forced to write lies or suppress what seems to him important news: the imaginative writer is unfree when he has to falsify his subjective feelings, which from his point of view are facts. He may distort and caricature reality in order to make his meaning clearer, but he cannot misrepresent the scenery of his own mind: he cannot say with any conviction that he likes what he dislikes, or believes what he disbelieves. (CEJL, iv.88)

The distortion and caricature of Orwell's savage, Swiftian, account of his prep school days represented the scenery of a mind that passionately believed the health and future of Britain depended more on the abolition of private education, and the privilege it entailed, than on the creation of a medical health service.

Despite – perhaps even because of – this justification for 'distortion', Orwell was obsessed by words and their proper use. He evidently enjoyed mastering foreign languages and in comparing their usages (see, for example, his note to the 1935 French edition of *Down and Out in Paris and London*, reproduced in the new English edition, I.170, in which he compares Hindustani *ap* and *tum* with the French use of *vous* and *tu*). He included lists of slang and argot in books (e.g. *Down and Out in Paris and London*, Chapter 32) and diaries (see CEJL, i.95–6); his notebooks have many lists of words and phrases, and, because he believed that society was controlled by mastery of language, what to many readers seems merely an appendage to *Nineteen Eighty-Four*, 'The Principles of Newspeak', is crucial to the interpretation of the novel. There is a certain irony, therefore, that two of his articles on words had difficulty getting into print. 'New Words' (CEJL, ii.17–27) was not published in his lifetime and its date of composition can only be guessed; much depends on what Orwell knew, or did not know, of *Finnegans Wake* in the early spring of 1940.

The much more important essay, and an essay that can still be read with advantage by writers and students, 'Politics and the English Language', was rejected by George Weidenfeld for his journal, *Contact: The Magazine of Pleasure*. The article has been reprinted many times. Its first two reprintings were private. One was for *The Observer*'s Foreign News Service and was given the title, 'What Do You Mean?'; the other was for journalists of the *News of the World*. A particularly unusual sequence of printings was for three Christmas Keepsakes published in Evansville, Indiana, 1947. Orwell had given his consent 'from Scotland', though whether he realised he was approving three Keepsakes, not one, is unclear.[18]

Orwell saw English civilisation as decadent and that the English language shared in 'the general collapse'. He was not the first author to think along these lines, of course. Henry James, in the *New York Times*, 21 March 1915, wrote of the First World War 'using up words', weakening them so that they deteriorated like car tyres. Edith Wharton's *A Son at the Feast* (1923) argued that, as a result of the war, 'The meaning has evaporated out of lots of our old words.'[19] Orwell goes much further. The problem was circular: our language becomes 'ugly and inaccurate because our thoughts are foolish, but the slovenliness of our language makes it easier for us to have foolish thoughts'. However, he believed the process was reversible: 'If one gets rid of these [bad] habits one can think more clearly, and to think clearly is a necessary step towards political regeneration' (CEJL, iv.157). What follows is, in effect, a short course on good, clear, honest writing. The conclusion is, alas, even more to the point today than it was fifty years ago: 'the present political chaos is connected with the decay of language. . . . Political language . . . is designed to make lies sound truthful and murder respectable, and to give an appearance of solidity to pure wind' (CEJL, iv.169–70).

Dickens, said Orwell, despised politics; he did not believe that any good could come out of Parliament (CEJL, i.460). Given Orwell's analysis of the use of language, especially by politicians, it is not surprising that his opinion was similar. Remarking in 1940 that 'All the old duds were back on the job' and that the shock of disaster had brought only a few able people to the fore, he concluded, 'A generation of the unteachable is hanging upon us like a necklace of corpses' (CEJL, ii.106). To Orwell the answer lay, fundamentally, though not exclusively, in the proper use of language. He also saw the art of Salvador Dali, and the willingness of a sophisticated public to buy his art, as 'a symptom of the world's illness'. Dali's art is 'a direct, unmistakable assault on sanity and decency; and even ... on life itself' (CEJL, iii.194,191,189). Since Orwell wrote these two essays, it might be argued that our language and our 'political health' have still further declined, and that the 'assault on sanity and decency' he found in the work of Dali has become far more widespread through what is purveyed by the mass-circulation newspapers and the video industry.

This trend is further and tellingly exposed in Orwell's examination of 'Raffles and Miss Blandish' (CEJL, iii.246–60). Orwell endeavours to show that in the half-century separating them there had been, in this kind of literature, a departure from a mood of 'boyishness' in which the norm, even among thieves, was an awareness of what was 'not done' (Orwell describes that as Raffles's and Bunny's 'key phrase'), 'for a header into the cesspool' (251). The 'whole theme' of this kind of literature 'is the struggle for power and the triumph of the strong over the weak.... Might is right: *vae victis*' – 'woe to the conquered' (253). What Orwell feared was the importation into England from America, along with its subliterature, the admiration of the successful criminal (255), the worshipping of power and successful cruelty, and the 'love of cruelty and wickedness *for their own sakes* (Orwell's italics; 258). Of course, he concludes, 'One ought not to infer too much from the success' of books such as *No Orchids for Miss Blandish*, but 'if such books should definitely acclimatize themselves in England ... there would be good grounds for dismay' (260). In our current adoration of power, violence, unrestrained market forces, and the idolisation in television series of criminals we have what Orwell deplored half a century ago and what he feared would result. As so often, Orwell has not only been proved right but there is a little kick in the tail of this essay:

> Comparing the schoolboy atmosphere of the one book [*Raffles*] with the cruelty and corruption of the other [*No Orchids for Miss Blandish*], one is driven to feel that snobbishness, like hypocrisy, is a check upon the behaviour whose value from a social point of view has been underrated.

Orwell wrote dozens of articles and over eight-hundred reviews but only three more can be touched on here. 'Benefit of Clergy' was originally intended for *The Saturday Book* for 1944. After the copies of the book had been bound, the publishers, Hutchinson, decided belatedly that the essay was obscene. Rather than reprint, the pages were sliced out, though the Table of Contents continued to list the essay's inclusion. (One or two copies escaped the butcher's knife so it is always worth checking second-hand copies of *The Saturday Book* for 1944 because a complete version has scarcity value.) There is, of course, nothing obscene about the essay but that it was thought so is a useful comment on the *mores* of that time. The essay was printed without arousing adverse reactions in *Critical Essays* (see below, pp. 109–10).

In 1949, the Ministry of Information obtained permision to re-print Orwell's essay, 'Reflections on Gandhi' (CEJL, iv.523–31) in *Mirror*, its publication for India. This was probably issued in July 1950, though printed almost a year earlier. Orwell did not wholly trust Gandhi. His suspicions are suggested by, for example, his juxtaposition of Gandhi's rejection of the machine to solve India's problems while 'he plays with his spinning wheel in the mansion of some cotton millionaire' in his review of *Beggar My Neighbour*, by Lionel Fielden (September 1943, CEJL, II.356). The 1949 essay re-dressed the balance, but not unequivocally. The MOI, almost certainly without reference to Orwell, who was very ill, quite skilfully cut and modified Orwell's original to use the article to bolster Anglo-Indian relations. In order to drive home the point it had thereby created, it advertised the 'garbled' essay as a 'new evaluation' by 'an English writer and critic well known for the independence and originality of his views'. This revision, coming so soon after Orwell had described the technique of rewriting to suit political ends in *Nineteen Eighty-Four*, and at a time when Orwell was dying, was particularly cynical.

P. G. Wodehouse broadcast five talks from Berlin to America in the summer of 1941. The first was rebroadcast to the Far East and all five to Britain in August 1941. For this he was unfairly but understandably publicly maligned, especially by Cassandra (William Connor) in the *Daily Mirror*. In due course an investigation by MI5 found no evidence of guilt and anyone who cares to read what Wodehouse broadcast (published by him in the second edition of *Performing Flea*, 1961) will wonder what the fuss was about. However, the texts were not available during the war and, before Wodehouse was cleared, Orwell wrote an essay in February 1945 in 'In Defence of P. G. Wodehouse' (published July 1945; CEJL, iii.388–403; 2624). He was, therefore, defending 'an outcast', at least, as seen by the press and the Establishment. Some libraries withdrew Wodehouse's books, Southport Public Library actually destroying its stock, and the BBC banned all his works. It is a nice irony that the general public had more sense. As Iain Sproat has pointed out, 450 000 copies of Wodehouse's books were sold in the United Kingdom between 1941 and the end of the war.[20] When Orwell went to Europe as a war correspondent for *The Observer* and *The Manchester Evening News* in 1945, he met Mr and Mrs Wodehouse in Paris. They were in straitened circumstances and he entertained them to a good meal. Wodehouse wrote Orwell two letters on 25 July and 1 August 1945. In these he thanked Orwell profusely. Everything Orwell had said about his work was 'absolutely right. . . . It was uncanny'; the criticism was excellent: 'It was a masterly bit of work and I agree with every word of it.' However, Wodehouse later revised his opinion of Orwell's essay. It was, he told Denis Mackail on 11 August 1951, 'practically one long roast. . . . Don't you hate the way these critics falsify facts in order to make a point?' (2625). But that was six years after Orwell had entertained him in Paris and Orwell had been dead for over eighteen months.

In March 1940, Gollancz published 'Charles Dickens', 'Boys' Weeklies', and 'Inside the Whale' under the title of this last essay. Gollancz wrote to Orwell early in 1940 telling him how much he had enjoyed reading the manuscript: 'It is, if I may say so, first rate.'[21] The book was sent for estimate on 1 January 1940 and 1000 copies were printed; there were 100 overs; the first 250 copies were bound on 29 February; despite the war, that was just two months after the estimate for printing was ordered. Copies were sold at 7s. 6d. ($37\frac{1}{2}$p). Orwell told Geoffrey Gorer that he had been paid an advance of £20 (607) but as some of the copies were destroyed in an air-raid, Orwell probably did not earn much above £30 from this book, including the advance. The type was distributed on 25 December 1940. (It will be noticed that public holidays were then no bar to work being undertaken by the publisher.) The rights reverted to the Orwell estate on 3 July 1950. There was no American edition but 'Inside the Whale' was published in Italian by Mondadori in 1949. A shortened version of 'Boys' Weeklies' was published by *Horizon* in March 1940.

The Lion and the Unicorn was the first in a series of Searchlight Books, edited by Orwell and Tosco Fyvel, and published by Secker & Warburg in February 1941, at 2s. 0d. (10p). The first 5000 copies sold out quickly and the first impression was increased to 7500 copies; a second impression of 5000 copies was ordered in March. The type was destroyed in an air-raid. There was no American edition. The section, 'The Ruling Class' appeared in *Horizon* in December 1940, possibly in place of 'How the Poor Die' (see p. 102). Seventeen Searchlight books were commissioned but seven were not written (including those by Michael Foot, Cyril Connolly, Tosco Fyvel, and Arthur Koestler). Orwell wrote forewords to T. C. Worsley's *The End of the 'Old School Tie'*, May 1941, and Joyce Cary's *The Case for African Freedom*, also 1941.

Orwell contributed two chapters to *The Betrayal of the Left: An Examination and Refutation of Communist Policy* which Victor Gollancz edited and published in March 1941: 'Fascism and Democracy' and 'Patriots and Revolutionaries' (originally published in *Left News* as 'Our Opportunity', to which he also contributed 'Will Freedom Die with Capitalism?'; see *737, 753, 755, 770* and *782*). Of the first printing of 1593 copies (including overs), 1300 were for sale to the public; the balance was for members of the Left Book Club. A second impression was published in May, 600 for the general public and 450 for the LBC.

In February 1946, Secker & Warburg published Orwell's *Critical Essays* at 8s. 6d. (42$\frac{1}{2}$p). This included reprints of the essays on Dickens and boys' weeklies, to which were added 'Wells, Hitler and the World State', 'The Art of Donald McGill', 'Rudyard Kipling', 'W. B. Yeats', 'Benefit of Clergy', 'Arthur Koestler', 'Raffles and Miss Blandish', and 'In Defence of P. G. Wodehouse'. The first edition of 3028 copies quickly sold out and a second impression of 5632 copies was published in May 1946. The first American edition, of 5000 copies at $2.50, was published by Reynal & Hitchcock in April 1946 with the title, *Dickens, Dali and Others: Studies in Popular Culture*. A Spanish edition was published on 20 July 1948; what, one wonders, did Spaniards make of Orwell on Dali?[22] Evelyn Waugh reviewed *Critical Essays* in *The Tablet*, 6 April 1946, under the heading 'A New Humanism'. He had (unsurprisingly, especially when Orwell touched on Roman Catholicism) criticisms, but found the essays formed 'a work of absorbing interest'. 'The Art of Donald McGill' was, he thought, 'the masterpiece of the book' and that, with 'Raffles and Miss Blandish', 'exemplify the method in which the new school' – the 'new humanism of the common man' – 'is supreme'. In a final reference to the initial suppression of 'Benefit of Clergy', Waugh, aware that he was writing 'in a journal largely read by the religious', commented that 'There is nothing in [Orwell's] writing that is inconsistent with high moral principles.'

Orwell continued to write essays as long as he had the strength to do so. As late as 24 August 1949 he wrote to Fredric Warburg from the sanatorium at Cranham, Gloucestershire, just before he transferred to University College Hospital, where he would die, listing six essays he wished to include in a new collection (*3679*).[23] These, indicative of what he particularly valued among his essays, were 'Lear, Tolstoy and the Fool', 'Politics vs. Literature' (on Swift), 'Reflections on Gandhi', 'Politics and the English Language', 'Shooting an Elephant', and 'How the Poor Die'. The book needed two more long essays and these were to be on Conrad and Gissing. Some indication of how ill Orwell was at this time is shown by a letter he wrote to David Astor the following day (*3680*). He said he could not write more than a scrawl because he felt so ghastly, 'really quite shaky', but wanted to thank Astor for sending him 'two nice vases and the flowers' and to tell him he might be moving to University College Hospital. Orwell had written an essay on Gissing for *Politics and Letters* in 1948 (CEJL, iv.485–93) but the magazine closed down before it could be published and it did not appear until June 1960 (in *London Magazine*). Presumably Orwell intended to expand it. Only a reading list (*3726*) and a few notes (*3724*) survive towards the proposed essay on Conrad. Orwell was also part-way through a long article on Evelyn Waugh. Part of this survives (*3585*), together with some notes (*3586*).

It is remarkable that so many of Orwell's essays, especially those on the politics of his time, which might be expected to be limited by temporality, and those on popular culture, the techniques for the analysis of which have become infinitely more sophisticated since he wrote, still speak to us directly, informedly and polemically.

6

Events Leading Up to the War and the BBC Years

In mid-March 1938, when he was living at The Stores in Wallington, Orwell was taken seriously ill. Precisely what happened is unclear (a detailed account of the evidence is given at 432), but he certainly bled profusely and the bleeding could not be stopped. It was suspected that he had pulmonary tuberculosis and he was dashed from Hertfordshire to Preston Hall Sanatorium, Aylesford, Kent, where Eileen's brother, Laurence (always called 'Eric', which can, especially in Eileen's letters, be confusing), was a consultant. Michael Shelden has unearthed Orwell's medical records and these show he had coughed up blood when ill in 1929 (possibly at the Hôpital Cochin), 1931 and 1934; had suffered from pneumonia in 1918, 1921, 1933 and 1934 (but not in 1929 as is stated in 'How the Poor Die' – see p. 102), and had Dengue Fever in Burma. With that record, he should certainly not have served in the bitterly cold trenches in Spain. In a report dated 7 November 1938 (475 n. 2), it was decided that 'in all probability' Orwell was suffering from 'bronchiectasis of the left lung', rather than tuberculosis. To add to the confusion, however, the Case Record carries a typed statement 'T. B. confirmed'. By then Orwell and Eileen were in North Africa, where it was believed (incorrectly) that the climate would aid his recovery. Their stay in Marrakech, from 12 September 1938 to the end of March 1939, was made possible by an anonymous gift of £300 from the novelist, L. H. Myers. Orwell regarded this as a loan and, when he could, repaid what he had received (see below, p. 129). It was arranged that Jack Common would take over the cottage in return for looking after the Orwells' goats and hens, a task he mis-managed. Despite being so ill, Orwell found time and energy to write a long letter, dated 5 August 1938, in defence of his POUM colleagues who were being tried by the Communists for espionage in Spain. Copies were sent to *The Manchester Guardian*, the *Daily Herald* (which supported the Labour Party), and *The New Statesman* (470). It was only printed by *The Manchester Guardian*.

Marrakech proved rather a disappointment and did nothing for Orwell's health that rest almost anywhere might have achieved. However, he was able to write some reviews, he assembled a fair amount of material in the diary he kept (later worked up into the article, 'Marrakech', *New Writing*, Christmas, 1939, CEJL, i.426–32), and he wrote *Coming Up for Air*.

Although this novel was written under the shadow of impending war, and ends with the RAF accidentally dropping a bomb on 'a little side-street off the High Street' of Lower Binfield, where the principal character, George Bowling is staying (VII.235), the novel is comic, reflective and nostalgic. George Bowling is a successful travelling salesman for an insurance company. Orwell probably got some of the information he needed about commercial travellers from Cyril Wright who, with his girlfriend Mikeal Smith (as she spelt her name), an assistant dispenser at Boots the Chemists, would drive over from Bedford, where he worked as a salesman, to see the Orwells at Wallington. Wright later moved to Coventry to work as a sales representative for Dean's, shop-blind manufacturers (*408 n. 4*). There is a passing reference to Boots in the novel (VII.136). In course of writing the novel, Orwell wrote two longish letters from Marrakech to John Sceats, an insurance agent, seeking further information (CEJL, i.395–9). The novel is, in effect, a long monologue, set in 1938 or 1939, but looking back to a wholly different world before the First World War. George Bowling takes French leave to visit the small agricultural town where he was brought up, Lower Binfield (a place-name also used in *Down and Out in Paris and London*, I.196, and representing, more or less, the world of Shiplake and Henley-on-Thames where Orwell spent his childhood). It is from this refreshing experience that the novel takes its title:

> The very thought of going back to Lower Binfield had done me good already. You know the feeling I had. Coming up for air! Like the big sea-turtles when they come paddling up to the surface, stick their noses out and fill their lungs with a great gulp before they sink down again among the seaweed and the octopuses. We're all stifling at the bottom of a dustbin, but I'd found the way to the top. (VII.177)

Even from this short extract, it can be seen how fluently and gracefully Orwell can now write. It is this ease which will be a marked feature of *Animal Farm* and many of his essays. So, despite Marrakech not realising the Orwells' hopes, the rest and the more-or-less un-interrupted time enabled him to make an important breakthrough in his writing technique. One incident, a parody of a Left Book Club meeting in Part III, Chapter 1, might have been expected to raise Gollancz's eyebrows, but he evidently found nothing objectionable in its fairly gentle satire.

Orwell and Eileen sailed from Casablanca in a Japanese ship, the SS *Yasukunimaru*, for a fare of £6 10s. each, arriving in England on the morning of 30 March 1939. In the afternoon Orwell handed in the manuscript of his novel to his agent. On 11 April (although two weekends had intervened) Gollancz sent the manuscript for an estimate for printing. The first 1250 copies were bound on 1 June. The first printing of 2109 copies (including overs) sold quickly, at 7s. 6d. (37½p) and a further 1000 copies (plus 50 overs) were or-dered on 30 June. Had it not been for the war, the book might have done even better and Orwell was keen that *Coming Up for Air* should be the first volume of the Secker & Warburg Uniform Edition. This was published in 5000 copies at 9s. 6d. on 13 May 1948. The price was reduced to 7s. 6d. in the month following Orwell's death, raised to 8s. 6d. in March 1951 and to 10s. 6d. in February 1952. Harcourt, Brace published an American edition of 8000 copies at $3.00 on 19 January 1950; a French edition was published by Amiot Dumont, Paris, in April 1952.[1]

An offer to reprint *Coming Up for Air* for the European English-language market comically reveals a certain naivety in Orwell. A contract survives for the publication of the novel by Albatross Verlag GmbH, either by themselves or on behalf of Bernard Tauchnitz Successors, Brandstetter and Company, Leipzig. Although the con-tract was issued from Paris, the company was obviously German. Negotiations began at the beginning of August (*561*) and the con-tract is dated 31 August 1939, four days before war between Ger-many and Britain broke out. In his Diary of Events Leading Up to the War for 4 August 1939 (*562*), Orwell notes that he must excise 'certain (though not all) unfriendly references to Hitler. Say they are obliged to do this as their books circulate largely in Germany. Also excision of a passage of about a page suggesting that war is imminent.'[2] Of course, the book was never published for circulation 'largely in Germany', yet on 8 December 1939. Orwell could write in remarkable innocence to his agent asking what had happened about the contract: 'Have [Albatross] gone west, I wonder?' (*581*). As was soon to be made only too clear, the answer should have been, 'Not for another month or two and then the Wehrmacht will set off.' With the fall of France it must have struck even Orwell that this contract would not be fulfilled.[3]

Looking back it is easy to see how the course of events in 1939 would inevitably lead to war, especially once Britain and France had failed to ally themselves with the Soviet Union and, instead, on 23 August 1939, the USSR and Nazi Germany became allies.[4] But, to the last, powerful forces were attempting to convince the British people that there would be no war. The *Daily Express* started off 1939 by stating, 'There will be no great war in Europe in 1939. There is nothing in our present situation which affords any ground to suppose that an upheaval must or will come' and almost up to the outbreak of war was assuring its readers there would be no war.[5] Although Orwell was convinced that war was coming, it is noticeable that he has George Bowling say, 'War is coming. 1941 they say' (VII.238). His and Eileen's reactions to the Munich crisis are revealing of their and also general responses, particularly Eileen's approval of Neville Chamberlain, who found few friends after his fall. On 27 September 1938, two days before Chamberlain, Daladier (the French Prime Minister), Hitler and Mussolini signed the Munich Agreement whereby the Czech Sudeten lands were ceded to Germany (without the agreement of the Czechs, who were not even invited to Munich), Eileen wrote to Orwell's sister, Marjorie (*487*):

> Eric, who retains an extraordinary political simplicity in spite of everything [presumably a reference to his experiences in Spain], wants to hear what he calls the voice of the people. He thinks this might stop a war, but I'm sure the voice would only say that it didn't want a war but of course would have to fight if the Government declared war. It's very odd to feel that Chamberlain is our only hope, but I believe he doesn't want war either at the moment and certainly the man has courage.

This passage deserves close attention, especially the last line. What precisely is the implication of Chamberlain not wanting war 'at the moment'? And what of her assessment (and she seemed more politically aware in 1938 than was her husband) that, certainly, Chamberlain had courage? How does this contrast with our pictorial impression of a cartoon-like figure, moustached, carrying a rolled umberella, waving a little piece of paper? Then, on 4 October 1938, writing to Geoffrey Gorer, she said (*493*):

I am determined to be pleased with Chamberlain because I want rest. Anyway Czecho-Slovakia ought to be pleased with us; it seems geographically certain that the country would be ravaged at the beginning of any war fought in its defence. But of course the English Left is always Spartan; they're fighting Franco to the last Spaniard too.

Czechoslovakia did not see things as did Eileen, but her caustic view of the Left and her determination to be pleased with Chamberlain, throw light on how things were seen fairly widely in Britain in the autumn of 1938.

Nevertheless, despite the reassurances of the press, on 2 July 1939 Orwell began his 'Diary of Events Leading Up to the War', closing in on 3 September. The title is the one he gave this diary and it is plain that he was in no doubt that war would soon break out. The 'diary' is an interesting culling of what Orwell read in newspapers and other journals, supplemented by opinions and items of information given him by friends and acquaintances. Some of the supplementary information is curious. For example, under 29 August, Orwell records, 'It appears from reliable private information that Sir O. Mosley is a masochist of the extreme type in his sexual life' (565). However, Orwell's chief concerns are political. What is intriguing, given his political inclination, are the newspapers from which he gained his information. Orwell quotes from 41 sources but 46.5 per cent of his references are to the *Daily Telegraph*. Its 138 items contrast with 20 from *The Sunday Times* (there was no *Sunday Telegraph* in those days), 16 from the *Daily Express*, and 13 from *The Manchester Guardian Weekly*. When Orwell went to stay with L. H. Myers for a few days, there is a noticeable increase in references to *The Times* and the *News Chronicle* (a Liberal-inclined daily), but even with them, there are only totals of seven and eight references respectively to these newspapers. One of the most interesting journals to which Orwell refers as frequently as *The Times*, though it is far harder to come by, is *Socialist Correspondence*, run by a group within the ILP known as 'the right-wing opposition' of this left-wing party. The group followed Nikolai Bukharin (1888–1938) and the issues from which Orwell quotes contained articles and supplements that would have undoubtedly interested and probably influenced him. For example, the supplement for August was a translation from the June 1939 German Communist Party paper, *Die Internationale Klassenkampf* ('The International Class Struggle') on the use of slogans to advocate war and the class struggle.[6]

On 9 September Orwell applied to undertake war work and he also tried to enlist. He was rejected for military service as medically unfit (he was eventually classified Grade IV on 3 June 1941) and his services as a writer were not taken up. While Eileen worked in the censorship department in Whitehall (an ironic twist) and then, more happily, in the Ministry of Food, Orwell disconsolately endeavoured to find some work more purposeful than filing reviews of run-of-the-mill films and plays. It was between the acts of *Portrait of Helen* at the Torch Theatre on 29 May 1940 that Orwell heard that troops were being evacuated from Dunkirk.[7] On 30 May he went to see Denis Ogden's *The Peaceful Inn*, which he described as 'The most fearful tripe' and, though set in 1940, 'contained no reference direct or indirect to the war'. In sad contrast, the next night he went to Waterloo and Victoria stations to see if he could get any news of Eileen's brother from those returning from the beaches of Dunkirk. As he records in his diary. 'Quite impossible of course', but he had to do what he could to console Eileen. Her brother, a Major in the Royal Army Medical Corps, was killed tending wounded awaiting evacuation from the beaches.

After many dismal and depressing months, enlivened only by his enthusiasm for the establishment of what he regarded as a citizen army, the Home Guard,[8] Orwell was appointed a Talks Assistant in the Eastern Service of the BBC on 18 August 1941 with responsibility for organising broadcasts to India.[9] He was paid £640 a year, a better salary than he had earned since he had served in Burma. The irony that he was only paid well when working, directly or indirectly, for the Raj would not have been lost on Orwell. He worked for the BBC until 24 November 1943. He certainly gave value for money. He worked incredibly hard and with great devotion on a task that he became increasingly aware was pointless. The intentions were good. Although the short, two-week, training course (cut down from three months) was referred to contemptuously by William Empson as 'The Liars' School', his and Orwell's training programmes have survived (845) and they are workmanlike, honest attempts to get across the basics of broadcasting.

One of Orwell's tasks was to produce commentaries on the progress of the war and, especially in 1942, it was extraordinarily difficult to present a sequence of ghastly disasters in a good light. In just over two years Orwell wrote 56 English-language, quarter-hour, newsletters (commentaries, not news bulletins) for India; 30 for occupied Malaya, and 19 for occupied Indonesia; he read 56 of these himself (892), using the name Orwell on the understanding that he would not be asked to say anything with which, in conscience, he disagreed. But, as he said, with delightful naivety, 'These commentaries have always followed what is by implication a "left" line, and in fact have contained very little that I could not sign with my own name' (1571). He also wrote English originals for at least another 115 newsletters for translation into vernacular languages. This made a total of some four newsletters a week, adjusting his commentaries to take account of widely different audiences: the British rulers of India, servicemen, the indigenous populations, and those suffering under Japanese occupation, listening in dangerous secrecy.[10] Orwell believed no one heard his broadcasts. Few did in India, where everyone was free to tune in, but evidence has come to light that he was avidly listened to by nuns in Malaya who then, at risk to their lives, passed on messages to others (1669). It is possible that he was also heard as far afield as occupied China and Hong Kong but, alas, the persons who could have confirmed this died just before I could talk to them.

Orwell devoted much more time and effort to educational and cultural programmes than to his commentaries. He ran what would now be called an Open University long before that concept was launched. He designed thirteen courses based on Calcutta and Bombay University syllabuses in English and American Literature, science, medicine, agriculture and psychology. The speakers were as eminent as any who now participate in the Open University's courses. They included T. S. Eliot, E. M. Forster, Joseph Needham, V. S. Pritchett, L. A. G. Strong, Stephen Spender, Ritchie Calder, Gordon Childe, Sir John Russell, and Harold Laski. These series were backed up by two booklets of talks given on literature, published by the Oxford University Press, Bombay, in October 1946. Alas, few seem to have heard these broadcasts and of the 4000 copies of the two booklets, only 713 had been sold by February 1949, modestly priced though they were at 12 annas (3102). Orwell also edited *Talking to India: A Selection of English Language Broacasts to India*, which George Allen & Unwin published in November 1943; the 2017 copies printed were sold out by 1945 (2359 and 2360). Orwell also ran a series of programmes introducing drama and the mechanics of its production, backed up with shortened versions of famous Indian plays. This had a direct effect in that two participants, Balraj and Damyanti Sahni, set up a travelling drama company in India on their return. When one looks at the kinds of programme Orwell organised, from talks on great books (including *The Social Contract, The Koran* and *Das Kapital*) to discussions of social problems (e.g. 'Moslem Minorities in Europe', and 'The Status of Women in Europe'), one can only conclude that, as war propaganda, it was idiosyncratic, remarkably enlightened, and its nature almost certainly unrealised by those in high authority.

The most specifically literary programme was 'Voice', described by Orwell as a 'poetry magazine'. There were six such programmes and scripts for five survive. There were many distinguished contributors, including Herbert Read, William Empson, Edmund Blunden, Mulk Raj Anand and Stephen Spender. Discussions were scripted and these are probably examples of what Orwell called faked discussions in his essay, 'Poetry and the Microphone' (probably written in the summer of 1943 but not published until March 1945, 2629). The scripting of discussions was to meet the demands of the censor. There were series of music programmes (performers included Myra Hess and Moura Lympany) and programmes in which European and Indian music were compared. There was a curious project which involved five writers, including L. A. G. Strong and E. M. Forster, completing a story begun by Orwell. Orwell made several adaptations for broadcasting to India, including Anatole France's 'Crainquebille', 'The Fox' by Ignazio Silone, and 'A Slip Under the Microscope' by H. G. Wells. He also made an important broadcast, 'The Rediscovery of Europe: Literature Between the Wars', on 10 March 1942, later printed in *The Listener* (CEJL, ii.229–40). Some talks were concerned with what Indian culture had given the West. Notable among these was E. M. Forster's 'My Debt to India', and two talks on philosophy by C. E. M. Joad, then a household name in Britain. None of this could be described as 'lying propaganda'.

Despite censorship, Orwell was allowed to organise talks by Reg Reynolds, a Quaker, on prison literature at a time when leading Indians, such as Gandhi and Nehru, were in prison in India. Even K. S. Shelvankar, whose Penguin Special, *The Problem of India* (1940), was banned in India, was commissioned to give a number of talks and, despite the protests of the head of the Indian section, Zulfaqar Ali Bokhari, who after the war was appointed Director General of Pakistan Radio, these were allowed to go ahead (see *1050*). There was also a series of what might be called politico-cultural talks. For example, Mulk Raj Anand spoke on 'The Fifth Column', 'Living Space', 'Propaganda', and 'The New Order'. In the series 'Their

Names Will Live', a variety of Asian speakers discussed important people, virtually all of whose names *have* lived. A few talks could be classed as propaganda though often of a fairly innocuous kind. R. R. Desai spoke in Gujarati about the Beveridge Report (the basis for the Welfare State); there was a seven-part series on the history of Fascism, all the talks being given by non-Europeans, and three talks on Japan's threat to Asia over the centuries. A series looked forward to India's problems in AD 2000 and this attracted very distinguished authorities, including Sir John Russell on agriculture and Richard Titmuss on population. Finally – from a remarkable range of titles which can only be touched on here – note might be made of a series with the disarming title, 'Today and Yesterday'. These broadcasts were given by the Indian writer Cedric Dover. They were far from milk-and-water affairs. They included 'The Importance of Minorities', 'Race Mixture and World Peace', The Problems of Cultural Expression', 'The Federal Idea' and 'Utopias and Federations', the last two being followed by discussions with C. E. M. Joad (*1029* and *1037*).

What caused Orwell to leave was his realisation that he was wasting his time and, as he had a puritanical belief that time was given us to be productively employed, he found that at first galling and then intolerable. Although there were a number of aspects of his work that distressed Orwell, two might be particularly picked out. The first was that no one had worked out just what was the likelihood of those in India listening to the broadcasts. There was not only the difficulty of reception itself (for in those days there was no communication by satellite and VHF transmission was subject to considerable interference and interruption) but the simple fact that, relatively speaking, there were very few radios in India. Whereas in Britain in 1939 there was one radio to 5.36 people, in India in 1940 there was one per 3875 people. Furthermore, broadcasts had not only to be in English but in Hindustani, Bengali, Marathi, Gujarati and Tamil. The chances of someone remembering, and being able, to tune in for a weekly quarter-hour of Gujarati were, to say the least, remote. Secondly, those who ran the service of which Orwell's section was a part, except for his immediate superior, Zulfaqar Ali Bohari, were the kind of people Orwell described as 'old duds', the 'unteachable' who hung on the nation's neck 'like a necklace of corpses' (see p. 106). In a memorandum located by Clive Fleay among the Sir Stafford Cripps's Papers at Nuffield College, Oxford, are thumbnail sketches of Orwell's superiors. Only Bokhari is thought worthwhile. The rest were variously described as 'suave, indecisive, conscientious, unimaginative', 'well-meaning, discouraged, tired out by routine; never been to India and knows nothing about it', 'obstinate, unimaginative, limited and very patronising to Indians. A joke' (*847*). It was not a joke that Orwell enjoyed. Needless to say, being a part of the Establishment, they remained in post unless they were promoted. On 14 March 1942, after six months at the BBC, Orwell described the atmosphere as 'something half way between a girls' school and a lunatic asylum, and all we are doing at present is useless, or slightly worse than useless. Our radio strategy is even more hopeless that our military strategy' (CEJL, ii.465) – and militarily, 1942 was a very bad year.

There was, possibly, a third reason for Orwell's leaving: exhaustion. When Orwell joined the Indian section, Bokhari, Orwell and three Hindu talks assistants, with three secretaries, produced twelve hours of broadcasting a week. A Marathi assistant, Miss Venu Chitale, joined in March 1943 but the transmission time was then increased. For many months Bokhari was away in India. It was an enormous burden of work. Orwell not only organised, and participated in broadcasts, but, in addition to writing four newsletters a week, wrote many feature programmes, including several drama features. The working week was then of $5\frac{1}{2}$ days and, apart from a fortnight's fishing at Callow End, Worcestershire (he only caught 18 dace, one perch and two eels, and the pubs ran out of beer, *1262* and *1261*), he had very little leave and several bad bouts of bronchitis. However, Orwell had not wholly wasted the little time left to him. The experience of such high-pressure writing, of a world of propaganda, and of the Ministry of Information, housed in Senate House, University of London, would provide part of the background for *Nineteen Eighty-Four*.

7

The Last Five Years

Orwell went to Paris for *The Observer* on 15 February 1945. He wrote thirteen articles for *The Observer* (two after his final return on 24 May 1945 – 'final return', because, very sadly, he had to return hastily when Eileen died on 29 March), and five for *The Manchester Evening News*. Orwell wrote from Paris, Cologne (where he was himself so ill that he had to be taken to hospital four days before Eileen died), Nuremberg, Stuttgart, and Austria. His articles discussed such things as the state of Paris newspapers (2627); the political aims of the Resistance (2632); an acrimonious debate about the continuation of state subsidies for Roman Catholic schools, which the Vichy Government, unlike the Third Republic, had paid (2633); the obstacles to Austrian recovery and joint rule of Germany presented by zoning, the four allies having separate areas of influence (2669, 2671); and the belief held by many French people that Britain had undergone 'an actual social revolution', leading to a 'flattering but somewhat exaggerated estimate of British political achievement during the war' (2637). He was much exercised by the problems facing the millions of displaced persons, how they would be fed and what was to become of them. He also tried hard to get across to British readers how desperately short of food were the Germans. In 1946 British rations were cut to feed the near-starving Germans and displaced persons, even bread being rationed, something that had not been necessary during the war.

The matter of revenge greatly exercised Orwell. Writing of the May Day celebrations in 1945 he described how the crowds chanted 'Pétain au Poteau!' (Pétain to the Stake!'; 2664). Earlier, in his first article from Paris for *The Observer* (2631), he put down the French lust for executions to the effect of occupation.

> The people who would like to see the 'purge' in full swing – and some of them say freely that they believe several thousand executions to be necessary – are not reactionaries and not necessarily

Communists: they may be thoughtful, sensitive people whose antecedents are Liberal, Socialist, non-political.

Your objections always get much the same answer: 'It's different for you in England'.

'Several thousand' implies fewer French people than were executed legally or illegally by the French themselves. According to Adrien Tixier, the postwar Minister of Justice, there were 105 000 executions between June 1944 and February 1945 in France. David Pryce-Jones concluded that 'the number of Frenchmen killed by other Frenchmen, whether through summary execution or rigged tribunals akin to lynch mobs or court-martials and High Court trials, equaled or even exceeded the number of those sent to their death by the Germans as hostages, deportees, and slave laborers'. But these figures exaggerate and underestimate. Officially 9–10 000 people were 'executed': the true number might have been about 20 000. The Mémorial des Martyrs et de la Déportation on the Ile de la Cité, Paris, commemorates 200 000 French men, women and children deported to their deaths in Germany.[1] It was this danger of national self-destruction, as much as what he saw as the threat of Soviet Communism, that motivated Orwell in writing *Nineteen Eighty-Four*: the capacity of human society to turn in upon itself and to destroy itself from within; see below, pp. 138–9 and 145.

Following his visit to Stuttgart in April 1945 Orwell wrote of the inefficiency of the French administration, its permissive attitude to widescale looting, and the pleasure the French took at the humiliation of Germans. 'I could not feel anything of that kind myself', he wrote (2661). Those on whom he was billeted longed for a quick end to the war and for occupation by Americans or British, rather than Russians or French. It was this that prompted the writing of 'Revenge is Sour', published in *Tribune*, 9 November 1945. What he witnessed in Stuttgart – he does not identify the place in the essay – led him to write:

Properly speaking, there is no such thing as revenge. Revenge is an act which you want to commit when you are powerless: as soon as the sense of impotence is removed, the desire evaporates also. Who would not have jumped for joy, in 1940, at the thought of seeing S.S. officers kicked and humiliated? But when the thing becomes possible, it is merely pathetic and disgusting. (CEJL, iv.21)

ANIMAL FARM

The success of *Animal Farm* in its own time and its continued popularity is in sharp contrast to the problems Orwell had in getting the
book into print. Gollancz said that though 'highly critical of many
aspects of internal and external Soviet policy', he could not possibly
publish 'a general attack of this nature'; Jonathan Cape was keen to
publish until dissuaded by 'an important official in the Ministry of
Information' (doubtless one of the unteachable old duds whom
Orwell found so shortsighted); T. S. Eliot turned it down for Faber,
as he had *Down and Out in Paris and London* (see p. 31); and so on.
In desperate straits, Orwell seemed intent on publishing the book
himself, going so far as to approach David Astor for a loan of £200.
In the end it was Warburg, publisher of another rejected book by
Orwell, *Homage to Catalonia*, who came to the rescue, a decision for
which his company should be for ever grateful, especially as it
brought in its train *Nineteen Eighty-Four*. The story is well told by
Professor Crick (pp. 452–63). In a letter to *Books & Bookmen*, dated
8 January 1973, Fredric Warburg, referring to Orwell's intention to
publish it himself, said that the likely disastrous consequences might
have been such that Orwell would 'never have had the morale or
strength to complete *Nineteen Eighty-Four*'. He goes on: 'Had that
happened the face of English literature in the second quarter of this
century would have a measurably different aspect.'[2] Even with
Warburg's help, the publication of the book faced problems. It
appeared on 17 August 1945, at 6s. 0d. (30p), two days after VJ-Day
(and the day Marshal Pétain's sentence of death for collaboration
was commuted to life-imprisonment). The proofs gave the date of
publication as February and the first impression, May. The second
impression gave the correct month of publication, August. These
delays were caused by shortage of paper. Only 4500 copies were
printed initially but a second impression of 10 000 copies was
published in November and in October 1946 a third impression of
6000 copies. In May 1949, 5000 copies of a 'Cheap Edition' at 3s. 6d.
(17½p) were published, and since then it has repeatedly been reprinted. It was published in America by Harcourt, Brace on 26
August 1946 at $1.75 in a print-run of 50 000 copies and then, as a
Book of the Month Club Edition in print-runs of 430 000 and 110 000
copies. Orwell received *an advance* of $37 500 from the Book of the
Month Club. There were then just over four dollars to the pound
and Orwell had to pay American income tax of 30 per cent and so

he could expect to receive £6500, ten times his BBC pay. He would also have to pay British income tax at the basic rate of 45 per cent and supertax on top of that. Nevertheless, as this was only the start of his American sales, from this moment, Orwell became financially secure, even relatively well-off as compared to his earlier life. These receipts contrast markedly with Warburg's advance of £100, paid in two halves. Orwell noted the receipt of the first £45 (£5 having been deducted by his agent as commission) in the record of monies received that he kept for his tax return, but he does not note precisely when the payment was made. The receipt of the second £45 is not recorded. A Canadian edition of 2000 copies appeared in November 1946 at $2.00 but the following year the price was reduced to 89 cents resulting in the edition selling out. Penguin Books published its first edition of 60 000 copies at 1s. 6d. (7½p) on 27 July 1951 and a second impression the following year of 40 000 copies at 2s. 0d. (10p). Translations had appeared in eighteen languages by the time Orwell died, ranging from Portuguese (the first) to Telugu. The title suggested by Orwell for the French edition was 'Union des Republiques Socialistes Animales' – URSA, The Bear – but it was tactfully changed to *Les Animaux Partout!* and Napoleon was renamed César. Not so much animals everywhere but the censorship *partout* that was to dog Orwell to his last days (see below, p. 138).[3]

Orwell wrote a Preface to *Animal Farm* and space was allowed in the proofs for it, the text then starting on p. 13. However, he changed his mind about its inclusion and so in the first edition the text begins on p. 9. Years later Ian Angus discovered the Preface and it is included as an appendix to the 1987 and 1989 editions. Its subject is 'The Freedom of the Press'. Both these editions include a second Preface, a back-translation from Ukrainian of the special introduction Orwell wrote at the request of Ihor Szewczenko, who wrote to Orwell on 7 March 1947 (*3187*) telling him that he had made a translation in his spare moments in order to read *Animal Farm* to Ukrainians living in Displaced Persons Camps in Germany. He movingly described the response of these men, former bolsheviks but later inmates of Siberian prison camps. He wished to publish a Ukrainian edition but thought that, though the book should be capable of being understood without a Preface, a Preface would ensure that there were no misunderstandings, especially among those who were half-educated, who read eagerly, but to whom 'it is better to say things twice' (*3197*).[4]

This Preface is important because it makes patently clear how

Animal Farm originated (from Orwell's experience in Spain), and the incident that suggested its genre: the little boy driving a huge cart-horse, which could easily overwhelm the child had it realised its own strength (VIII.113; Penguin VIII.112). Orwell's concern for those so eager to read *Animal Farm* led to his specifying that he should receive no royalties from editions for political refugees and those who could not afford to pay royalties (such as those for whom the Telugu edition was published). Unfortunately, the Ukrainian edition did not reach the Displaced Persons Organisation. The 5000 copies were intercepted by the American Military Government in Munich and handed over to the Soviet Repatriation Commission. Presumably the copies went the same way as people forcibly repatriated by the Allies to the USSR. Orwell endeavoured to ensure that the same thing did not happen with the Russian-language edition, 1949. He had hoped that the British government would finance this (the Iron Curtain then being firmly in place), especially as, in addition to an issue on ordinary paper, one was published on thin paper for circulation behind the Iron Curtain. Even this was beyond the 'old duds' and Orwell himself paid for the edition.

Although the book is invariably called simply *Animal Farm*, that is not its full title. Orwell added a sub-title: *A Fairy Story*. That was too much for most publishers. The American editions have always dropped these embarrassing words. (Dial Press, one of the American publishers to whom it was originally offered, is reported to have rejected it on the ground that there was no market for animal stories, itself a failure to assess correctly a new market.) Of the editions published in Orwell's lifetime, only the British publishers and the Telugu translation respected the author's wishes. Perhaps had others been offered royalty-free rights they would have done likewise. Orwell found some shops placed *Animal Farm* among children's books and he took it upon himself to move them surreptitiously.[5] The early Swiss-German and German editions could not settle on a description. The first, October 1946, called it 'Eine Fabel' and explained that it was 'eine politische Satire im Gewand einer Fabel'; the second, published in three issues of the American-sponsored *Der Monat*, February–April, 1949, consolidated this as 'Eine satirische Fabel'; and the third, October 1951, as 'Eine Zeitsatire'.[6]

'*Fairy Story*' is important, of course. Why, otherwise, should Orwell so describe the book? Orwell was fascinated by fairy stories and similar highly-imaginative books for children. As already mentioned, one of his childhood favourites was Beatrix Potter's *Pigling Bland* (see above, p. 9). A glance at the frontispiece showing two pigs walking on their hind legs overrides any lingering feelings that Jacintha Buddicom, who recalled his love of this book, was herself romancing.[7] When at the BBC he adapted Hans Christian Andersen's *The Emperor's New Clothes* for broadcast to India, 18 November 1943 (*2361*); on 24 April 1946, Roger Senhouse, a Director of Secker & Warburg, told Orwell that he had accumulated 'a further stock of Source books on Nursery Rhymes' (note 'further'; *2982 n. 2*); on 9 July 1946, his adaptation of *Little Red Riding Hood* was broadcast in the BBC's *Children's Hour* (*3033*); and on 25 January 1947 he told Rayner Heppenstall, who produced the first two radio adaptations of *Animal Farm*, 14 January 1947 and 3 March 1952, the first made by Orwell himself, that he was interested in adapting fairy stories for radio and that *Cinderella* was 'the tops as far as fairy stories go' (*3163*). So not only must the sub-title be included it must also be considered by readers. The sub-title is ironic, as are the titles, *Burmese Days* and *Keep the Aspidistra Flying*. The essence of the fairy story is that the hero or heroine triumphs over the most untoward circumstances. It would, indeed, be a fairy story were a revolution founded on violence to end peacefully and equitably, but this farmyard revolution does not do so any more than did those in Soviet Russia or Spain. The tone of *Animal Farm* is akin to the description Orwell gave of Thomas Mann's *Royal Highness* in a review of 18 May 1940 (*624*); it was, he said, 'one of those eighteenth-century tales in which fairy story and social satire are combined'.

What happens in this Fairy Story was outlined by Orwell at about the time he first conceived of *Animal Farm*, the year after he had returned from Spain. He was reviewing Jack Common's *The Freedom of the Streets* (CEJL, i.372):

> It would seem that what you get over and over again is a movement of the proletariat which is promptly canalized and betrayed by astute people at the top, and then the growth of a new governing class. The one thing that never arrives is equality. The mass of the people never get the chance to bring their innate decency into the control of affairs, so that one is almost driven to the cynical thought that men are only decent when they are powerless.

Once again, that key word, 'decent'.

Many sources have been suggested for *Animal Farm*, recently and intriguingly, a cartoon in *Punch* of 23 May 1934, by E. H. Shepard, illustrator of the Christopher Robin stories. This shows Sir Oswald Mosley, dressed as a Blackshirt, standing in a farmyard addressing the animals. With his arm raised in the Nazi salute he is saying, 'Conservatism has chosen the financier. Fascism has chosen the British farmer.'[8] The prime source, however, is Orwell's experience of 'the Revolution Betrayed' in Spain. George Woodcock (a close friend of Orwell's), has described *Nineteen Eighty-Four* as enunciating a theme central to 'classic anarchist criticism of Marxism' and exemplified in Trotsky's *The Revolution Betrayed*. I have not been able to trace whether Orwell knew this book (also seen by some as a source for Emmanuel Goldstein's 'The Theory and Practice of Oligarchical Collectivism'); it does not appear among his list of books, nor is it in his pamphlet collection.[9] However, the theme is inherent in revolutionary movements – the French Revolution spawned an interminable series of bloody betrayals – and a later pamphlet that Orwell did own, *The Philosophy of Betrayal*, published by the Russia Today Society in 1945, indicates the persistence of the idea. And, of course, he had contributed to Gollancz's *The Betrayal of the Left* (p. 109).

Inevitably *Animal Farm* and *Nineteen Eighty-Four* were pretty thoroughly misunderstood, although noticeably not by those like Szewczenko and Joseph Czapski[10] who had bitter experience of the Soviet system. Even as intelligent and sympathetic a man as Dwight Macdonald was puzzled. Orwell had to explain to him that he did mean the book to be, primarily, a satire on the Russian Revoution:

> But I did mean it to have a wider application in so much that I meant that that kind of revolution (violent conspiratorial revolution, led by unconsciously power-hungry people) can lead only to a change of masters. I meant the moral to be that revolutions only effect a radical improvement when the masses are alert and know how to chuck out their leaders as soon as the latter have done their job. The turning-point of the story was supposed to be when the pigs kept the milk and the apples for themselves (Kronstadt). If the other animals had had the sense to put their foot down then, it would have been all right (3128).

By Kronstadt Orwell meant the 1921 mutiny of the sailors at that naval base in support of strikers in Leningrad over shortages of food. As the sailors were folk-heroes of the revolution for initiating events in 1917, this was a cruel blow to their leaders. Trotsky and

Tukhachevsky put down the rebellion, bloodily, but concessions in the form of the New Economic Policy were introduced. (Tuchachevsky was made a Marshal of the Soviet Union in 1935 and was executed in Stalin's 1937 purge.)

When Orwell adapted the novel for radio, he took care to make this turning-point of the novel (at VIII.23) clearer by introducing four lines of dialogue:

> CLOVER: Do you think that is quite fair [the appropriation of the apples]?
> MOLLY: What, keep all the apples for themselves?
> MURIEL: Aren't we to have any?
> COW: I thought they were going to be shared equally.
>
> [1987 edn, p. 153]

It hardly needs to be said that the BBC producer cut out these lines.

Another who misunderstood Orwell's standpoint was the Duchess of Atholl, author of the Penguin Special, *Searchlight on Spain*, (1938; reviewed by Orwell, 469). She invited him to speak for the League for European Freedom on 13 November 1945. Orwell replied two days later (2795) saying he was not in agreement with the League's ultimate objectives: 'I cannot associate myself with an essentially Conservative body which claims to defend democracy in Europe but has nothing to say about British imperialism', and he concluded, 'I belong to the Left and must work inside it, much as I hate Russian totalitarianism and its poisonous influence in this country.'

The literature on *Animal Farm* is enormous and it is not my purpose to review it here. One quotation from an early review does deserve mention, however. After saying that a story about farmyard animals did not sound very promising, Edmund Wilson wrote in *The New Yorker*, 7 September 1946:

> But the truth is that [*Animal Farm*] is absolutely first-rate. As a rule, I have difficulty in swallowing these modern fables.... But Mr. Orwell has worked out his theme with a simplicity, a wit, and a dryness that are closer to La Fontaine and Gay, and has written in a prose so plain and spare, so admirably proportioned to his purpose, that *Animal Farm* even seems very creditable if we compare it with Voltaire and Swift.

For this high praise Eileen must take some credit. Orwell did not usually allow others, even Eileen, to read what he was writing before he had finished. Professor Crick says that Eileen told friends that she was 'always a bit disappointed that he did not want her to read through and criticize his manuscripts before typing them out; only rarely, even back in Wallington days, did he even ask her to type for him'. *Animal Farm* was the exception. Each evening

> he read his day's work to her in bed, the warmest place in their desperately cold flat, discussed the next stage and actually welcomed criticisms and suggestions, both of which she gave. Never before had he discussed work in progress with anyone. Then the next morning Lettice Cooper and Eileen's other women friends at the Ministry of Food waited eagerly for a paraphrase of the latest episode.[11]

On 19 February 1946, Orwell wrote to Dorothy Plowman, the widow of Max Plowman, the man who had helped get Orwell's first articles for *The Adelphi* published (see p. 30 above). Dorothy Plowman had acted as L. H. Myers's intermediary in making the Orwells the anonymous gift of £300 so they could winter in Marrakech. Myers did not want Orwell to know his name and Orwell accepted the money as a loan (see above, p. 111). With royalties for *Animal Farm* coming in, Orwell quickly set about repaying what he regarded as a debt. He sent the first instalment of £150 to Dorothy Plowman. In his covering letter Orwell wrote,

> It was a terrible shame that Eileen didn't live to see the publication of *Animal Farm*, which she was particularly fond of and even helped in the planning of. I suppose you know I was in France when she died. It was a terribly cruel and stupid thing to happen.[12]

Animal Farm is a last, and worthy, tribute to Eileen's beneficial influence on Orwell.

NINETEEN EIGHTY-FOUR

There are grounds for complaining that great writers spawn industries dedicated to the examination of their work and the furtherance of academic careers. There is a Shakespeare industry, a Joyce industry and, as a mark of his stature I suppose, an Orwell industry of which, alas, I must be a part. There is even a *Nineteen Eighty-Four* industry. Much that has been written on this novel, its origins and its implications is excellent and genuinely helpful. A great deal of ground was covered by William Steinhoff in *George Orwell and the Origins of '1984'* (1975); Peter Stansky edited a collection of essays, *On Nineteen Eighty-Four* (1983), which includes, for example, a study of 'Zamyatin's *We* and *Nineteen Eighty-Four*' by Edward J. Brown; Irving Howe edited another volume of essays, *'1984' Revisited: Totalitarianism in Our Century* (1983), which includes 'The Disintegration of Leninist Totalitarianism in Our Century' by the Yugoslav author and dissident, Milovan Djilas; in 1984, Oxford University Press published an annotated edition of *Nineteen Eighty-Four*, with a critical introduction by Bernard Crick; less accessible, but worth digging out, is Roy Harris, 'The Misunderstanding of Newspeak', *The Times Literary Supplement*, 6 January 1984; and more recently, W. J. West has put forward new theories in *The Larger Evils* (1992), which, as the book's subtitle states, attempt to dig out 'The Truth Behind the Satire', and there is a chapter on 'Orwell at the BBC'. Here I shall content myself, and I hope the reader, by pointing to one or two minor items that have arisen in the course of editing Orwell's work that may throw a little more light on the novel and its author.

First, a seeming non-source. It is curious that Orwell nowhere in his writings or letters mentions *Swastika Night* by Katherine Burdekin, published under her pen-name, Murray Constantine. This was first published in 1937 and Orwell might in that year have easily missed it. It was republished in July 1940 as the 157th Left Book Club volume. The book has certain outline similarities to *Nineteen Eighty-Four* (though far fewer than to Zamyatin's *We*), and occasional local likenesses. For example, the manuscript book in which Winston keeps his diary and the volume containing Friedrich von Hess's 'hand-written terribly fragmentary history' (which has a general parallel with Goldstein's *Theory and Practice of Oligarchical Collectivism*) is introduced thus in *Swastika Night*:

> The Knight put his hand again under the desk and this time drew forth a huge book of deep yellow colour. As he opened it the leaves made a peculiar thick crackling sound, unlike the rustling of paper.

Goldstein's book is described quite differently (IX.191); the book in which Winston keeps his diary is kept in a drawer and is initially described as 'a thick, quarto-sized blank book with a red back and marbled cover', but then as 'a peculiarly beautiful book. Its smooth creamy paper, a little yellowed by age, was of a kind that had not been manufactured for at least forty years past' (IX.7,8). There is nothing here (the yellowed pages, for example) that is not of the common stock of all writers, and I am not convinced that Orwell knew *Swastika Night* in any detail. However, I should not be surprised if he had come across it very briefly. I wonder whether it was sent to him for review in *Tribune* with Jack London's *Iron Heel*, and *The Sleeper Awakes* by H. G. Wells, both of which influenced Orwell. He describes these as 'prophecies of Fascism' in his review of 10 July 1940 (CEJL, ii.45–9). *Swastika Night*, a futuristic book, is much concerned with Hitler and the 'Hitler Book' and a Twenty Years War, and a reference to *Swastika Night* would have fallen naturally into place in his review. Of all those listed above, only W. J. West mentions *Swastika Night* but it is taken as a source by Daphne Patai in *The Orwell Mystique: A Study of Male Ideology* (1984), an important feminist critique of Orwell. I am not inclined to accept that lack of reference to *Swastika Night* by so many scholars is a male plot (but, of course, it might be said that that would be my position). However, it should be noted that neither the excellent and comprehensive *Feminist Companion to Literature*, edited by Virginia Blair, Patricia Clements and Isobel Grundy (1990), nor the more recent *Bloomsbury Guide to Women's Literature*, edited by Claire Buck (1992), makes any allusion to Katherine Burdekin or Murray Constantine. I guess that Orwell may have seen the book but thought it so inferior to *The Iron Heel*, *The Sleeper Awakes* and *Brave New World* (which he also discusses in his review), that he did not think it worth the briefest space. It is a pretty turgid book. W. J. West sums up neatly: 'Orwell found it quite impossible to keep silent about books that interested him or which he had been given to review'; he makes no reference to *Swastika Night*, though he refers repeatedly to Zamyatin's *We*.[13]

The influence of C. K. Ogden's Basic English on the creation of Newspeak has been well documented, especially Ogden's 'translation' of part of H. G. Wells's 'Language and Mental Growth' in Book V ('The Modern State in Control of Life') of *The Shape of Things to Come*, and is discussed by William Steinhoff. Steinhoff finds less convincing the suggestions that Orwell was influenced by 'cablese' but he gives an example from Eugene Lyons's *Assignment in Utopia*, which Orwell reviewed on 9 June 1938 (CEJL, i.368–71). Orwell commissioned a broadcast for India on Basic English by Leonora Lockhart. This was transmitted on 2 October 1942 and the script survives in the BBC's Archives at Caversham. On 16 December 1942 Orwell wrote to Ogden about the lack of response to that broadcast (see *1393* and *1747*). He wrote to Ogden again on 1 March 1944 and referred to the problems Ogden had had with 'the Esperanto people' (*2427*).[14] Such influence as 'cablese' might have had could have been prompted by its satiric use by Evelyn Waugh in *Scoop* four years earlier, for example, the two words, 'ADEN UNWARWISE' that the London office of William Boot's newspaper was expected to expand to 'Aden the focal point of British security in the threatened area still sunk in bureaucratic lethargy'.[15] Orwell devotes particular attention to the use of *un* and *wise* in *Nineteen Eighty-Four* (IX.315); see also 'unproceed constructionwise' (176) which Orwell 'translated' for the Danish translator of the novel as 'Do not proceed with the construction' (IX.341 of the hardback edition). Another possible influence on the deliberate restriction of language, also stemming from 1938, is T. H. White's *The Sword in the Stone*, where communication between ants is only through words associated with duty, compliance, and conformity. But the search for sources and parallels is almost without limit.

'Doublethink' could have had an equally long period of gestation. It may stem from Orwell's interest in *Macbeth*, Orwell's favourite play by Shakespeare, in which the Porter refers satirically to equivocation. Standing as if at the Door of Hell, the Porter asks who knocks: 'Faith, here's an equivocator that could swear in both the scales against either scale, who committed treason enough for God's sake, yet could not equivocate to Heaven: O come in [to Hell], equivocator' (II.2.6–10). The particular equivocator was probably Henry Garnet, Superior of the Order of Jesuits in England, who was associated with the Gunpowder Plot and hanged in 1606. Orwell told Eleanor Jaques, 'I so adore Macbeth' (presumably the play) on 18 November 1932 and he was keen to take her to see a production at the Old Vic (CEJL, i.130–1) when he was teaching at The Hawthorns. This was a time when he was conscious of equivocation within himself, telling Eleanor just four weeks earlier that to please a friend, the curate of the local church, he would have to take Holy Communion, even though that would be hypocritical: 'It seems rather mean to go to H.C. when one doesn't believe, but I have passed myself off for pious & there is nothing for it but to keep up the deception' (CEJL, i.128). Orwell gave a half-hour broadcast to India about the play on 17 October 1943 and his talk was accompanied by extracts he had selected to illustrate the story (2319; the extracts do not include the Porter). It is *Macbeth* that Dorothy teaches the children in *A Clergyman's Daughter*. At the end of the novel she discusses with Warburton the hypocrisy of pretending to believe. Warburton asks her whether she fears that the consecrated bread of the Communion might stick in a disbelieving throat. She admits it might be better to be a hypocrite, pretending to believe being less selfish than an open declaration of unbelief which could adversely influence others (III.276–7). At the very end of the novel, her pondering upon equivocation becomes virtually doublethink: 'faith and no faith are very much the same provided that one is doing what is customary, useful and acceptable' (III.295, and see p. 64 above). Julia puts it much more crudely in *Nineteen Eighty-Four*: 'Always yell with the crowd . . . It's the only way to be safe' (IX.128).

Orwell completed typing the final draft of *Nineteen Eighty-Four* at Barnhill, Jura, in great pain, on 4 December 1948. He sent copies off to London and managed only another month at Barnhill before being driven to Cranham Sanatorium, Gloucestershire, on 6 January 1949. From there he was transferred to University College Hospital on 3 September. A bedside marriage to Sonia Brownell, an editorial assistant on *Horizon*, was arranged by special licence on 13 October. He died on 21 January 1950, aged 46. By then he knew that *Nineteen Eighty-Four* had, literally, taken the world by storm.

Warburg recognised from the outset that the novel would be successful. He published 26 575 copies (an enormous increase on the initial printing-runs of Orwell's two earlier books that he had published – *Homage to Catalonia*, 1500 copies, and *Animal Farm*, 4500 copies). Harcourt, Brace published 20 000 copies on 13 June 1949; the book was translated into many languages and it has been reprinted time after time.[16] In order to rush out the American edition it was not set from the English edition but prepared for printing by Robert Giroux simultaneously with the English edition from a carbon copy of the typescript. The Americans wished to excise Goldberg's 'Testament' and the Appendix on Newspeak; Orwell refused point blank. Without consulting Orwell, they changed Orwell's metric measurements into miles, yards, etc., to make them comprehensible to American readers. On 1 March 1949, Orwell asked

Moore to see they were changed back and this was done (3556). There were, inevitably, differences in styling and some differences in readings, a number of which stem from Orwell. The 1987 edition endeavours to sort out these variants and its Textual Note gives lists of variant readings. That edition also includes a passage of Newspeak in Standard English that Orwell prepared to assist the Danish translator (IV.341). 'A Note on the Text' to the Penguin edition of 1989 reproduces a passage cut from the facsimile (IX.xix) and explains how it came about that from 1950 to 1987 all English editions gave the formula '2 + 2 = 5' on p. 303 as '2 + 2 = '. This was because the leading of the Monotype in which it was set loosened in the forme and the five dropped out.[17] This alters the 'meaning' of the novel in that, with the five, Winston conforms; without it he maintains vestiges of independence. So far as I know, no critic noticed the significance of this typographical error.

Room 101, which arouses such fear, is one of Orwell's private jokes. It was the number of the room where BBC Eastern Service Committee meetings were held at 55 Portland Place and these Orwell was required to attend. To the last Orwell retained a sense of humour.

The year 1984 has often been interpreted as deriving solely from a reversal of the last two digits of the year when he completed the novel, 1948. Certainly Orwell saw this link, but as late as 22 October 1948, Orwell told Warburg that he was hesitating between 'Nineteen Eighty-Four' and 'The Last Man in Europe' as the book's title (CEJL, iv.507). Orwell was then seeking to have Warburg send him a typist to make a fair copy. The manuscript, he said, was 'unbelievably bad' so that 'no one could make head or tail of it without explanation'. No one could be found and Orwell, racked with pain, typed the fair copy himself. In this letter he said, self-deprecatingly,

I am not pleased with the book but am not absolutely dissatisfied. I first thought of it in 1943. I think it is a good idea but the execution would have been better if I had not written it under the influence of T.B.

The year 1984 is a little arithmetical puzzle (perhaps one might call it 'arithmetical wit'). First of all, it is important to note that what survives of the original draft manuscript of *Nineteen Eighty-Four* shows that the year was not to be 1984 but 1980 (see *Facsimile*, p. 23). Although he had first thought of the idea for the book in

1943 (his last year at the BBC), it was only on 25 June 1945 that
Warburg would report that Orwell had told him that the first twelve
pages had been written (*2677, n. 4*). As it took longer and longer to
complete the novel, Orwell changed 1980 first to 1982 and then to
1984. Consequential advances were simultaneously made to other
dates. When war broke out in 1939, Orwell was 36. He adopted his
son, Richard, in 1944 and I believe that when he started the surviving draft he was looking forward to a time when his son would be
36: that is, 1980. As time passed he kept advancing the date so that,
when the novel was finished, in 1948, the addition of 36 years produced 1984. A little clue to support this will be found in 'As I
Please' for 2 February 1945, where he records the explosion nearby
of a V-2 (a 'Steamer' in the novel, IX.87): 'in the next room the 1964
class wakes up and lets out a yell or two' (CEJL, iii.373). The reference is to the few-months-old Richard. In 1964 he would be twenty
and, as the 'Class of 1964', graduating, a trifle early, perhaps, but
that is Orwell's calculation; arithmetic was not his strong point (see
above p. 71).

In 'As I Please', 48, 17 November 1944, Orwell remarks that 'One
favourite way of falsifying history is to alter dates' (CEJL, iii.315–
16). He then recounts how Maurice Thorez, the leader of the French
Communists, fled to the USSR (then an ally of Nazi Germany) when
he was called up at the outbreak of war in 1939. However, when
Thorez returned to Paris, after it was liberated by the Allies, in
order to continue his activities on behalf of the Communist party,
it was claimed that he had been in the Soviet Union for six years,
not five. This made it appear that he had not deserted France in
order to side with the allies of the Nazis, but, at the time war was
declared, had already been in the Soviet Union for a year. 'This',
says Orwell, 'is merely one act in the general effort to whitewash
the behaviour of the French and other Communists during the period
of the Russo-German Pact', and he claims he could name other
similar falsifications.

Orwell makes use of the falsification of dates for a like purpose
in a memorable moment in *Nineteen Eighty-Four*. Into Winston
Smith's hands falls a newspaper cutting showing a photograph of
the triumvirate of alleged traitors, Jones, Aaronson and Rutherford.
They are shown at a Party function in New York. What immediately
strikes Smith is that at that time, according to the evidence laid
against them, they were betraying military secrets to the Eurasian
General Staff in Siberia: 'There was only one possible conclusion:

the confessions were lies' (IX.81). This falsification of history was made possible by altering dates. The origins of this incident in *Nineteen Eighty-Four* might seem to depend on Orwell's article of 1944, but they go back long before and are more personal.

The passport issued on 19 October 1922 for his journey to Burma (No. 280033) gave his correct date of birth. Passports then only lasted five years but no passport application can be traced for his journey to Paris in 1928. His passport would still have been valid for his return from Burma. However, in the light of the absence of a passport application for the journey to Paris, it is probable Orwell took the precuation of renewing his 1922 passport in Burma because it would soon be out of date. Passports were essential in those days and Orwell makes the point in *Down and Out in Paris and London* that he needed his passport to pawn his and Boris's overcoats (Ch. VII, especially p. 40). Although one cannot take what is said in a fictionalised autobiography as evidence for what happens in life, Boris and most of the events of *Down and Out* are factual (see pp. 35–6). Orwell does admit that 'Many of the waiters had slipped into France without passports, and one or two of them were spies' (I.72), but it was far easier to slip into France from Italy or Switzerland than from England and, in any case, Orwell would have needed his passport at the Hôpital Cochin and there his date of birth is given as 1902. When he registered with the consul in Marrakech in 1938, Orwell gave his date of birth as 1902 (*483*); this date is in Orwell's own handwriting. These two dates would have had to tally with his passport. When he married on 9 June 1936, Orwell's age was registered as 33 but he would not have been 33 until 25 June. And, on 12 February 1938 (CEJL, i.336), Orwell wrote to A. H. Joyce at the India Office in connection with an offer he had received to join the staff of *The Pioneer*, Lucknow. He told him he was born in 1903 but 'by mistake this has been entered as 1902 in my passport'. Now, Orwell's passport application for his journey to Spain, made on 8 December 1938 (no. 157953, three weeks before he set off), also gives his date of birth as 1902. A final passport was issued on 10 May 1949 (No. 1243051), the time when, though very ill, he was hoping to go abroad for the winter (see his letter to Anthony Powell, 11 May 1949, CEJL, iv.562). This last passport gave his correct year of birth, 1903.[18]

Orwell certainly gave a wrong year of birth when applying for a passport in 1936, but he was in haste to travel to Spain and to get the records corrected would, according to the Passport Agency, have required a fair amount of time-consuming paperwork. Orwell was in the final stage of completing *The Road to Wigan Pier* and presumably took the simple course of acquiescing in the false date on his second passport. There is no reason why Orwell should have falsified his age and his statement to Joyce that 'by mistake' this had been entered incorrectly into his passport – but in 1927, not 1936 – was probably true. However, this clerking error, probably made in Burma, meant that for ten years Orwell had passports showing the 'falsification' of his dates of birth. His sensitivity towards this was what, in all probability, drew his attention to the political uses of such falsification.

When Winston Smith accidentally comes across the photograph of Jones, Aaronsen and Rutherford, he knows that the dates alleging their treachery have been falsified. But the photograph itself seems to have had a specific source. David Astor (at the time the distinguished editor of *The Observer*, for which Orwell wrote) asked Orwell why he had given up writing for *Tribune*. Orwell seemed embarrassed but told him that he no longer felt at ease with its semi-honest attitude to the Soviet Union. Aneurin Bevan, whom Orwell liked better than any other British politician, had no illusions about the true character of the Soviet regime but, Orwell told Astor, Bevan would not say publicly what he really thought about the USSR. Then he added, as an aside, that he had seen a photograph of Bevan in 1930, standing proudly by the Dnieperstroi Dam workings that conveyed the opposite of his real opinion of the regime. Although he gave up writing for *Tribune*, he never turned against Bevan nor wished to harm him.[19] Was Orwell's coming across the photograph of Bevan, with its inversion of truth, the origin of the picture of the triumvirate in the novel which also contradicted what had happened? And did he link that with the accidental falsification of the dates of his passports and the deliberate falsification of the dates of Thorez's flight to Russia to avoid serving in the French army when the Nazis invaded?

Like *Animal Farm*, Orwell's last novel was misunderstood. It was particularly galling to him that right-wingers saw (and still see) *Nineteen Eighty-Four* as arguing against socialism. When Warburg went to see Orwell at Cranham (and he, and many other friends, especially David Astor, were assiduous in their kindness to Orwell, making the journey to Gloucester when, in those days, that meant a tedious trek by public transport) on 15 June 1946, he wrote down notes of a statement Orwell wished to have circulated. In this, Orwell made it plain that he was not attacking the Labour Party ('Members of the present British government, from Mr Attlee and Sir Stafford Cripps down to Aneurin Bevan will *never* willingly sell the pass to the enemy'), and most especially he stressed that he was *not* prophesying what would happen in forty years' time. What he had written, he said, was a warning: 'The moral to be drawn . . . is a simple one: *Don't let it happen. It depends on you*' (3646).[20] The full history of the part-letter to Francis A. Henson, published in CEJL, iv.564, has now been established. In brief, the New York *Daily News* interpreted the novel as an attack on the Labour government. Warburg telephoned a refutation to *Life*, which ignored that but published part of the version sent to Francis A. Henson. A slightly different version was published by the *New York Times Book Review* and a full version in *Socialist Call* (New York).

Despite these efforts, the book is still sometimes interpreted as an attack on socialism, rather than on its perversion, and as a prophecy, with the comforting delusion that 'We have got through 1984 so we are safe'. Though he did not intend prophecy, Orwell did, in fact, accurately predict so much that has happened: metrication, deforestation (in Vietnam), the treatment of dissidents in mental hospitals, the breakdown of the nuclear family, the distribution of habit-forming drugs, the disappearance of those who oppose a brutal regime (especially in South America), the degeneration of language (how can people be so insensitive as to say 'weatherwise' and the like, if they have read the Appendix?), and perhaps especially the waging of wars on the fringes of the World Powers but never between them: Chad, Somalia, Iran/Iraq, The Falklands, Lebanon, Afghanistan, Grenada, Panama, Yugoslavia, Haiti, Ruanda . . . the list is endless. There is even a Lottery with 'enormous prizes' each week which, for the Proles, was 'their delight, their folly, their anodyne, their intellectual stimulant' (ix. 89).

Orwell had fought and suffered from censorship all his working life so it was incongruously appropriate that the last letter to him from his agent (on 27 November 1949) was about censorship. A Spanish translation was proposed for Argentina. The publishers wished to cut about 140 lines which they feared the police would object to on moral grounds. This would serve as an excuse to ban the book without stating that the objections were political. The full details, and the passages to be cut, are given at 3710. Needless to say, they would not offend the most delicate sensibility.

In *Orwell's Message*, George Woodcock argues that the danger that Orwell warns against might, paradoxically, stem from the very institutions set up to protect the individual in the welfare state. The creation of state dependency, the intrusion into the privacy of individuals, the necessary regimentation of society that welfare demands, and the replacement by bureaucratic initiative of those generous impulses that characterise free societies, will, despite their originally benevolent intent, weaken 'our ability to resist the more malevolent assaults of governments that may come in harsher times. We are all there, meticulously registered, awaiting their attention.'[21] The year 1984 may be receding into the past, but Orwell's onetime anarchist friend and colleague suggests why Orwell's warning should still be heeded.

8
Conclusion

Orwell died of a massive haemorrhage of the lung at University College Hospital in the early hours of Saturday, 21 January 1950. Death came quickly and, although Sonia had been with him much of the day, he died alone. He was buried according to the rites of the Church of England, as he had requested in the Will he made on 18 January 1950, at All Saints, Sutton Courtney, Berkshire, the arrangements having been made by David Astor. At his death he seems to have had savings of £2500; anticipated royalties of £8800 (spread over a year); effects worth £300; an insurance for Richard of £150; and was owed £520, a total of £12 270. A statement of account he drew up 'on the assumption of my dying in 1949' shows a slightly larger figure (3725). When probate was granted in May 1950 his estate came down to £9908 14s. 11d. (3729). In terms of the value of the pound that is approximately equivalent to £150 000 today. The pre-probate figures took no account of hospital bills. The interesting figure here is the amount he was owed. Those he had helped were George Kopp, £250; Paul Potts, £120; Sonia, £100; Inez Holden £75; Jack Common £50 (see 3666); and Humphrey Slater, £25. These sums in terms of the value of the pound today total almost £8000. Probably few people with assets today of £150 000 (the value of a house that someone with Orwell's income might reasonably expect to own) have lent friends £8000. As we know from other sources, Orwell was particularly generous in giving to 'good causes'.

In his obituary of Orwell published in *The Bookseller*, 11 February 1950, Warburg said that at his death, Orwell had two new novels 'simmering in his mind, and a long essay on Joseph Conrad'; Orwell told Sonia that he had two novels in mind. After his visit to Orwell at Cranham on 15 June 1949, Warburg told his fellow directors that Orwell had formulated 'a nouvelle of 30 000 to 40 000 words – a novel of character rather than of ideas, with Burma as background' (3645). This must be 'A Smoking-Room Story', for which a section in the form of an unfinished draft, with further notes and a lay-out, survive (3721–2). From the notes it is clear that this is set in 1927, the year Orwell returned from Burma. It looks as if the draft was

140

written in the spring of 1949. On 15 April 1949, Orwell told Tosco Fyvel, 'I have a novel dealing with 1945 in my head now, but even if I survive to write it I shouldn't touch it before 1950' (*3598*). Shortly before he died, plans were being made for Orwell to recuperate in Switzerland. Although that was a forlorn hope, to Orwell it seemed genuine enough. There is no doubt that, although, in a fashion typical of him, he would say 'if I survive', he was expecting to live and continue writing. This should be borne in mind when attempts are made to apply a sense of impending death to his writing, especially to *Nineteen Eighty-Four*.

This study is not intended to be a full-dress biography, nor is it primarily a critical assessment of Orwell as writer and man, nor does it set out to review all that has been written about Orwell and his work. Its scope is limited to the publishing history of Orwell's work, his relations with publishers, and to what influenced him. In passing, of course, some assessments have been offered. In conclusion, it might be appropriate to look briefly at Orwell more broadly.

There is a first-rate account of the process by which a literary reputation is created that pays particular attention to Orwell: John Rodden's *The Politics of Literary Reputation: The Making and Claiming of 'St. George' Orwell* (1989). Despite the sub-title, this is not a dismissive exposure of Orwell but a well-informed and perceptive analysis of postwar literary trends and attitudes. Rodden is not only concerned with the vicissitudes of Orwell's literary reputation but also how his legend as a man has been created. One of the characteristics he points to is the divergence of critical attitudes within 'Orwell's standing as a "canonized" author'. He says, for example:

One coordinator of an American academic conference on Orwell's work in 1984 told me that, of more than a dozen academic symposia she had organised in the previous three years, no figure or issue had attracted so many international participants as the Orwell symposium. Such testimony stands in apparent opposition to the verdict of several U.S. English professors in a 1983 interview. They agreed that Orwell was a 'journalist' and 'didactic writer' who 'failed to live up to top literary standards', with *Nineteen Eighty-Four* in particular 'lacking in literary sophistication'.[1]

In 1969, Keith Alldritt maintained that 'With the possible exception of *Nineteen Eighty-Four*, Orwell created no valuable work of literary art; rather his contribution was to literary culture.'[2] Even the novel Alldritt excepts, with reservations, was by 1990, dismissed. John Torode, admittedly in a weekend newspaper magazine, stated flatly in the headline to an article, '1984 is no good in 1990'. He argued that the 'destructive Orwell myth, honed and polished during the Cold War decades, came to embrace three false beliefs': that the 'great moralist was also a great novelist'; that he was 'a perceptive political analyst as well as an outstanding political reporter'; and that *Animal Farm* 'got it right' about the history of the Russian Revolution. He concluded, 'It is time we reclaimed Orwell from the Cold War Warriors.'[3]

Feminists have castigated Orwell for ignoring women workers in *The Road to Wigan Pier* (and I have tried, not to pretend it is not so, but to put into the context of its time, pp. 73–5), and that he was a misogynist; but unless the word is being given a meaning other than I believe it to have, his life and behaviour demonstrate that he did not have 'a contempt for women', as Deirdre Beddoe claims.[4]

Brenda Salkeld, the gym mistress at St Felix Girls' School, Southwold, and a friend of Orwell's in the 1930s, spoke as vehemently as anyone about Orwell and women. 'He never understood people', she claimed, 'He didn't really like women. . . . He was a sadist and that was why he had this feeling towards women.'[5] However, Kay Ekevald, who also knew him well, thought Orwell 'liked women well enough', even though he was 'ultramasculine' towards them, but yet 'he didn't treat you like that when you met him. He was very equalitarian in discussion.'[6] It was, however, 'we cruel girls' who mocked Orwell's attempts to become a writer – 'like a cow' (note the sex) 'with a musket', according to the poet, Ruth Pitter. She thought he had a cruel streak, but, interestingly, she put that down to his mother: 'His mother, you see, was waspish. He's bound to have inherited a touch of that.'[7] However, it was not Orwell but his sister Avril who caused Susan Watson, who looked after Richard, to pack up and leave: 'At no time did I blame him for what happened. Our relationship was a good one, bound on mutual respect. I miss him very much and think of him as a fine and completely irreplaceable person.'[8] Katie Darrod, who lived nearby Orwell on Jura, found him 'a good neighbour . . . willing to help anyone'.[9] Had he had so much contempt for women, Mikeal Smith would hardly have accompanied Cyril Wright to see him at

Wallington on a number of occasions (p. 112), and Orwell would not have bothered to write long letters about Spain and current problems to Amy Charlesworth in 1937 and 1944 (the years for which letters survive: *384, 393, 2493*, and *2569*; she died in 1945). Amy Charlesworth lived at Flixton, near Manchester, and had been forced to leave her husband with her two children because of his brutality. She and Orwell seem never to have met. Especially telling is a letter from one of his BBC secretaries, sent him on 8 December 1949 (*3713*). Nancy Parratt left the BBC to join the WRNS in 1943. She served for some time in the USA and married. She had heard of the success of *Nineteen Eighty-Four* but seemed unaware that Orwell was ill. Her letter is so obviously friendly, telling Orwell of her new life and her reactions to America, that it is inconceivable that, had Orwell been contemptuous of women, she would have bothered to correspond with him six years after she finished working as his secretary. And one could go on, but those who believe Orwell was a misogynist and contemptuous of women are unlikely to be convinced otherwise by evidence.

To Daphne Patai, 'Orwell and the cult that arose around him in the mid-twentieth century will eventually be viewed as a problem in intellectual history and intellectual consumption.'[10] Lest this be thought exclusively a feminist view, John Rodden's conclusion does not expect 'the Orwell centennial in 2003 to be more than an academic affair',[11] and I am certainly uneasy when I see him likened, however well-meaningly, to Solzhenitsyn.[12]

And yet, is Orwell so easily dismissed? I suppose I have spent as much time as almost anyone – Ian Angus and Bernard Crick would be obvious exceptions – 'in company' with Orwell, plodding away at producing reasonably accurate texts of his books and preparing for the printer everything else he wrote, from the most seeming trivia to his best essays. In the decade and a half that that has taken me, the man and his writing have increasingly enthralled me. Of course, that might be a limitation in me, but I am not sure that, even if it is, it isn't the same kind of limitation that vast numbers of people share who don't have an axe to grind.

Orwell's virtues are at their most attractive in his incredible determination to be a writer, whatever the difficulties and disappointments; in his passion for what he saw as social justice – in, to use three of his favourite words, to strive against the 'beastly' for 'decency' and, in writing to achieve that, to fight against the insistence of censors and publishers to 'garble' what he said. Of course he had his limitations and he certainly made mistakes. In that he was human (his most endearing characteristic). Only the Pope and literary and social critics can claim infallibility, at least, in their own eyes. But, perhaps because he started so late, and was not conditioned by an orthodox university education, but rather that his first experience of work was in a milieu he quickly rejected, he remained ready to change and develop throughout his life. An appealing trait was his ability find error in what he had written – he devotes his London Letter to *Partisan Review* of December 1944 to what he had got wrong in earlier letters (CEJL, iii.335–41) – and in himself (notable in his ability to turn those whom he had attacked into lifelong friends).

Orwell may not be a novelist of the first rank, although even the potboilers he himself dismissed have a curious capacity for touching the readers' sensibilities and causing them to see the world, especially the dispossessed, in a new and sympathetic light. The topographical, social, and personal journeys of *The Road to Wigan Pier* also speak to people new to the book to this day, removed though its specific context is from our experience, and naive though is his personal struggle to come to terms with socialism. Presumably no one now reads *Amiel's Journal* and that fate may still overtake *The Road to Wigan Pier*, but I doubt if it is yet, or even by 2003. *Homage to Catalonia* is not an important introduction to the facts of the Spanish Civil War as is, say, Thomas's history, but it is one of the very few books in English, perhaps the only book, still read *from that period* for a personal and passionate account of the Spanish experience. *Down and Out in Paris and London* and *A Clergyman's Daughter*, for all their structural infelicities, convey the experience of poverty vividly, and so long as we have people sleeping in doorways, which seemingly will be for ever, that remains important. Successful comic novels are rare, but *Coming Up for Air* is one; it probably suffers because prospective readers unfortunately bring to Orwell no awareness of his wit and humour and so fail to spot those elements. *Burmese Days* remains a good, and very enjoyable, novel of the second rank; it is more than a simple romance and, in my experience, most readers understand its subtext, if not all its ironies. *Animal Farm* is *not* restricted to the Russian Revolution: its lesson that power-hungry leaders of violent, conspiratorial revolutions should be chucked out as soon as their initial work has been done (see pp. 127–8) will, unfortunately, always need to be learned. As for *Nineteen Eighty-Four*, I could wish its warnings were no longer necessary. It is not a book I warm to because its warning is a reminder of the blight that may affect our futures and those of our children. Three years after the year 1984, Colin Thubron's brilliant account of his long journey through China was published. It offers a terrible reminder that the lesson of *Nineteen Eighty-Four* can never be well enough learned. He wrote:

> In the anarchy of the Cultural Revolution, between 1966 and 1976, the Chinese people had not merely been terrorised from above, but had themselves – tens of millions of them – become instruments of their own torture. The land had sunk into a peculiar horror. A million were killed; some thirty million more were brutally persecuted, and unknown millions starved to death. Yet it was less the numbers which appalled than the refinements of cruelty practised – in one province alone, seventy-five different methods of torture were practised. . . .[13]

Were we able to hope that such regimes had no place in the modern world, and that they would never arise in Britain, the 'necessity' for *Nineteeen Eighty-Four* would disappear and the novel itself could become a footnote, a mere 'problem in intellectual history'. Until that happy and unlikely state occurs, it will remain an essential warning. It is ironic that, despite his various passages of arms with those in authority, and his suspicions of such institutions as the India Office, the BBC and the Ministry of Information, in his final years, when he was too ill to contribute directly, the Foreign Office consulted him from time to time on the publication of factual articles and books by reputable experts to counter the threat of Communism.[14]

Orwell's achievement in establishing a truly enterprising series of 'open university' courses is now, happily, a footnote to history, for things have advanced, but it remains socially important, as do his attempts to raise the level of debate in the kinds of talks he organised for the BBC. What will, I believe, remain important in any circumstance are Orwell's essays. It is undoubtedly true that he was a journalist, though at a time when journalists were worthy of more respect than they are today. As a result, many of his articles and reviews are hasty in thought and execution. They are often still lively and, in the context of the debates that ensued, even the most workaday of his contributions to *Tribune* played a part in the political and social debate of his time.[15] What will last are what can properly be called 'the great essays'. These are of two kinds. Those that are concerned with political, moral, linguistic and social issues that will always be important, and those that are a delight in themselves, such essays as 'Some Thoughts on the Common Toad'. It is, I think, particularly surprising that some essays that one would have thought could no longer interest us, because of the passage of time and the increased critical techniques with which we have become familiar, can still speak directly to us; for example, 'Raffles and Miss Blandish', 'Benefit of Clergy' and 'Notes on Nationalism'. Without any question, Orwell's constant concern for language is still important. Did we only take note of what he argued! The relationship of language to democracy (not mere representative government, which is all we can seem to achieve) is still vital to the establishment of healthy societies.

In his final years, Orwell suffered at least four major disappointments, two personal, one social, one political. The death of Eileen, though he spoke and wrote little of it, affected him deeply, the more so because it was unexpected and he was out of the country. She was an excellent letter-writer and her last letters, *2638, 2640, 2642*, and *2647*, are very moving. It was a great cause of regret to Orwell that not only did he not live to see his son, Richard, grow up, but that in his last year he could spend so little time with him for fear of giving him tuberculosis; see especially the last paragraph of his letter to Sir Richard Rees from Cranham Sanatorium, 3 March 1949 (CEJL, iv.540). Orwell believed passionately that the 'health of the nation' would be better served by ridding England of its private schools than by Aneurin Bevan's National Health System (see p. 104 above), which was ironic given his own sickness. Lastly, he was saddened by the failure of the attempt to reveal the true culprits of the Katyn and Starobielsk massacres.

With Arthur Koestler, Orwell tried hard to get an English translation published of Joseph Czapski's *Souvenirs de Starobielsk* (Paris, 1945). Orwell had met Czapski in Paris a short time before Eileen's death. Though Czapski had suffered severely at Stalin's hands, it was Czapski who persuaded Orwell to make a last-minute change to the proof of *Animal Farm*. Instead of, as Orwell had originally written, 'all the animals, including Napoleon' falling down in fear during the attack on the windmill, Czapski had him write, 'all the animals, except Napoleon' (VIII.69/22) because that, as Orwell explained to his publisher, 'would be fair to Stalin, as he did stay in Moscow during the German advance' (*2635*). It was Czapski who brought home to Orwell and Koestler that it was the Russians, not the Germans (as was widely then believed) who had massacred 15 700 Polish prisoners at Katyn, Starobielsk, and other camps (*Souvenirs de Starobielsk*, p. 18). In *The Inhuman Land* (1951), Czapski described how a further 7000 Polish prisoners from the Komi Peninsula were packed into barges and then drowned in the White Sea (pp. 35–6). Orwell failed to persuade any publisher to risk offending the Russians in 1945 by making the truth known. Although in 1952 a United States congressional inquiry had established Russian responsibility for these massacres, successive British governments, Labour and Conservative, connived at concealing the Russians' guilt, and to such an extent that, when a memorial to those murdered at Katyn was dedicated at Gunnersbury Cemetery in London in 1976, the Labour government threatened any British officers who attended in uniform with court-martial. Only in September 1988, at a ceremony at the memorial to mark the Russian invasion of Poland in 1939, were British officers allowed to attend in uniform (ironically following a change of policy instigated by Mrs Thatcher). The book has never been translated into English and it took over forty years for British and Russian governments to acknowledge a truth that Orwell and Koestler had tried to make known shortly after the end of the war.

It is too easy to claim that Orwell's novels do not accord with what are taken to be the canons of high literature; Orwell is central to the developments that have challenged such notions and, especially through his essays, he has been instrumental in broadening and redefining concepts of culture. His influence in so doing is still felt and it will continue. There is no doubt his future significance is assured. It is fair to say, I think, that Orwell is most influential with younger rather than older and more sophisticated readers. This is no bad thing. The fact that he is accessible to younger people is of the greatest importance, prompting, infuriating, enlightening, nagging and warning his readers in so many areas of thought and action. Thereafter a kind of cultural snobbism sets in. What has been learned, directly or indirectly, is dismissed, and the failure to read Orwell (among many other writers) in context means that what they have to offer is too readily scorned, even sneered at.

The one characteristic of Orwell's writing that, it seems to me, is too often overlooked is his wit and his wry humour. The impression of a grim prophet, a forbidding Old Testament figure, is too easily conjured up. He had a marvellous gift of humour and I suspect that, in the last analysis, he will have the laugh over those who would belittle him.

Notes

Introduction

1. Jacintha Buddicom, *Eric and Us: A Remembrance of George Orwell* (1974), p. 11. Hereafter as *Eric and Us*.
2. See Tables 2.1 and 5.1, pp. 32 and 92–3, and, for full details, my 'Orwell: Balancing the Books', *The Library*, VI, 16 (1994), 77–100.

1 Getting Started

1. Sir Richard Rees, *George Orwell: Fugitive from the Camp of Victory* (1961), pp. 144–5. Hereafter as 'Rees'. Mabel Fierz's report is quoted by Shelden, p. 127.
2. *Eric and Us*, pp. 13–14.
3. CEJL, iv.412.
4. Rees, p. 145.
5. See Bernard Crick, *George Orwell: A Life*, (third, Penguin, edition, 1992), p. 107; Michael Shelden, *Orwell: The Authorised Biography* (1991), p. 73; US pagination differs. Hereafter as 'Crick' and 'Shelden' respectively.
6. Stephen Wadhams, *Remembering Orwell* (1984), p. 44. As 'Wadhams' hereafter. Wadhams's interviews, conducted in 1983, are a particularly valuable source of information.
7. Rees, p. 145. Mabel Fierz gave Wadhams a similar account, pp. 44–5.
8. Crick, pp. 48–9; Shelden, pp. 22–3.
9. VII.37. See also Crick, pp. 54–5; he identifies Kate of the novel with Elsie of the Anglican Convent Orwell attended from 1908 to 1911, with whom Orwell says in 'Such, Such Were the Joys' he 'fell deeply in love' – when aged about 6.
10. *Eric and Us*, p. 19. A footnote on that page reproduces part of a letter from Avril to Jacintha, 14 March 1973, in which Avril, having read a draft of Jacintha's book, says that she 'is making a very fair assessment of Eric's boyhood'. Her brother, she wrote, was 'essentially an aloof, undemonstrative person, which doesn't necessarily mean to say that he had a blighted childhood and developed a "death wish" as so many biographers seem to think'. Avril's use of 'necessarily' is intriguing.
11. See the second paragraph of 'Why I Write', CEJL, i.23.
12. 'My Brother, George Orwell', BBC Third Programme broadcast, 1960; printed in *Twentieth Century*, March 1961; reprinted in *Orwell Remembered*, ed. Audrey Coppard and Bernard Crick (1984), p. 27. As *Orwell Remembered* hereafter.
13. *Eric and Us*, pp. 68–9, 78–80. Jacintha reprints five letters from Mrs Blair.
14. *Eric and Us*, p. 39.

15. *Eric and Us*, pp. 39–41, 94. *The Twilight of the Gods* and *The Fairchild Family* are among books mentioned in Orwell's letter to Brenda Salkeld, September 1932 (CEJL, i.125–6).
16. Wadhams, p. 96.
17. *Eric and Us*, pp. 143–5.
18. Cyril Connolly, *Enemies of Promise* (1938), p. 213; Penguin Books, 1961, p. 179.
19. Laurence Brander, *George Orwell* (1954), p. 4. As Brander hereafter.
20. 'Some Are More Equal Than Others', *Penguin New Writing*, 40, September 1950; partially reprinted in *Orwell Remembered*, as 'That Curiously Crucified Expression', pp. 171–6. Morris failed to realise that Orwell was often 'setting him up'.
21. Private communication from David Astor.

2 Foreign Fields

1. Three of Orwell's colleagues, George Stuart, Roger Beadon, and L. W. Marrison have left useful information about Orwell in Burma, the former in a recording held by the Orwell Archive and the latter two in *Orwell Remembered*, pp. 62–6. See also Peter Stansky and William Abrahams, *The Unknown Orwell* (1974), Part Three: Burma; Crick, 139–75; Christopher Hollis (who was two years behind Orwell at Eton), *A Study of George Orwell: The Man and his Works* (1956), Ch. 3: Burma; Shelden, 101–23 and 506 n. 2. Shelden doubts Stuart's testimony but this has been shown by Crick to be genuine, pp. 586–9. For a fuller account than that given here, see *Complete Works*, 63.
2. Maung Htin Aung, 'George Orwell in Burma', *Asian Affairs*, 57 (ns 1), Pt I, February 1970 (the passages referred to are from pp. 23, 24 and 25); 'Orwell and the Burma Police', *Asian Affairs*, 60 (ns 4), Pt II, June 1973 (the passages referred to are from pp. 182 and 183). The first article is reprinted in *The World of George Orwell*, ed. Miriam Gross (1971), pp. 20–30; this also includes John Gross, 'Imperial Attitudes', pp. 32–8.
3. *Enemies of Promise*, 1938, p. 213; 1961, p. 179.
4. *Enemies of Promise*, 1938, pp. 207–8; 1961, p. 175, R. D. Pearce's 'The Prep School and Imperialism: The Example of George Orwell's St Cyprian's', *Journal of Educational Administration and History* (Jan. 1991), pp. 42–53; and his 'Orwell and the Harrow History Prize' (with sample questions), *N&Q*, 235 (ns 37), (Dec. 1990), 442–3, are both very illuminating on this topic.
5. Although Newbolt, and this line in particular, might now be regarded with suspicion, even contempt, it echoes a passage in Wordsworth's 'Character of the Happy Warrior': '. . . the Man, who, lifted high . . . Or left unthought-of in obscurity, . . . Plays, in the many games of life, that one / Where what he most doth value must be won' (lines 65, 67, 70–1), another poem regularly learned in the heyday of imperialism. To Orwell, Wordsworth was an 'English institution', like tea, cricket, kindness to animals, Nelson, etc., at which 'professional' Roman Catholic columnists such as 'Beachcomber'

(J. B. Morton) and 'Timothy Shy' (D. B. Wyndham Lewis) endlessly gibed; see 'As I Please', 30, 23 June 1944, CEJL. iii.205–6.

6. Brander refers to Orwell as a preacher on, for example, pp. 4, 14–15, 17, 51, and 151; the passage quoted is from p. 127 of his *George Orwell*. See also above, p. 72, where the last lines of Brander's account are quoted.

7. See Crick, pp. 160–2 (which prints 'The Lesser Evil', *69*, and 'Romance', *65*) and pp. 170–1 (where 'When the Franks have lost their sway', *66*) is reproduced. 'Romance' is also reproduced by Shelden, p. 108.

8. Crick, p. 195.

9. Shelden, p. 127.

10. For Orwell's time in Paris, see Crick, pp. 188–210; Shelden, pp. 135–47. Peter Lewis, *George Orwell: The Road to 1984* (1981), has illustrations of the Rue du Pot de Fer (p. 20), the Hôpital Cochin (p. 19), and a typical small bistro of the period (pp. 24–5), as well a number of other evocative pictures illustrating Orwell's life.

11. Wadhams, pp. 41, 81 and 84. Milton was the unnamed American sentry who was standing by Orwell when he was shot through the throat (VI.138). Adam gave up the Esperantist movement when he separated from his wife and left Paris in 1936. According to Bannier, their marriage was not happy: 'She had no character. She was soft, without backbone, without willpower' (Wadhams, p. 42). In 1945, towards the end of the war, when Orwell was working as a war correspondent in Paris, he took tins of canned meat to Bannier on behalf of his Aunt Nellie Limouzin (Wadhams, 42).

12. Alok Rai, *Orwell and the Politics of Despair: A Critical Study of the Writings of George Orwell* (1988), p. 53.

13. For a full discussion of this problem, see my 'George Orwell: Dates and Origins', *The Library*, VI, 13 (1991), 137–9.

14. From Orwell's later correspondence with Plowman, 22 September 1929 (CEJL, i.37), and 1 November 1930 (CEJL, i.50–1), it looks as if the article sent from Paris was a longer version of 'The Spike', which Plowman asked Orwell to shorten.

15. Rees records that after being picked up, he reappeared the next day, 'very crestfallen. He had duly got drunk and been taken to a police station. But once there he had received a fatherly talk, spent the night in a cell and been let out the next morning with a cup of tea and some good advice', p. 144. Compare Ch. IX of *Keep the Aspidistra Flying*.

16. For a detailed analysis of how these and later figures for earnings are calculated, and also the possibility that Orwell was paid 200 francs for another article just before starting as a dishwasher (I.19–20), see my 'George Orwell: Balancing the Books', *The Library*, VI, 16 (1994), 77–100. In a BBC Third Programme broadcast in 1960, Brenda Salkeld recorded that Orwell, 'summing up his life at twenty-eight – financially' (i.e. in 1931), said he had earned £100 from writing; £200 from teaching and tutoring; £20 from dishwashing; £20 from other jobs; and £2000 in the Indian Police (printed in *Orwell Remembered*, p. 68).

These figures depend on two peoples' memories and cannot be relied upon, despite their sources. Orwell certainly earned more than £2000 in the Police and it is difficult to see where he earned £200 from teaching and tutoring before he had even started at The Hawthorns. In 1937–38, piano lessons in the provinces from a qualified teacher might be had at 1s. 6d. per half-hour lesson, or, for even less, at 10s. 6d. a term. (At 1994 prices £200 was roughly equivalent to something like £8000; 1s. 6d. to £3.00.)

17. See letter to Leonard Moore, 26 April 1932, CEJL, i.101–2, and Crick, p. 621 n. 44. The usual commission taken by a literary agent from an author is 10 per cent; Moore seems to have taken 12¼ per cent, except for the first advance for *Animal Farm* from which 10 per cent was deducted.

18. In 1929, *Sleeveless Errand* by Norah C. James was seized at the instigation of Sir William Joynson-Hicks of the Home Office. It was banned by the Bow Street Magistrate for having too many swearwords. It was then printed in France. (Nicholas Parsons, *The Book of Literary Lists* (1986), pp. 236–7.)

19. Wadhams, pp. 47–8. Adrian Fierz said that his chief memory of Orwell was of the calmness, 'of his whole attitude and way of speaking and way of treating subjects' despite the strength of his feelings (p. 48).

20. Edwin Muir, review of *Pleasure of New Writing*, commenting on a reprint of John Morris's essay, 'Some Are More Equal than Others' (first published 1950 and abstracted in *Orwell Remembered*), *The Observer*, 3 February 1952; Meyer's letter in response was published on 10 February. Orwell's relations with working-class people will be discussed later in connection with *The Road to Wigan Pier*.

21. David Smith and Michael Mosher, *Orwell for Beginners* (1984), pp. 95–105.

22. See Keith B. Williams, 'The Will to Objectivity: Egon Kisch's *Der Rasende Reporter*', MLR, 85 (1990), 92–106, an early draft of which was kindly lent to the author. An edition of *Der Rasende Reporter* was published at Köln in 1983 by Verlag Kiepenheuer und Witsch. Although I have not been able to establish any direct link (and Orwell did not speak German), it would be premature to suggest one did not exist.

23. Shelden, pp. 145–6. I am grateful to Michael Shelden for making a copy of the annotations he located available to me.

24. For full details, see 157.

25. Wadhams, pp. 27–9.

26. Wadhams, pp. 29–30.

3 The Profession of Author

1. 'Stories and Voices in Orwell's Early Narratives', in *Orwell: Views from the Left*, ed. Christopher Norris (1984), p. 164.

2. Bernard Gensane, *George Orwell: Vie et écriture* (Nancy, 1994). Gensane's analysis, though his work is imaginative and sympathetic,

is very dated in its range of reference. He does not refer to Lynette Hunter's work in the same field, Shelden's biography receives only a fleeting reference in a single footnote (with the author's name misspelt), and he is unaware that Orwell's works, which he analyses so carefully, were issued in corrected editions in 1986 and 1987. Thus he can write of *A Clergyman's Daughter*, 'l'amnésie de l'héroïne n'est qu'un grossier procédé narratif' (p. 93), having no awareness that the book's narrative line was grossly disturbed by censorship. However, despite that, there are valuable insights into Orwell's characters and voices.

3. Rai, p. 54. In his note to this passage he directs the reader to Jenni Calder, *Chronicles of Conscience: A Study of George Orwell and Arthur Koestler* (1968), p. 33; and Peter Stansky and William Abrahams, *The Transformation* (1974), p. 16.

4. Wadhams, pp. 36–8.

5. See Penguin Twentieth-Century Classics Edition, 1989, 'A Note on the Text', pp. xvi–xix, and, for Mabel Fierz's remembrance, Dervla Murphy's introduction, p. viii.

6. Maung Htin Aung, 'Orwell of the Burma Police', *Asian Affairs (Journal of the Royal Central Asian Society)*, 60 (ns 4), Pt II (June 1973), 186.

7. David Lodge argues it matters little: see 'A Hanging' in *The Modes of Modern Writing* (1977), pp. 9–17.

8. Maung Htin Aung, 'George Orwell and Burma', *Asian Affairs*, 57 (ns 1), Pt I, February 1970, p. 27.

9. See 326.1. The tape is in the Orwell Archive, UCL. Although doubts have been expressed about its authenticity, Professor Crick has established that it is genuine (587–8). In 1993, an Indian judge awarded the owner of an elephant killed in a road accident 465 000 rupees (£10 000) damages, the highest compensation then paid in such a case (*Daily Telegraphy*, 27 August 1993).

10. Stansky and Abrahams, *The Transformation*, thought there had been only one printing and of that 976 copies had been remaindered (p. 57).

11. *The Transformation*, pp. 58–60.

12. Maung Htin Aung, in 'Orwell of the Burma Police', records that U Po Kyin was a probationer with Orwell at the Police Training School, Mandalay. In the seniority list, U Po Kyin was number 79 and Orwell slightly his junior at 81. This U Po Kyin, far from being villainous, had 'an absolutely clean service record' (pp. 184–5).

13. For a full account, see the Appendix and Textual Note to the Secker & Warburg edition, 1986, pp. 302–22. A shorter Textual Note is given in the Penguin edition, 1989, pp. v–viii. See also the headnote to 236.

14. From the records of Victor Gollancz, Ltd.

15. Ian Willison, pp. 6–11.

16. For some account of this and other related issues, see my 'What Orwell Really Wrote', *George Orwell & 'Nineteen Eighty-Four'* (1985), pp. 3–19.

17. Full lists of both classes of words are given in the 1986 edition, pp. 312–13. The distinction between alien and assimilated words provides an interesting commentary on Anglo-Indian characteristics. To the

OED, 'syce', a groom, was not regarded as alien, whereas 'sahib' was.

18. 'George Orwell and Burma', p. 20. Elizabeth wears tortoise-shell spectacles, which Mrs Lackersteen believes 'all the – er – *demi-mondaines* in South America' are wearing (II.100), which, if she knows what she is saying, is more insult than compliment.

19. Tacitus, *Agricola*, 30. Note also how Orwell refers ironically to those who can spout Latin tags: when Flory expresses his disgust to Veeraswami at the way 'honourable English gentlemen' talk, he includes 'Macgregor with his Latin tags and please give the bearer fifteen lashes', II.36.

20. Vizetelly died in 1894. One of his earliest successes was a cheap edition of *Uncle Tom's Cabin*, 1882. The 'rapid spread of demoralizing literature' was debated in the House of Commons and the National Vigilance Association published a transcript of the debate and the trial, together with extracts from the newspapers, as a pamphlet. In Parliament it was argued that 'Such garbage was simply death to a nation'. The text is conveniently reprinted in *Documents of Modern Literary Realism*, ed. George J. Becker (1963), pp. 350–82.

21. Rosalind Wade wrote over thirty novels, some under the pseudonym Catherine Carr, and edited the *Contemporary Review* from 1970–88. In 1985 she was awarded the OBE. She died in 1989.

22. Records of Victor Gollancz Ltd. For details of editorial changes and a list of variants, see the Secker & Warburg edition, 1986.

23. See Textual Note to *Keep the Aspidistra Flying*, especially in the hardback, 1987, edition and *267, 268, 279, 283*, and *284*.

24. Sheila Hodges, *Gollancz: The Story of a Publishing House, 1928–1978*, (1978), p. 107.

25. Records of Victor Gollancz Ltd. For details of editorial changes and a list of variants, see the Secker & Warburg edition of 1987.

26. Reprinted in *George Orwell: The Critical Heritage*, ed. Jeffrey Meyers (1975), p. 63. The section devoted to criticism of *Keep the Aspidistra Flying* is very good. It should be borne in mind that American critics only wrote after Orwell's death, by when his reputation following *Animal Farm* and *Nineteen Eighty-Four* was established. There is a good and often amusing account of the time Orwell, Sayers and Rayner Heppenstall shared a flat (especially Ch. 11 which describes Orwell knocking out a drunken Heppenstall) in Rayner Heppenstall, *Four Absentees* (1960). The absentees, all dead by 1960, were Orwell, Eric Gill, Dylan Thomas, and J. Middleton Murry.

27. Introduction to Mark Rutherford, *Autobiography and Deliverance*, The Victorian Library (1969), pp. 8–9.

28. *Autobiography*, p. 115; Essay on 'Principles', p. 306; edition cited.

29. Christopher Small, in *The Road to Miniluv* (1975) identifies Orwell with Dorothy (p. 41).

30. Patrick Reilly, *George Orwell: The Age's Adversary* (1986), p. 120.

31. Edition cited, p. 17.

32. *Hudson Review*, Summer 1956; reprinted in Meyers, *The Critical Heritage*, p. 88.

33. Ibid., p. 89.

4 The Turning-Point: Wigan and Spain

1. The phrase is that used by Stephen Wadhams, p. 50. Professor Crick, relying on information from Geoffrey Gorer, gives the figure of £500 but he states categorically that the book was commissioned by Victor Gollancz and 'not commissioned, as has often been said, for the (Communist-dominated) Left Book Club', pp. 278 and 279.

2. See *341* and Peter Davison, 'Orwell: Balancing the Books', *The Library*, VI, 16 (June 1994), pp. 77–100, particularly pp. 86–8. For a good account of the Left Book Club, see Gordon Barrick Neavill, 'Victor Gollancz and the Left Book Club', *The Library Quarterly*, 41 (1971), 197–215.

3. See his advice to Nadine Gordimer, Hodges, p. 187.

4. Crick, pp. 307–8.

5. Ruth Dudley Edwards, *Victor Gollancz: A Biography* (1987), pp. 246–7.

6. Records of Victor Gollancz, Ltd; Willison, pp. 17–20; Textual Note to 1986 edition, V.227–32; and the Introduction to *Complete Works*, volume I.

7. For further details see a reproduction of the contract at *358* and Davison, 'Orwell: Balancing the Books', pp. 85–6.

8. Wadhams, p. 60; see 60–6 for interviews. See also interviews and Jack Common's reminiscences in *Orwell Remembered*, pp. 130–43.

9. Brander, p. 127.

10. Penguin Twentieth-Century Classics edition, 1989, p. vi. Arnold Bennett, writing from within a culture well-known to him, notes the 'steamy whiff of humanity' of a Sunday School procession and the nauseating smell of a theatre crammed with striking pottery workers in *Clayhanger* (1910; Book 2, ch. X.2 and ch. XX.3).

11. Included in *Inside the Myth; Orwell: Views from the Left*, ed. Christopher Norris (1984), pp. 126–38 (as 'Norris' hereafter); the passage quoted is from p. 128. The form 'mysogynist' avoids, presumably deliberately, the 'i' of the prefix 'miso', on the assumption that the prefix is 'mis' and thus too alike to 'Miss' and therefore offensive to women. Compare the serio-comic form 'herstory' to draw attention to 'history' being male-orientated. (Intelligent feminists are, of course, well aware that the first syllable of 'history' has nothing to do with the male sex. The first syllable is derived from the Greek for 'knowing' and in many languages the word is feminine, as is *l'histoire* in French.) John Rodden, *The Politics of Literary Reputation: The Making and Claiming of 'St. George' Orwell* (1989), quotes Beatrix Campbell's use of the phrase 'toxic scorn' from her *Wigan Pier Revisited: Poverty and Politics in the 1980s* (1983), p. 436, n. 103.

12. I ought to make my own position clear. I am firmly middle-class with all the weaknesses and virtues (as I see them) of that class. When I was younger – much younger – I played cricket for two seasons with a small club made up, except for myself, entirely of working-class men. It was perfectly friendly but it was made plain, despite my best efforts to be companionable, that I was not sufficiently 'one of them' for more than utilitarian purposes. Class distinction, I have found, works in more than one direction. Like Orwell, I found when serving

on the lower deck of the Navy, 1944–48, class distinctions could readily melt away in that context and relationships that developed then continue to this day.

13. George Woodcock, *The Writer and Politics* (1948), p. 176. There is also an essay on Orwell and one on English hymns, which Orwell admired and which, he told Koestler, he had 'always been meaning to write something about' (24 May 1948, CEJL, iv.480).

14. Ibid., pp. 182–3.

15. Thus Frank Frankford, who served in the same unit as Orwell in Spain, told Stephen Wadhams that he was suspicious of Orwell; 'it was his condescending attitude that got me' (Wadhams, p. 83). Frankford made charges against his colleagues which were written up and elaborated in the *Daily Worker*. He was roundly condemned by John McNair, Orwell, and 14 members of the contingent. When asked if he was angry that the *Daily Worker* had put words into his mouth, he replied that that was 'Quite legitimate in politics, I am a realist' (Crick, pp. 346–8; see also 635. n. 63 for further examples of Frankford's belief that Orwell despised his colleagues).

16. Term might sometimes have started after this Sunday, which could fall between 14 and 21 January.

17. Information from W. J. West, 22 July 1994.

18. See also Conclusion, pp. 142–3.

19. Orwell described the POUM in *Homage to Catalonia* as 'one of those dissident Communist parties which have appeared in many countries in the last few years as a result of the opposition to "Stalinism". . . . Numerically it was a small party, with not much influence outside Catalonia, and chiefly important because it contained an unusually high proportion of politically conscious members. . . . It did not represent any block of trade unions.' The POUM claimed 10 000 members in June 1936, 70 000 at the end of that year, and 40 000 in June 1937, but 'a hostile estimate would probably divide [these figures] by four' (VI.202–3). Orwell gives an account of the competing factions in Appendix I (Chapter V of the original edition) of *Homage to Catalonia*.

20. Rees, p. 147. Much the same account is given in his *For Love or Money* (Southern Illinois University Press, Carbondale, 1960), p. 153. This is quoted by Michael Shelden in his biography of Orwell, p. 302. The passage begins 'She seemed not so much surprised, as *scared*, to see me'. For Burnett Bolloten's application of the word 'terror', see his *The Spanish Civil War: Revolution and Counterrevolution* (1991), pp. 570–1. The word 'magisterial' is sometimes loosely applied to bulky academic studies, but it may truly be given to Bolloten's lifelong work.

21. Bob Edwards, who led the ILP contingent in Spain for a only few weeks and later became a Labour MP, accused Orwell of being 'a bloody scribbler' whose chief concern was to gather material for a book rather than fight. This has been exposed by Michael Shelden as a travesty of the facts. Edwards was only at the front from 2 February to 17 March and on his return home he wrote at least seven articles for *The New Leader* in the first eight months of 1937, so that 'It is odd that *he* should have named Orwell a 'bloody scribbler.' He continued to traduce Orwell's motives as late as 1970 in his introduction

to a special edition of *Homage to Catalonia* (Shelden, pp. 289–90). Stafford Cottman thought Edwards's attitude unreasonable, a product of 'inverted snobbery, class prejudice' (*Orwell Remembered*, p. 152).

22. Wadhams, pp. 80 and 82 respectively.
23. *Orwell Remembered*, p. 147.
24. Kimche, recalling his and Orwell's experiences of Spain, Wadhams, p. 95.
25. Wadhams, 94–5.
26. As Bernard Crick points out, Orwell's point of view was shared by Willy Brandt, then serving in Catalonia and later to be West German Chancellor. Orwell, when 'on the run' just before escaping from Spain, met Brandt, who was in a similar predicament (Crick, pp. 330, 338). No attempt is made in this short study to tease out the complicated history of the Spanish Civil War, nor how it has been represented, except in so far as these impinged upon Orwell. Although few contemporary accounts of the Spanish Civil War, apart from Orwell's, have continued in print, there are a number of excellent historical studies. In addition to Bolloten (see n. 20), Hugh Thomas, *The Spanish Civil War* (1961; third edition, quoted here, 1977) is particularly recommended. A good, short, illustrated account is that by Paul Preston, *The Spanish Civil War, 1936–39* (1986).
27. Crick, p. 326.
28. Bill Alexander, 'George Orwell and Spain', in Norris, p. 94; David Corkhill and Stewart Rawnsley (eds), *The Road to Spain* (1981), p. xii.
29. Wadhams, p. 96.
30. William Rust, *Britons in Spain: The History of the British Battalion of the XVth International Brigade* (1939). Neither Rust nor Alexander's *British Volunteers for Liberty: Spain, 1936–1939* (1982), list POUM casualties. Valentine Cunningham in his introduction to *The Penguin Book of Spanish Civil War Verse* (1980), gives a different total; he says that '2,762 Britons . . . fought with the International Brigades' and that about 80 per cent of these were working-class men (p. 33).
31. See Thomas, *The Spanish Civil War*, p. 798, n. 2. He records Tapsell's death but only hints at its cause by referring to Col. Bielov as 'more of an NKVD specialist than an engineer'. Charlotte Haldane, who worked for the Communists in Spain, seems in no doubt that Tapsell and Reid were 'sold down the river' by their own side (*Truth Will Out*, 1949, pp. 127 and 137). Thomas does not mention Reid.
32. David Smith and Michael Mosher, *Orwell for Beginners* (1984), p. 131, cite *Pravda* as declaring that in Catalonia 'the elimination of Trotskyites and Anarcho-Syndicalists has begun. It will be carried out with the same energy as in the Soviet Union' – a reference to the Purge Trials of 1936.
33. Brander, pp. 140–1.
34. See Shelden, pp. 306–7.
35. The letter and Gollancz's response are given in full in Crick, pp. 343–5. For Gollancz's rejection of *Animal Farm*, see Hodges, 109–11.
36. Fredric Warburg, *An Occupation for Gentlemen* (Secker & Warburg, 1959), see Ch. 10; Willison, pp. 21–7.

37. Orwell never met Madame Davet but they had corresponded from before the war, particularly over a translation of *Down and Out in Paris and London*. Their correspondence is included in the *Complete Works*. Madame Davet was for a long time secretary to Gide and she was honoured by the Académie Française for her translations of books from English into French. When I met her in the mid-1980s she was very old and had, sadly, lost her English. She had never seen either of the French translations of *Down and Out* but she was, at last, able to hold one in her hands.

38. I mentioned this in the Orwell Lecture, 1984. Stafford Cottman was in the audience and when his hand shot up at the end of the lecture I feared I had made some terrible error. But no, he told me I was quite right about that meaning of DSO and that Thomas Parker was alive and well and running a carousel in the East End of London.

5 Orwell as Reviewer and Essayist

1. I am grateful to Mr Croft for making a copy of this letter available to me, and also Nancy Cunard's covering letter when she sent it to Randall Swingler. He published the letter in *The New Statesman*, as part of an article, 'The Awkward Squaddie', 18 March 1994. It is *386A* in the *Complete Works*.

2. Rees, p. 147.

3. Crick, p. 305.

4. W. J. West, *The Larger Evils: 'Nineteen Eighty-Four' – The Truth Behind the Satire* (1992), esp. 171–2, 176, and plate.

5. An account of the pamphlet collection is given at *3732*. A copy, with a transcript of Orwell's catalogue of part of the collection, fully annotated, has been deposited in the British Library with the collection (the call number of which is 1899 ss. 1–21, 23–48), and in the Orwell Archive, UCL.

6. See p. xx of Introduction to *The Facsimile*, ed. Peter Davison (1984).

7. The first 'As I Please' was published on 3 December 1943 and Orwell wrote eighty of these columns, the last, and his final contribution to *Tribune*, on 4 April 1947. Orwell was given a free rein to write on what he liked; in this he was stoutly supported by *Tribune*'s editor, Aneurin Bevan. Many protesters threatened to cancel their subscriptions but the circulation manager reported that, despite the huffing and puffing, they rarely did so. The title may have been suggested by that for a short series written by Raymond Postgate in *Controversy*, edited by C. A. Smith, in 1939. Jon Kimche told me in 1990, a little over three years before he died, that he had suggested the title to Orwell, but there were other similar titles that Orwell might have known. Lord Elton gave a series of broadcasts in 1937–38 under the title, 'It Occurs to Me'; and Joseph Duranty, foreign correspondent of the *New York Times*, 1913–39, whom Orwell included in his private list of Crypto-Communists and Fellow Travellers (*3731*), wrote a column, 'I Write As I Please'. Kimche handled much of Orwell's copy. It was, he said, punctual, accurate, of the correct length, and

required virtually no sub-editing. In other words, it was thoroughly professional. One characteristic of 'As I Please' was the lively correspondence it attracted. The *Complete Works* will include many of the letters published (and a few that were not); they give a rare experience of a writer and the audience he wrote for. See headnote 2378.

8. For Orwell with one of his favourite goats, Muriel – the name he gave the goat in *Nineteen Eighty-Four* – see Crick, plate 19.

9. Crick, p. 577.

10. Sir Charles Napier wrote a single-word despatch following his victory at Hyderabad in the Indian province of Scinde, 1843: 'Peccavi' (I have sinned) (CEJL, i.516 and *599 n. 1*).

11. For a fuller account, see Peter Davison, 'George Orwell: Dates and Origins', *The Library*, VI, 13 (June 1991), 139–42.

12. On 25 November 1971, the Hospital provided Sonia Orwell with details of Orwell's admission. He was admitted to the Hospital's Salle Lancereaux on 7 March 1929 'pour une grippe' and discharged on 22 March. There is an excellent analysis of this essay by David Wykes in his *A Preface to Orwell* (1987), pp. 112–18, but he does not discuss Tennyson's poem in detail. Wyckes is good in distinguishing between non-instrumental and instrumental criticism of Orwell's essays: the former analysing a work in the traditional 'poem on the page sense', as art; the latter, Orwell's writing as an interpretation of life (pp. 118–20). As he puts it, 'Orwell's best criticism is the search for meaning in the life of society' (p. 118). President Mitterrand underwent surgery at the Cochin in September 1992. Presumably attitudes had improved since 1929.

13. Crick, pp. 78–9.

14. Robert Pearce, 'Truth and Falsehood: George Orwell's Prep School Woes' (1992), pp. 367–86. See also his 'The Prep School and Imperialism: The Example of Orwell's St Cyprian's' (1991), pp. 42–53; and 'Orwell and the Harrow History Prize' (1990), pp. 442–3.

15. See 'George Orwell: Dates and Origins', pp. 147–50 for a detailed explanation.

16. Tosco Fyvel, *George Orwell: A Personal Memoir* (1982), pp. 146–7. Fyvel comments that, looking back, he regretted persuading Orwell not to write this article: 'Orwell was of course right, as he so often was: the expensive, fee-paying schools have remained the divisive factor in British society.' See Crick, p. 519. Tom Dalyell, MP, reviewing Tim Card's *Eton Renewed* (1994) in the *Daily Telegraph*, 14 May 1994, states that 'Orwell in 1945 warned Attlee that Labour would get nowhere unless it first abolished [public schools], together with the House of Lords.' I can find no evidence to support this claim and upon inquiry, Dalyell could produce none; he had probably confused Attlee and Bevan. Fyvel maintains that Orwell 'decidedly did not respect Clement Attlee', p. 126.

17. Streptomycin was only available then in the USA. David Astor obtained supplies but the drug had terrible side-effects when given to Orwell. It would be a year or two before a technique would be worked out for administering the drug to someone in his condition. By then

he was dead, but two women, to whom the drug meant for him was given, lived.

18. For the essay, see CEJL, iv. 156–70; for details surrounding the publication of the article and its reprinting, see notes to *2815*; for the notes Orwell made in preparation for the essay, see *2816*.

19. Quoted by Peter Buitenhuis, *The Great War of Words: Literature as Propaganda 1914–18 and After* (1987; 1989, edition referred to), pp. 61 and 152.

20. Iain Sproat, *Wodehouse at War* (1981), p. 78. Sproat prints the five broadcasts and gives a full account of the background and investigation by MI5; he includes Major E. J. P. Cussen's report on behalf of MI5 to the Home Office. Details of the broadcasting dates, and Wodehouse's interview with Harry Flannery of CBS, are given on p. 160.

21. Hodges, p. 108.

22. Information for Gollancz from the publisher's records and Willison, pp. 33–5 and 40; for Secker & Warburg from Willison, pp. 36–9. Willison's figures for *Betrayal of the Left* differ slightly from those in the Gollancz records.

23. See also Crick, pp. 561–3, for Warburg's confidential report on his visit to Orwell at Cranham, 15 June 1949. This describes Orwell's poor state of health, the work he was hoping to write, and Orwell's financial prospects.

6 Events Leading Up to the War and the BBC Years

1. Publication details from Willison, pp. 28–32; Gollancz figures checked against their records.

2. Probably the paragraph starting 'War is coming, 1941, they say', VII.238, about half a page, and the final paragraph of that section, which includes the sentence, 'The bad times are coming, and the streamlined men are coming too', another eight lines, VII.239.

3. The contract is held by the Harry Ransom Research Centre, The University of Texas at Austin. It is listed as item 5371 in William B. Todd and Ann Bowden's *Tauchnitz International Editions in English 1841–1955* (1988).

4. In his 'Diary of Events Leading Up to the War', Orwell noted under 3 September that the Labour-inclined Sunday paper *Reynold's News* had published letters extolling the Pact 'but have shifted the emphasis from this being a "peace move" to its being a self-protecting move by U.S.S.R.' (*570*).

5. Quoted by Robert Kee, *The World We Left Behind: A Chronicle of the Year 1939* (1984), p. 87. On p. 118 he remarks, 'Goebbels in the *Völkischer Beobachter* was running a peace campaign rather like that of the London *Daily Express*'. My father-in-law, an insurance claims manager in Manchester, was one of many totally convinced by the *Daily Express*, as late as August 1939, that there would be no war.

6. See *533* for a description of the Diary and its n. 1 for details of *Socialist Correspondence*.

7. For Orwell's review, see 636. Orwell kept most of the programmes of the plays he reviewed, and the handouts issued for those reviewing films, and these are with his collection of pamphlets in the British Library.

8. Orwell served in C Company (St John's Wood) of the 5th County of London Battalion from 12 June to 23 November 1943 as a sergeant. His corporal was Fredric Warburg (who had served as an officer in the First World War and fought at Passchendaele). Warburg gives a very amusing account of Orwell in the Home Guard in *All Authors Are Equal* (1973), pp. 35–9, including the incident when, accidentally, Orwell allowed a live instead of a practice shell to be fired indoors from a spigot mortar. One soldier lost most of his teeth and another was unconscious for 24 hours. There was a Court of Inquiry but no disciplinary action seems to have been taken. In the light of the self-inflicted casualties described by Paul Fussell in *Wartime: Understanding and Behavior in the Second World War* (1989), this was a minor mishap. Orwell took Home Guarding very seriously and his 'Lecture Notes for Instructing the Home Guard' have survived (730 to 736). He discusses street-fighting (in great detail), field fortifications, smoke mortars, the Northover Projector, and, of course, the spigot mortar.

9. Orwell's time at the BBC bulks very large in the *Complete Works*, taking up some 2000 pages.

10. W. J. West has edited two volumes of Orwell's BBC broadcasts: *Orwell: The War Broadcasts* and *Orwell: the War Commentaries*, 1985. He provides introductions and notes (often with valuable insights) and a selection of letters, but unfortunately both volumes are inaccurate. Passages are unaccountably omitted (a whole page from the newsletter of 12 September 1942), some newsletters are not Orwell's, and some are omitted. Mr West also believed that Orwell was not allowed to write newsletters after 13 March 1943, whereas he wrote at least 165 newsletters thereafter in his last eight months at the BBC. Indeed, he wrote newsletters until the very last moment he was employed by the BBC, his last two being broadcast a couple of days after his departure. With the exception of extracts from two newsletters, the English versions of vernacular newsletters have been destroyed.

7 The Last Five Years

1. David Pryce-Jones, *Paris in the Third Reich: A History of the German Occupation 1940–1944* (1981), pp. 144 and 206. I am indebted to Professor Michael Foot for pointing out the inaccuracy of Tixier's and Pryce-Jones's figures.

2. Warburg was responding to a criticism made by Evelyn Waugh in the December 1973 issue of *Books & Bookmen*. Waugh had said that 'a more painstaking publisher' than Warburg might have found someone to tidy up the second half of *Nineteen Eighty-Four*. Warburg thought no tidying up was necessary: 'Orwell certainly did not think so.' Waugh had a point, however. For example, when Julia is dragged

off after she and Winston are arrested, Orwell states, 'and that was the last he saw of her' (IX.232). The meaning could imply 'on this occasion', but that would be superfluous. It must mean that they would never meet again, but, of course, they do, very sadly, in the Chestnut Tree, after both have been released (IX.304–6).

3. For full publication details, including the many translations published in Orwell's lifetime, see Willison, 43–73. See also Textual Note to the 1987 edition and the Note on the Text to the 1989 Penguin edition. For details of the arrangements to have the book published in America and for Orwell's initial receipts, see *2982 n. 2*. Orwell's very clean typescript of *Animal Farm* has survived and is held by the Orwell Archive, UCL.

4. Szewczenko is now, as Ihor Sevcenko, Professor of Byzantine Literature at Harvard University. I am grateful to him for making his letters to Orwell available.

5. For the Dial Press and reshelving references, see Shelden, p. 425.

6. Willison, p. 59.

7. *Eric and Us*, pp. 39–40.

8. Suggested by John Herbertson, in the *Daily Telegraph*, 31 October 1992. His letter was accompanied by a detail from the cartoon.

9. For Woodcock, see his *Orwell's Message: 1984 and the Present* (1984), p. 106; William Steinhoff, *George Orwell and the Origins of 1984* (1975), finds the link with Goldstein tenuous at best, p. 201; it was suggested by Isaac Deutscher in *Russia in Transition*. There are many parallels between the history and personalities of the Soviet Union from 1917 to 1944 and *Animal Farm*. In *A George Orwell Companion* (1982), J. R. Hammond lists 18 (p. 161). The less obvious are Minimus – Mayakovsky; Moses – Russian Orthodox Church; Mollie – White Russians; Pilkington – Britain; Battle of the Cowshed – the allied invasion of 1918; Battle of the Windmill – the German invasion, 1941; and the windmill itself – the Five-Year Plans.

10. Joseph Czapski and Orwell met in Paris in 1945 when *Animal Farm* was in proof. Though he had suffered terribly under Stalin, and thousands of his fellow Polish prisoners had been slaughtered by the Russians, he persuaded Orwell to alter page 69, line 22, so that Napoleon alone did not fall to the ground. See 1987 edn, p. 202; 1989 edn, p. xix. Orwell and Arthur Koestler tried hard to persuade English publishers to bring out an English translation of Czapski's *Souvenirs de Starobielsk*. This shows the extent of the mass murders committed by the Russians on Poles in what is now familiarly known as 'the Katyn Massacres', although the slaughter spread wider than Katyn. No English publisher would issue a translation though it appeared in French and Italian (as well as the original Polish). Until the last year or two, British governments of all complexions had refused to admit that the Russians committed these atrocities. For some indication of what Czapski and his compatriots suffered at the hands of the Russians, see his *The Inhuman Land* (1951). Among the killings it describes (and to which, I believe, no attention was paid when the perpetrators of the Katyn murders were exposed), was the

packing into barges of 7000 Poles imprisoned in the Komi Republic; the barges were then deliberately sunk in the White Sea. This method of disposing of one's enemies was not new. The French so treated the Vendéans who opposed the Revolution.

11. Crick, p. 451.
12. CEJL, iv.131. Eileen died of a heart attack in the course of an operation for cancer on 29 March 1945. For her last, often very moving, letters and her Will, see *2639–40*, and *2642–7; 2640* is to Lettice Cooper.
13. *The Larger Evils*, pp. 185–6. For a useful appraisal of Daphne Patai's *The Orwell Mystique*, which pays tribute to her perception and insight whilst recognising her weaknesses, especially failing to cite with approval favourable critical comment on Orwell's work, see Rodden, pp. 214–18.
14. Steinhoff, pp. 167–9. See also W. J. West (ed.), *Orwell: The War Broadcasts*, pp. 47–8 and 62.
15. Evelyn Waugh, *Scoop* (1938), Bk 1, Part 5, Section 4.
16. Willison, pp. 87–105 gives a full account of editions and translations in Orwell's lifetime.
17. When the 1987 edition was set, '2 + 2 = 5' appeared as '2r 29 5'; this was not noticed by the printers or publishers.
18. I am grateful to Barry Bloomfield for checking details of Orwell's date of birth in the India Office records and to the UK Passport Agency for its courteous help.
19. Private communication from David Astor, 18 December 1992.
20. It also transpired from this meeting that Orwell had in mind sending Richard to a boarding school. Richard was enrolled to enter Westminster School in 1957. Because Orwell died, Richard went to school in Scotland. That Orwell should make such an arrangement in the light of his views about private education is intriguing.
21. *Orwell's Message*, pp. 159–61.

8 Conclusion

1. Rodden, p. 19; the relevant footnote states, '"Professors Rate *1984* A Good Book, But Say It's Not an Outstanding Novel", *Binghampton Sun Bulletin* (N.Y.), 30 December 1983' (n. 21, p. 410).
2. Keith Alldritt, *The Making of George Orwell: An Essay in Literary History* (1969), p. 2.
3. *Independent Saturday Magazine*, 19 May 1990.
4. Rodden discusses Daphne Patai's assertion of Orwell's 'generalized misogyny', as she terms it, and she is not alone in so describing Orwell (see p. 85). He comments: 'No biographical or historical evidence linking Orwell's alleged misogyny to his reception is adduced to support this claim, exemplifying the frequent tendency among literary critics to let textual analysis do the work of historical and biographical investigation' (p. 215). Jane Mills, in *Womanwords* (Virago Press edition, 1991), offers no alternative to 'misogyny' to indicate that it means something to feminists other than 'woman-hater'. Deirdre Beddoe describes Orwell as having a 'contempt for

women' and being 'not only anti-feminist but . . . totally blind to the role women were and are forced to play in the order of things'; his female fictional characters, she says, include 'some of the most obnoxious portrayals of women in English fiction' ('Hindrances and Help-Meets: Women in the Writings of George Orwell', in Norris, pp. 140 and 141). I find some of his male characters singularly (and rightly) unpleasant, more so than any of his principal women characters, even Elizabeth. Rodden devotes a section of his study to feminist criticism of Orwell, pp. 211–26.

5. *Orwell Remembered*, p. 68.
6. Wadhams, p. 58.
7. *Orwell Remembered*, pp. 68–74.
8. *Orwell Remembered*, pp. 70 and 225.
9. Wadhams, p. 175.
10. Daphne Patai, *The Orwell Mystique: A Study in Male Ideology* (1984), p. x.
11. Rodden, p. 403. Perhaps we can dispense with even genuine academic symposia. I for one would be glad; and I am sure Orwell would rejoice.
12. So his friend of BBC days, Henry Swanzy (who gave Orwell his copy of *Tempête sur l'Espagne*, 1936). Orwell and Solzhenitsyn shared, he thought, 'the same wonderful capacity to mould details, and this rather mixed-up basic attitude' – an ability 'to turn the world into his own world' without it linking 'entirely onto the reality' (Wadhams, p. 125).
13. Colin Thubron, *Behind the Wall: A Journey through China* (1987), p. 2.
14. Information kindly provided by the Library and Records Department of the Foreign Office, 13 September 1994.
15. For an assessment of Orwell's journalism, see Julian Symons on his column, 'As I Please'. This he found 'often quite amusing, sometimes really infuriating, and sometimes silly. . . . But those columns read much better now, and this is the most impressive tribute one can pay to them as works of journalism . . . the best of them . . . are marvellously good' (Wadhams, p. 148).

Bibliography

This bibliography does not set out to list all that has been written on Orwell and his work. It is chiefly confined to those books, memoirs, and essays that I have found helpful in writing this study. Place of publication is London unless specified otherwise.

Bill Alexander, *British Volunteers for Liberty: Spain, 1936–1939*, Lawrence & Wishart, 1982.

Keith Alldritt, *The Making of George Orwell: An Essay in Literary History*, Edward Arnold, 1969.

John Atkins, *George Orwell: A Literary Study*, John Calder, 1954.

Maung Htin Aung, 'George Orwell and Burma', *Asian Affairs*, 57 (ns 1), Pt 1, February 1970, 19–28.

——, 'Orwell and the Burma Police', *Asian Affairs*, 60 (ns 4), Pt II, June 1973, 181–6.

George J. Becker (ed.), *Documents of Modern Literary Realism*, Princeton, NJ, 1963.

Deirde Beddoe, 'Hindrances and Help-Meets: Women in the Writings of George Orwell', in Norris, pp. 139–54.

Burnett Bolloten, *The Spanish Civil War: Revolution and Counterrevolution*, Harvester, Wheatsheaf, New York and London, 1991.

Laurence Brander, *George Orwell*, Longmans, Green & Co., 1954.

Jacintha Buddicom, *Eric and Us: A Remembrance of George Orwell*, Leslie Frewin, 1974.

Peter Buitenhuis, *The Great War of Words: Literature as Propaganda 1914–18 and After*, University of British Columbia Press, 1987; Batsford, London, 1989 (edition referred to).

Beatrix Campbell, *Wigan Pier Revisited: Poverty and Politics in the 1980s*, Virago, 1983.

——, 'Orwell – Paterfamilias or Big Brother?', in Norris, pp. 126–39.

Cyril Connolly, *Enemies of Promise*, Routledge & Kegan Paul, 1938; Penguin Books, Harmondsworth, 1961.

Murray Constantine (= Katherine Burdekin), *Swastika Night*, Gollancz, 1940.

Audrey Coppard and Bernard Crick (eds), *Orwell Remembered*, Ariel Books, BBC, 1984.

David Corkhill and Stewart Rawnsley (eds), *The Road to Spain*, Borderline, Dunfermline, 1981.

Bernard Crick, *George Orwell: A Life*, 1980; 3rd edition, Penguin Books, Harmondsworth, 1992.

——, *Nineteen Eighty-Four*, with a Critical Introduction and Annotations, Clarendon Press, Oxford, 1984.

Valentine Cunningham, *The Penguin Book of Spanish Civil War Verse*, Penguin Books, Harmondsworth, 1980.

Peter Davison, *Nineteen Eighty-Four: The Facsimile of the Extant Manuscript* (ed.), Preface by Daniel G. Siegel, Secker & Warburg, London; M&S Press, Weston, Mass.; Harcourt Brace Jovanovich, New York, 1984, pp. 5–21.

——, 'Editing Orwell: Eight Problems', *The Library*, VI, 6, September 1984, 217–28.

——, 'What Orwell Really Wrote', *George Orwell & 'Nineteen Eighty-Four': The Man and the Book*, Library of Congress, Washington, DC, 1985.

——, 'Bangkok Days: Orwell and the Prisoner's Diary', *Manuscripts*, 41, Fall 1989, 303–10.

——, 'George Orwell: Dates and Origins', *The Library*, VI, 13, June 1991, 137–50.

——, 'Orwell: Balancing the Books', *The Library*, VI, 16, June 1994, 77–100.

Ruth Dudley Edwards, *Victor Gollancz: A Biography*, Gollancz, 1987.

Elisaveta Fen, 'Orwell's First Wife', *The Twentieth Century*, 168, April 1960, 114–26.

Paul Fussell, *Wartime: Understanding and Behavior in the Second World War*, Oxford University Press, New York, 1989; 'Behavior' spelt with a 'u' on the dust-jacket of the American-printed edition circulated in England.

Tosco Fyvel, *George Orwell: A Personal Memoir*, Weidenfeld and Nicolson, 1982.

Bernard Gensane, *George Orwell: Vie et écriture*, Presses Universitaires de Nancy, Nancy, 1994.

Miriam Gross, *The World of George Orwell*, Weidenfeld and Nicolson, 1971; includes a shortened version of Maung Htin Aung's, 'George Orwell and Burma' (though the origin and abbreviation are not noted).

J. R. Hammond, *A George Orwell Companion*, Macmillan, 1982.

Rayner Heppenstall, *Four Absentees*, Barrie and Rockliff, 1960.

Sheila Hodges, *Gollancz: The Story of a Publishing House, 1928–1978*, Gollancz, 1978.

Christopher Hollis, *A Study of George Orwell: The Man and his Works*, Hollis & Carter, 1956.

Irving Howe (ed.), *'1984' Revisited*, Harper & Row, New York, 1983.

Lynette Hunter, *George Orwell, The Search for a Voice*, Open University Press, Milton Keynes, 1984.

——, 'Stories and Voices in Orwell's Early Narratives', in Norris, pp. 163–82.

James Joll, *The Anarchists*, 2nd edn, Harvard University Press, Cambridge, Mass., 1980.

Robert Kee, *The World We Left Behind: A Chronicle of the Year 1939*, Weidenfeld & Nicolson, 1984.

Pat Kirkham and David Thoms (eds), *Social Change and Changing Experience in World War Two Britain*, Lawrence & Wishart, 1995.

Peter Lewis, *George Orwell: The Road to 1984*, Heinemann, 1981.

David Lodge, *The Modes of Modern Writing*, Edward Arnold, 1977.

Jeffrey Meyers (ed.), *George Orwell: The Critical Heritage*, Routledge & Kegan Paul, 1975.

Gordon Barrick Neavill, 'Victor Gollancz and the Left Book Club', *The Library Quarterly*, 41, 1971, 197–215.

Christopher Norris (ed.), *Inside the Myth; Orwell: Views from the Left*, Lawrence & Wishart, 1984.

Nicholas Parsons, *The Book of Literary Lists*, Sidgwick & Jackson, 1985; Fontana, 1986.

Daphne Patai, *The Orwell Mystique: A Study in Male Ideology*, University of Massachussetts, Amherst, 1984.

Robert Pearce, 'Truth and Falsehood: George Orwell's Prep School Woes', *RES*, ns 43, No. 171, 1992, 367–86.

——, 'The Prep School and Imperialism: The Example of Orwell's St Cyprian's', *Journal of Educational Administration and History*, January 1991, 41–53.

——, 'Orwell and the Harrow History Prize', *N&Q*, ns 37, Vol. 235, December 1990, 442–3.

Paul Preston, *The Spanish Civil War, 1936–39*, Weidenfeld & Nicolson, 1986.

David Pryce-Jones, *Paris in the Third Reich: A History of the German Occupation, 1940–44*, Collins, 1981.

Alok Rai, *Orwell and the Politics of Despair: A Critical Study of the Writings of George Orwell*, Cambridge University Press, Cambridge, 1988.

Sir Richard Rees, *George Orwell: Fugitive from the Camp of Victory*, Secker & Warburg, 1961.

——, *For Love or Money*, Southern Illinois University Press, Carbondale, 1960.

Patrick Reilly, *George Orwell: The Age's Adversary*, Macmillan, 1986.

John Rodden, *The Politics of Literary Reputation: The Making and Claiming of 'St George Orwell'*, Oxford University Press, New York, 1989.

William Rust, *Britons in Spain: The History of the British Battalion of the XVth International Brigade*, Lawrence & Wishart, 1939.

Mark Rutherford, *Autobiography and Deliverance*, The Victorian Library, Leicester University Press, Leicester, 1969.

Michael Shelden, *Orwell: The Authorised Biography*, Heinemann, London; Harper Collins, New York; 1991. The American pagination differs from that of the English edition, which is used here.

David Smith and Michael Mosher, *Orwell for Beginners*, Writers and Readers Publishing Cooperative Ltd, 1984.

Christopher Small, *The Road to Miniluv*, Gollancz, 1975.

Iain Sproat, *Wodehouse at War*, Milner and Co., 1981.

Peter Stansky (ed.), *On Nineteen Eighty-Four*, W. H. Freeman & Co., New York, 1983.

Peter Stansky and William Abrahams, *The Unknown Orwell* and *The Transformation*; first published in Britain by Constable, 1972 and 1979; editions referred to here, Granada, St Albans, 1981.

William Steinhoff, *George Orwell and the Origins of '1984'*, University of Michigan Press, Ann Arbor, 1975.

Hugh Thomas, *The Spanish Civil War*, 3rd edition; Hamish Hamilton, London, and Penguin Books, Harmondsworth, 1977.

Colin Thubron, *Behind the Wall: A Journey through China*, Heinemann, 1987.

William B. Todd and Ann Bowden, *Tauchnitz International Editions in English 1841–1955*, Bibliographical Society of America, New York, 1988.

Stephen Wadhams, *Remembering Orwell*, Penguin Books Canada, Markham, Ontario; Penguin Books, Harmondsworth, 1984.

Nicolas Walter, 'Orwell and the Anarchists', *Freedom: Anarchist Review*, 42, 30 January 1981, pp. 9–12.

Fredric Warburg, *An Occupation for Gentlemen*, Houghton Mifflin, Boston, Mass., 1959.

Courtney T. Wemyss and Alexej Ugrinsky, *George Orwell*, Hofstra University, Westport, Conn., 1987.

Gary Werskey, *The Visible College*, Allen Lane, 1978.

W. J. West, *Orwell: The War Broadcasts* and *Orwell: The War Commentaries*, Duckworth/BBC, 1985.

——, *The Larger Evils: 'Nineteen Eighty-Four' – The Truth Behind the Satire*, Cannongate Press, Edinburgh, 1992.

I. R. Willison, *George Orwell: Some Materials for a Bibliography*, Librarianship Diploma Thesis, University College London, 1953. A copy is held by the Orwell Archive, UCL.

Keith B. Williams, 'The Will to Objectivity: Egon Kisch's *Der Rasende Reporter*', *MLR*, 85, 1990, 92–106.

George Woodcock, *The Crystal Spirit: A Study of George Orwell*, Jonathan Cape, 1967.

——, *The Writer and Politics*, Freedom Press, 1948.

——, *Orwell's Message: 1984 and the Present*, Harbour Publishing, Madeira Park, BC, 1984.

David Wykes, *A Preface to Orwell*, Longman, 1987.

Alex Zwerdling, *Orwell an the Left*, Yale University Press, New Haven, 1974.

Index

The Chronology is not indexed and the notes only if they provide substantial information not given in the main text; the reference number of notes is given in parentheses after the page number – e.g. 160(18). Literary works are listed under the names of their authors. Lists (as that on p. 99) are not individually indexed.